W9-BNT-511

WITHDRAWN

# a song
# for you

also by

# betsy thornton

# a song for you

## BETSY THORNTON

THOMAS DUNNE BOOKS
ST. MARTIN'S MINOTAUR
⚏ NEW YORK

THOMAS DUNNE BOOKS.
An imprint of St. Martin's Press.

A SONG FOR YOU. Copyright © 2008 by Betsy Thornton. All rights reserved. Printed in the United States of America. For information, address St. Martin's Press, 175 Fifth Avenue, New York, N.Y. 10010.

www.thomasdunnebooks.com
www.minotaurbooks.com

Library of Congress Cataloging-in-Publication Data

Thornton, Betsy.
    A song for you / Betsy Thornton. —1st ed.
        p.   cm.
    ISBN-13: 978-0-312-38062-5 (alk. paper)
    ISBN-10: 0-312-38062-3 (alk. paper)
    1. Newcombe, Chloe (Fictitious character)—Fiction.   2. Victims of crimes —
Services for—Fiction.   3. Arizona—Fiction.   I. Title.
    PS3570.H6645S66   2008
    813'.54—dc22                                              2008024869

First Edition: October 2008

10  9  8  7  6  5  4  3  2  1

TO ALEX

# acknowledgments

*Thanks again to Tom Glass of the Cochise County Attorney's Office for his weapons expertise.*

a song
for you

# prologue

*I'D HEARD STORIES AND THERE IS ALWAYS* something worse than what you are going through right now but it was the wettest monsoon in my memory. Day after day waking up to dark skies, the greenish light that thickened as the foliage grew and grew, sunflowers lining the roads like golden sentinels, and waterfalls dripping down the craggy hills that lined Highway 92 as you approached the Mule Pass Tunnel. The trip between Dudley and Sierra Vista now resembled a passage through some third-world paradise where they grew lots of rice.

At first it was a hoot, like a free trip to another country without the hassle of plane rides. But after a while the water that ran down the drainage ditches turned from a trickle to a muted but ominous roar. Gardens vanished, smothered by ferocious vines of blue morning glories that twined around everything like kudzu. Down on the Gulch, the entire road was blocked off by fast-flowing reddish brown water, Zacatacas Canyon was impassable, and the people who lived back there had to hike downtown over the mountains.

Out in the Sulphur Springs Valley a local woman who should have known better drowned in a flash flood in a low spot on the normally dry dirt road leading to her house, and a young couple from Colorado had to be rescued when their car got stuck in a running wash.

California Bert, a local drinker, lurched out of the St. Elmo's Bar and into the street as usual but this time the rushing water swept his feet out from under and carried him, arms flailing, to the underpass, right down the big hole at the bottom of the Gulch and into the drainage system. His body was found a few days later, a couple of miles away where the system emptied out.

People joked, "Too drunk to notice, probably" and "He didn't feel a thing" as a way of deflecting the image of poor Bert's final, fatal journey through the drains. The monsoons that year created that dark image and that same year unearthed another. But that comes a little later.

My name is Chloe Newcombe and at the time all this was going on I was employed as a victim advocate at the Cochise County Attorney's Office.


Six months ago Don Barnett and his wife, Cici, had moved from the Phoenix suburb of Glendale to 703 Ocotillo Canyon in Dudley, Arizona, a mountainous former mining town transformed years ago into something quaint and artsy.

"One of the top twenty small art towns in the country!" Cici had said excitedly to Don when they had begun to think about moving there.

And their new house was certainly charming. A two-bedroom renovated miner's shack, it was set halfway up a hill with a great view looking down on the 125-year-old town, plus it was cheap compared to what houses were going for in the Phoenix area—only two hundred fifty thousand. They'd bought it from an adorable younger couple who'd completely remodeled it all by themselves and it was full of the sweetest little arty touches:

scalloped trim, old windows some with stained glass created by local artists, Saltillo-tiled floors the colors of a ripe peach, and Talavera tile in the bathroom shower.

But then it started to rain. Don and Cici knew all about the monsoons, since they were old-time Arizonans, but this year it had rained so much more than usual it had broken records for the month of July and was headed for the same in August. Every ceiling in every room in the goddamn charming little house leaked. The grout between the Saltillo tiles in the kitchen, not set quite right, began to chip and some of the Talavera-style Mexican tile on the wall in the bathroom fell right off.

Don and Cici had paid cash for the house and as Don liked to say, that young couple was damn lucky they'd moved to Hawaii where he couldn't get his hands on them.

They had a lot of trouble even reaching any local roofers and finally in desperation they paid a guy's gas to come over from the bigger, newer neighboring town of Sierra Vista just to take a look. He pulled up in a resassuringly newish truck, a big bald guy with a full beard. He told them he could probably get someone over in a couple of weeks to put some temporary tar on the roof and then in three or four months, well, maybe five, he could get a crew together to put on a whole new roof. Lots of other jobs already lined up right now.

They stood outside in the yard while the roofer explained all this. The yard was charming too, with its pots of red and yellow marigolds and the concrete retaining wall studded with handmade tiles by yet another local artist. When the roofer had finished explaining, he walked over to the wall, gave it a little pat, then hoisted himself up and looked over the edge.

"Son of a bitch!" he said. "Excuse my French."

"What?" said Don.

"I hate to tell you folks," he said. "You got a problem with your roof, but we'll tar it up, should be okay for a little bit—but this here retaining wall, all the rain we been having, this wall don't look too good. Lots of junk behind there, been filling probably for years and it's starting to crack. Pressure, you know? This here wall could be a real problem. Lawsuits, even. Better do something."

"What should we do?" cried Cici.

"Get yourself a good cement guy—shit." The roofer looked down at the ground as if he couldn't bear to look at Don and Cici directly. "It'll take a while, finding a cement guy. They ain't got too many around and they're real busy. Damn monsoon—just won't stop." He scratched his head. "You're kind of stuck right now. Got nothing much but prayer."

"Prayer!" said Cici unbelievingly.

"Unless . . ." The roofer paused.

"What?" said Don.

"There's this halfway house for alcoholics and the like. The Verhelst House. Got a brother-in-law stayed there once."

"A halfway house?" said Don faintly.

The roofer nodded. "You could get yourself a crew from there. They can't redo the wall for you but they can dig out all this dirt's been building up behind it—take off the pressure till you get yourself a cement guy. They're not the fastest but they work real cheap. Got the phone number right here somewhere."


Twenty miles away the residents of Sierra Vista, a flat and rapidly growing town anchored by a military base at one end and a pretty new mall at the other, were unafraid of monsoons, but Brian Flynn, ex-cop and owner of Flynn Investigations, had his own problems. First was a growing caseload, almost too much to handle. The second was just about to materialize as Flynn, in his office working on reports, happened to glance out the plate-glass window to see a car pulling in beside the green Volkswagen that belonged to the CPA next door; a Ford Escort.

Why anyone in their right mind would buy a Ford Escort was beyond him—even if it was because you wanted to Buy American you could still do better than that. The car door opened and a woman got out—a blonde in big sunglasses, jeans, and a red shirt, her hair cut very short and tousled. She moseyed rather than walked out of his line of sight.

A second later his phone rang. Lois, his office manager. The space Flynn rented across from the Sierra Vista Mall was large enough for a reception area in front where Lois had her desk, a reasonably sized office for Flynn, and another smaller office that was presently being used as a storage area. It also had a convenient back-door exit for clients Flynn wasn't ready to deal with.

"Someone's here to see you, she walked right by me, didn't give her name," Lois said.

Flynn looked up. The woman he'd seen outside was standing at the door to his office. Too late for the back door. *"Val?"* he said.

"Do you mind?" His ex-wife Valentine took off the sunglasses, sat down in the client chair next to Flynn's desk, and reached in her purse. Out came a pack of cigarettes and a NASCAR lighter. She took out a cigarette and flicked on the lighter.

"Uh," said Flynn, "there's no smoking in here."

"You're kidding me." Val had gotten the cigarette lit and she squinted at him from behind a puff of smoke. Her hair was a punk kind of style probably supposed to be young and cool, but it made her look older.

"I'm not kidding you," Flynn said.

Val stared at him in disbelief. "You're telling me you have nervous clients, people with serious problems coming in here, and you don't even let them smoke?"

He did let clients smoke, of course he did, but he couldn't see why that applied to Val. "I thought you stopped smoking when we were still together," he said accusingly.

"I did."

"So the *coach* likes it that you smoke?"

Val moistened her fingers and pinched the cigarette out. She put it back in the pack. "You always give me such a hard time," she said. "Harry hates me smoking, I don't do it around him."

Flynn had been so proud of her when she'd quit smoking. Now it occurred to him for the very first time that the reason she had quit smoking back then was because she was getting involved with the coach.

"So what the hell *are* you doing here?" he asked.

"Wow," said Val. "My God. You're so *hostile.* What did I *do?*"

Flynn couldn't believe she was even asking that question. He could think of no answer that wouldn't draw him into something he wanted to avoid.

"Anyway," said Val, "smoking's not the only thing Harry gives me a hard time about. Seems like it's anything and everything lately." She sighed. "I heard you were doing really good."

"I'm doing okay," said Flynn. "Why aren't you in Portland, Oregon?"

"Because I'm here." Val stood up. "I'm staying at the Best Western. Look"—she leaned over his desk, found a pen—"I'll write it on this Post-it note, twenty-three, my room number, and my cell phone number. Give me a call if you feel like it—we could go out to dinner or something, talk about old times. I think of you, I really do." She paused. "Are you seeing anyone special?"

Flynn thought of Chloe instantly, Chloe Newcombe, who worked for the county attorney's office as a victim advocate. They'd been involved in a case together when he was still with law enforcement and it had kind of turned into more than that. But he hadn't seen her for several months actually so he wasn't sure why he thought of her so fast. "Not really," he said.

"Well," said Val, "think about it, okay? We could go to the Outback Steakhouse. It might be—"

The phone rang.

"—fun."

"Flynn Investigations," said Flynn. "Can I help you?"

Val paused at the door, looked back at him. She gave him a big toothy smile and a little wave.

Tucson was a good place for a gardener because you could work the entire year except for the monsoon season. The gardener hated the monsoons though he knew he shouldn't. After all, he was a gardener. When the monsoons came the desert blossomed and grew green. Everything he'd planted during the spring and early summer and that was just struggling along got a chance to really make it. But when the monsoons came he could only work in the mornings, because the rains tended to come in the afternoons. Or worse, he couldn't work at all because the ground would be too wet.

When he worked, he worked so hard he was too tired to think when he got home but when he wasn't working he thought. So he got other jobs, fixing things, outside things: fences and ramadas and gazebos.

He'd started off interested in horticulture, he liked the idea of calling himself a horticulturist, but he hadn't studied long enough for credentials for that or for Master Gardener. So he was a gardener. Until the monsoon, then half the time he was just a handyman.

It used to bother him, but he'd gotten so used to his life it didn't bother him anymore. Just his thoughts bothered him, he tried not to think because it didn't do any good, but even when his mind was blank, he could feel his thoughts pressing on that blankness trying to get through.

# part one

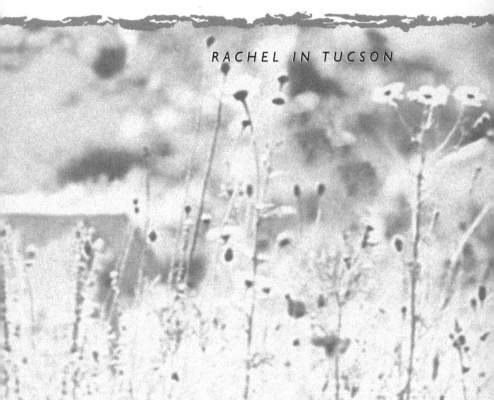

*RACHEL IN TUCSON*

# chapter one

RACHEL AND HER MOTHER, THE SINGER, were at the mall, at Dillard's, or was it Macy's? They didn't have the same taste, not at all, but her mom kept pointing out clothes she thought would be nice for Rachel—bright print tops, too bright and with sequins; Indian cotton gauzy skirts, floaty and see-through; ridiculous tie-dyed wide pants. "Try something on," her mom kept insisting, grabbing more and more stuff. "Just try one thing. You might even like it."

Heaps of stuff, mountains, and her mother kept on piling the bright happy clothes in her arms till Rachel could hardly see her anymore. "You need something new," her mother, the singer, said. "We have to find a song for you."

In the dark, Rachel opened her eyes. "Mom?" she whispered.

She knew better, it was just that little space before she woke up completely—sometimes when she dreamed of her mom it wasn't like that, her mother would be just at the edge of her vision, not quite real, but this time she was so sharp, so clear. This dream had started out, she and her mom, just like she wanted her mother to be, shopping with her now that she was lost to her, gone, gone forever and ever, then everything suddenly felt so crazy with the ending.

Rachel took a few deep yoga breaths. Even though she couldn't think why—it was just a bunch of piled-up clothes—that ending disturbed her; filled her with dread, dread that something awful was about to happen. When she was younger she'd had dreams like this a lot but as time went by she'd had them less and less—in fact, she hadn't had one in several months, maybe longer. Oh, God, were they starting up again?

*Why?* She'd tried so hard to allow no stress into her life whatsoever. Rachel took a few more yoga breaths, counting to ten on the in breath, ten on the out.

*You're fine.*

But she wasn't.

Beside her, her husband Scott lay sleeping on his stomach, wearing just a pair of plaid boxers, covers thrown off though it was a little chilly—the air-conditioning was set too high. *Scottie,* she thought, *at least I have Scottie, so handsome, so perfect*; an attorney, working as a misdemeanor prosecutor with the Pima County Attorney's Office. Mustn't wake Scottie—he tried so hard to be supportive that sometimes in a weird way she felt as though she were working even harder supporting him at being supportive.

The muscles in Rachel's neck and upper back were all tensed up, *no.* What time was it? The red numerals of the black digital clock showed 2:47. She slipped out from under the covers and went barefoot, out of the bedroom, through the living room, out the sliding glass doors to the pool.

She sat down on the edge and let her feet dangle in the water, swishing them back and forth, making little waves. For the first time in quite a while it hadn't rained yesterday or during the night. Late summer in Tucson, a cloudy night; the moon shining soft silver behind clouds and thunder grumbling somewhere over the mountains. Mingled with the chlorine from the pool was the smell of rain. The monsoons had been pretty active this year.

Somewhere in Tucson it would be raining right now probably, raining outside of Tucson maybe in one of the little desert towns, over in Cochise County. In Willcox, or Douglas, or even Dudley.

Rachel sighed. Except for one brief afternoon to testify at the trial, she hadn't been back to Dudley since her dad came and took her away right after her mom was killed. Now her mom had been dead for fifteen years, no—more like seventeen. At this point, Rachel didn't know if her memories of her mother were even real or just memories of something she'd been told or even seen in a movie and connected with.

Palm trees rose beyond the cinderblock wall that bounded the yard, their silhouettes looking strangely like . . . like Sideshow Bob from *The Simpsons*. It should have been funny but it wasn't, it was creepy. She took some more deep yoga breaths, ten counts in, ten counts out, but the muscles in her back kept tensing and her head felt light, bright, something whined like the sound of a saw far away but it wasn't real and she knew no one else could hear it.

Suddenly she smelled the sharp licorice tang of fennel, the fennel that grew in the drainage ditches in Dudley—it always happened during the rainy season when the fennel was almost as tall as she was, ten years old, and what was the song that played everywhere that summer? Madonna sang "Like a Virgin," but her mom liked Sade, "Is It a Crime," "The Sweetest Taboo." But no, weren't those songs earlier?

The whining grew louder, like a pack of hornets, why worry, it was so long ago, no one was going to come and get her, it wasn't real fear, it was anxiety. Did she still have some Ativan? She hadn't needed it for a while. She pushed herself up and went back inside, down the hall to the bathroom. She opened the medicine cabinet. Thank god—there it was, the amber-colored prescription bottle. But when she took it down it was empty.

*What the fuck?* Seeing it empty made her realize just how much she needed it right now. Why would you keep an empty bottle in the medicine cabinet? *Why?* Rage made her light-headed. Empty. It was so stupid, so unbelievably stupid, she threw the bottle as hard as she could against the wall. The bottle was plastic and light, it didn't even break, just fell harmlessly onto the tiled floor.

"Rachel?"

She turned around.

Scottie was standing in the doorway, blinking. "You okay?"

Her anger had dissipated some of the anxiety. It was still there but bearable. "Oh, Scottie, I'm sorry." She felt guilty. "You have to get up early for work. I didn't mean to wake you."

"What's *wrong?*"

"The usual," said Rachel.

Scottie rubbed his eyes. He looked so sweet standing there, so concerned and so tired. He must be so sick of this, she thought. *How can he stand me?*

"Your mom?" he said.

Rachel nodded.

"Sweetheart." She knew he didn't mean to, but he let a note of exasperation creep into his voice. "What can I *do?*"

What could he do? She could see all his good qualities; he was there for her when she needed him, a nice-looking man who worked hard. She saw him standing there but he was on a par with the porcelain sink, the pink towel left to dry on the shower rod, the open medicine cabinet. She couldn't feel his presence, as if she had just conjured up a hologram. *In fact,* she thought, *that's my whole life, not real, a hologram.*

"Nothing," she said. "There's nothing you can do. Go back to bed, sweetie, okay?"

# chapter two

DON CALLED THE NUMBER FOR THE HALFWAY
house the roofer had given him and made all the arrangements
with the director. Around nine the next morning a rust-colored
pickup truck arrived, dropped off three men and some tools, and
drove away. One of the men was young, very thin, and almost
frail, and the other two were older guys with scruffy beards and
hard muscles and multiple tattoos.

Don took them around back to the patio and showed them the
problem. Then he and Cici watched from the windows as the
men raised picks and shovels and hacked away at the dirt and
debris that had built up behind the retaining wall without quite
the vigor Don thought they might have displayed had they been
making more than minimum wage. Some kind of boom box blared
out as they worked, a country station—Trace Adkins, Toby Keith
singing about getting drunk and being somebody.

Their daughter Lisa had called that morning around eight to
say she and the kids were coming for their first visit next week.
Cici was thrilled. With any luck these relentless rains would finally
be over and surely the men would have finished digging out behind the wall. She understood that most of the men were down on
their luck, having been in the grip of an addiction they couldn't

control, and the director of the halfway house had assured Don that the crew he sent over were all DUI offenders and not real criminals, but still Cici thought they looked a little rough with their grubby T-shirts and tattoos to be hanging around her grandchildren. Or her daughter either for that matter.

They worked steadily till noon, you had to give them credit—no sloughing off—then the pickup truck came back and the driver, who turned out to be the director, a nice man called Pat, said he was taking the men to lunch at the Burger King. Don and Cici had Chinese chicken salad at home on the patio, enjoying the return of silence.

When the men came back, carrying big paper cups with the Burger King logo, Cici was in the guest room trying to figure out a way to fit Lisa and both kids in there, or maybe the kids would like to sleep out on the patio?—but what if it was still raining?—and Don was searching the closets for the air mattress.

She had a good view of the men from the guest room as they wielded their picks and shovels, smoked and talked and swore. Cici could hear every word because they hadn't brought back the boom box and the window was half open. They swore so much Cici just didn't know what she'd do if they were still working when the kids got here.

"Hey, man, what the fuck!"

"Son of a bitch!"

"*Jesus fucking* Christ!"

The swearing seemed to be escalating.

Cici wished they would stop. "Don," she called urgently. "Could you ask them to maybe tone it down?"

Feeling reluctant, Don went outside to see what the commotion was all about. The three men were standing behind the wall, so all he could see was their upper torsos, but they were all staring down at something, something unpleasant, by the looks on their faces. What *now*? Then the three men looked up at him simulta-neously, like three puppets pulled by the same string.

"Hey, uh . . . Mr., uh . . . you better come take a look at this."

Don walked over to the wall. "What is it?"

One of the older men guffawed. "You tell me," he said.

"I ain't touchin' it, man," said the other old guy. "You couldn't pay me. In fact, I think I quit."

The young thin one poked at the ground with his shovel, clearing away dirt. "Oh, man," he said. "Ronnie, you was right." He started shaking his head back and forth. "Man, oh, man," he said. "Man, oh, man. Better call the cops on this one. Lookee here, mister."

Don peered down and saw a human skull.


Rachel's cell chimed.

"Hello?"

"Hi, sweetie," Scottie said. "Feeling any better?"

"Much," Rachel lied, but she'd just taken an Ativan, so it was only half a lie.

"I would have stuck around, but I had court at eight. Don't cook tonight, I'll bring takeout. Special takeout. A surprise."

"Great! 'Bye."

Rachel closed her cell. She'd called her doctor at ten, when his office opened, and they'd called her prescription in, but it had taken till twelve-thirty for it to be ready. She'd paced around the pool for two hours, staving off the anxiety as best she could. Now she sat in her car in the parking lot outside Walgreen's, where she'd gotten the prescription, holding a bottle of water, watching the shoppers go in and out of Fry's next door and listening to the Dixie Chicks; Natalie Maines singing "Not Ready to Make Nice." She loved the Dixie Chicks, especially Natalie.

The Ativan hadn't really kicked in yet, but knowing it was going to was practically enough in itself. She took another sip of water and squeezed her eyes shut tight, disgusted with herself, which she often was. Once Scottie finished law school, she'd planned to go to graduate school, get a master's though she wasn't sure in what, but she'd chickened out because of the panic attacks. She didn't even have a real job, just looking decorative in an art gallery.

*You're stupid, you're boring, not even Scottie will love you anymore if you keep this up.*

Natalie Maines, on the other hand, was courageous, not afraid to criticize the President even if it alienated her fans and hurt her career. And here Rachel was—a woman sitting in a white Honda in a grocery store parking lot; a tiny speck, if that even, on Google Earth. Rachel, a woman who had seen counselor after counselor and still had anxiety attacks. She was sick of being Rachel, with nothing better to do than watch shoppers go in and out of Fry's.

What had she ever done for anyone? What had she even done for Kurt, for instance, for poor Kurt? He'd always been her pal. But most of all, what had she done for her mom? Cried for her, yes—but not even as much as Annie's mother, Rachel's grandmother, had cried. When Annie's parents were still alive, living up in Seattle, Washington, Rachel would go visit two weeks every summer. And every single night after dinner, her grandmother would still sit out on the screened-in porch in front and weep for her only child Annie.

They'd left Rachel fifty thousand dollars when they died. It sat in the bank making more money because Rachel had never touched it. It wasn't really hers—it was Annie's.

"I'm sorry, Rachel," Scottie had said, for once driven beyond his own limits from exasperation, "but that's the dumbest thing I've ever heard."

\* \* \*

Two police cars pulled up in front of Don and Cici's, red and blue lights flashing, and four policemen got out and went around the side of the house to the back yard, two in uniform and two in plain clothes. While the two in uniform strung yellow crime scene tape along the concrete wall with the hand-painted tiles and a ways up the hill behind, one of the men in plain clothes walked around aiming a camera at things that Don and Cici couldn't see.

The other man, who seemed to be in charge, walked over to them as they stood, appalled, on their patio with the pots of red and yellow marigolds. He was in his late forties with a full and handsome brown mustache.

"Sergeant Jack Nelson, investigator with the Dudley Police Department," he said.

They shook hands all around.

"Guy with the camera is Manny Rodriguez," he went on, "and the two uniforms are Pete Clark and Will Leuthe."

Cici and Don nodded as the names went through and exited swiftly from their minds. Cici had goose bumps on her arms though it wasn't cold. She rubbed them.

"I'd like you folks inside if you don't mind," said Sergeant Nelson. "Don't want any more contamination than we already have."

So they went inside to the living room and waited and waited. And waited. Cici kept thinking about Lisa and the kids. A body behind their retaining wall? A human skeleton? How could that be?

Finally Sergeant Nelson knocked on the patio door and Cici ran to open it.

"My . . . my daughter and her kids are coming next week," she said. "Do you think they'll be done with everything by then?"

"I sure hope so," said Sergeant Nelson. "Gee, this is hard on you folks. This place was up for sale, if I remember correctly, not that long ago."

Behind the photographer, Cici could see one of the uniformed policemen putting something into a brown paper bag. She tried not to see what it was.

"Six months." Don's voice came out gruff. He cleared his throat. "We bought it six months ago from Lulu and—what was his name, hon?"

"Vince," said Cici. "Lulu and Vince Biggars. They moved to Hawaii."

"How long they live here, you know?"

"Yes," said Don. "Five years. I remember Vince telling me."

"Got an address for them, by any chance?" asked Detective Nelson.

Don shook his head. "We paid cash," he said, "from the sale of our place in Glendale."

"What are you saying?" asked Cici excitedly. "That nice young couple—"

"Nice?" snorted Don. "They robbed us blind."

"—were *murderers*?" said Cici.

"Yes," said Don. "That's what we're wondering, Officer. Are we talking about a murder here?"

"In answer to your first question," said Sergeant Nelson, "body's been there a lot longer than five years, is my guess. Way before they were here. It was down pretty deep, would've taken a while for that much dirt to build up behind the wall."

"Oh. Maybe it's historical?" Cici said, suddenly hopeful. "Like an Indian or a miner."

"I really shouldn't comment on an ongoing investigation," said Detective Nelson. "But between you and me, folks, I think I'd categorize it more as a suspicious death."

Cici sat down abruptly on one of the attractive wrought-iron chairs. "So it *is* murder."

Sergeant Nelson looked away modestly. "It's a strong possibility."

"Someone was murdered right behind our house?" Cici covered her eyes. "All these years people must have lived here and didn't even know."

She wished she didn't know either. She wished Lisa and the kids weren't coming quite so soon. Maybe they could all meet in Tucson—off-season summer rates were quite cheap now for the fancy resorts. And Tucson was so much closer to Phoenix and there were so many beautiful retirement places around there, she'd seen the ads on TV—Green Valley, SaddleBrooke, Sun City, Heritage Highlands—sunny, clean, and welcoming places, full of active smiling people who looked like they were in their late thirties except with white hair. Funny, even though she'd never really paid any attention to those ads, she could see them so clearly now, all those tanned smiling people all waving, calling out, *Don and Cici, come on over!*

The Ativan was wearing off a bit by the time Scottie walked in with takeout, looking frazzled but handsome—because he'd had court today he wore a tie, askew now. Rachel did all the cooking but two or three times a week they ate takeout, sitting in the living room in front of the TV news.

"Aha," said Rachel just the way anyone would say aha. Normally, a hint of a lilt at the end. A*ha*. "AJ's Fine Foods. Expensive."

"Not cheap," said Scottie, "but I figured you needed a lift."

"Work!" said Rachel brightly. "How was work today?"

Scottie tugged off his tie and threw it across the room. "It was a bitch—that same domestic violence asshole I had a couple of weeks ago that I let plead out if he got counseling, he's back again, some people would rather destroy their lives . . ."

Rachel nodded sympathetically and tuned out, while Scottie

went on and on. He complained all the time but he loved his job, it gave him all the excitement he needed in his life, which meant, Rachel thought sadly, she didn't have to supply any.

They ate sushi, and grilled chicken with tropical fruit salsa, chili-crusted salmon fillet, and something with chipotles. Rachel ate carefully. It had cost, what? Probably fifty, sixty dollars, and she had no appetite. Scottie reminded her of her father sometimes, the way they both thought spending money would fix anything.

The first thing her father had done after he'd come to get her after her mother's murder was take her shopping for a whole new wardrobe.

As they ate they watched the news, the tail end of the national and then the local.

"In the wake of the drowning of a popular Dudley local, Bert Asher, now more breaking news from Dudley," said the anchorwoman on Channel Thirteen. "This afternoon, a body was unearthed from behind a retaining wall . . ."

The scene shifted to a picture of the Channel Thirteen crime reporter in front of a little hillside house.

Rachel exclaimed, "No! *No.*"

She closed her eyes on the memory of the news crews coming down to Dudley from Tucson after her mother's murder, acting all polite and concerned; *prying.* Alice, the good neighbor, had kept them away until Rachel's father came.

"What?" Scottie said.

". . . as yet unidentified," said the anchorwoman. "More on this later . . ."

"Switch, switch," said Rachel, her eyes still closed. "I don't want to hear about Dudley."

"It's okay," said Scottie. "Look, I changed the channel. *What Not to Wear.* Stacy and Clinton. You always like that."

# chapter three

SUCH A SUMMER OF DISASTER—FIRST THERE
was poor drowned Bert swept into the main drainage ditch and
then I heard on the six o'clock news they'd found a skeleton, human, buried behind a retaining wall on Ocotillo Street. They
showed a couple of shots of the wall and the hill beyond, it looked
like it was pretty far up the Gulch. A renovated place, by the looks
of the patio. The spokesman for the Dudley PD, and also the investigator, was Jack Nelson, whom I knew slightly.

"The investigation is ongoing," he said. "Couldn't even tell you
the sex of the victim right now."

As if all that weren't bad enough, my job as a victim advocate
for the Victim Witness Program at the county attorney's was kind
of going to hell. A few months before while she was still the Victim
Witness Program manager, my former boss Lucinda had walked
into her Tucson house late in the evening after a volunteer meeting in Dudley and was accosted by two men wearing ski masks and
brandishing guns. They tied her to a chair, took everything in her
apartment of any value, loaded it into a truck parked outside, and
drove away. The men were never caught. There were rumors they
might have done other things too but if they had, Lucinda wasn't
telling.

As a Victim Witness person Lucinda encouraged victims of crime to talk it all out, however she herself disliked appearing vulnerable in any way. Shortly after the incident she quit the job and moved away to California to be near her daughter in one of those L.A. suburbs—Downey, or Reseda.

"Safety plans, Chloe." Wearing dark stiff jeans, a light blue dress shirt, and a red tie, my new boss leaned back in his chair and regarded me over steepled fingers. He had a crew cut, blond, and resembled a jolly aging Marine.

"What?" I said.

Larry sighed with extreme patience. He'd just returned from a Victim Witness workshop in Phoenix. "Safety plans," he said again. "They came up several times at the workshop and I had to ask myself, are we doing enough to help all our victims develop a safety plan? In fact, are we doing anything at all?"

I hated Larry's bushy eyebrows and his close-cropped hair and his wire-rimmed glasses. Especially I hated the way he said *we* when he meant *you.* My dislike even extended to his extremely confident perky blond wife, a school nurse over in Sierra Vista, who occasionally popped in.

I took a deep breath. "Safety plans are more Linda's area," I said. Linda was our recently hired victim advocate for the misdemeanor court. "They're mainly for domestic violence cases—stuff like how to get out of the house, keeping the car gased up, important documents to take with you, et cetera, et cetera."

"Something to think about," said Larry. "Let's keep open minds, be creative in our thinking. It's easy to fall into ruts."

"Let me put it this way," I said. "In the serious felonies, which are what I deal with, when the defendant is most likely in custody, what would be the point of a safety plan?"

"Anyway." Larry coughed. "Let's move on to resources, I noticed reading over the old reports that we don't do as many referrals as we might. You might want to work on that. If a resource is out there it's wasted if we don't use it."

"What resources are you referring to specifically?" I asked.

He looked at me in mock surprise. "You've been with the program for a while, surely you must be familiar with them."

"We don't have many resources," I said between my gritted teeth, trying to keep the *you idiot* out of my voice. "This is a *rural* county."

Larry and his wife had moved here quite recently but surely he had noticed this was a rural county for god's sake.

He cocked his head. "No need to get defensive, we're both on the same side here—working together as a team to help victims." Actually, at work he didn't spend much time with victims, mostly he was gone at networking meetings, and when he was here he stayed in his office clinging to his computer. "How about that grant report, coming along all right?"

"I've been in a trial all week," I said. "Remember? It was that homicide where the victim was stabbed twenty-six times by her meth-addicted boyfriend."

The light dimmed in Larry's eyes. He had no interest in the details of crimes.

"And," I went on, "the report's not due for a month."

"Always good to finish early, though." He rubbed the palms of his hands together. "I like to review things pretty thoroughly before they go out."

"Oops," I said. "Was that my phone? I'll get on that grant report right now." I stood up. "Are we done?"

"For now," said Larry. "Is Linda here yet?"

"Uh, don't know," I said.

God, I missed Lucinda. She had had her faults but at least she wasn't all form and no content; and she had a brain. She didn't mouth catchphrases from some management book, she knew what a safety plan was, and she didn't go over my grant reports to correct the spacing.

Then mercifully Kelly, our secretary, called out to me, "Phone, Chloe."

"Got it." I scurried past her toward my office.

Victim Witness had been expanded a lot even before Lucinda left; we had our own secretary now, and we had Linda. Linda had a desk next to mine but there was no sign of her—she'd probably gone directly to justice court. She'd only been here six weeks, hired to do the misdemeanor cases plus fill in for me in superior court when necessary. I work twenty hours a week, with full benefits, which is about as much as I want to, but Larry had been making noises about needing someone who would be willing to work forty.

I sat down at my desk and picked up the phone.

"This is Chloe. Hello? Hello?"

But there was no one on the line.

"Kelly!" I called. "They hung up. Who was it?"

"Flynn! He said his name was Flynn."

"*Brian* Flynn? Are you sure?"

"I think so."

Flynn and I had been an item once for a while several months ago when he was still a cop, which was somewhat hard to figure out, because we didn't get along. He was basically an arrogant know-it-all pain in the ass and I was glad I'd missed the call, though not quite as glad as I should be. I guess a few memories still lingered.

Flynn had been with the Sierra Vista branch of the Cochise County Sheriff's Department for twenty years, and the whole time he'd chafed at the restrictions involved in being a cop. He liked to go his own way and now he'd done so—set up in his own investigation business; quite a successful business, from what I'd heard. He'd always been good at generating publicity, I thought scornfully—back when he was a cop in narcotics he was in the news all the time: Super Narc, they called him.

Why had he called anyway? I hoped he didn't think because we'd slept together a few times (*why?*) that he could call me whenever he felt like it for information, because whatever I dealt with involving victims was confidential.

Out the window it looked like more rain, gray clouds hovering over the little wooden houses. It was still morning, early for rain, but this year wasn't following the usual rules. And now Flynn was hovering. What did he want? What was it that had finished us off anyway, the last straw? *Deadwood*. Aha. It was *Deadwood*. The entire series was on my Netflix queue. It was all about the old Wild West so I'd thought he'd like it.

"I don't get it," he grumbled halfway through the second episode, Season One. "Why do they have to say fuck all the time, what's the point of that?"

"Realism," I said.

"Realism? What? You grew up in a house where people said fuck all the time?"

"No. But this is the *Wild West*."

"I get enough crap as a cop, why would I want to sit down and watch it on TV? Anyway, it's not realism, you know what it is?"

"No, what?"

"It's a frigging *liberal's* idea of realism."

"Well, that's what I am," I said, stung. "I'm a liberal and proud of it."

"Well, I'm a conservative," said Flynn. "A Republican. You know that."

"How could you be?" I cried, unable to help myself. "How could you have voted for that *idiot*?"

Flynn rolled his eyes in exasperation, looking up at the ceiling or possibly beyond to that pro-life, hardworking Lord. "What the hell was I doing here?" he muttered just before he stormed out. *Was*.

To distract myself from thinking about him anymore, I checked my e-mail. Netflix had received *Deadwood: Season Two,* disc three. I looked around at the familiar office, at my desk, at Linda's opposite me and the one in the corner for volunteers; the office plant, a leather-leafed viny thing that thrived on fluorescence; the cartoon above my desk that had been there for years, yellowed with age, two guys in a prison cell, one saying to the other, "I've tried victimless crimes but I'm a people person."

I'd always liked my job a lot, had almost lost it once, but that had worked out. Now with Larry in charge I had a nasty little vision of the future: victims would be calling but getting a recording, *Welcome to the Victim Witness Program, we care about your call and we care about you. If you are the victim of a misdemeanor, press one, if you are the victim of a felony, press two. Thank you. The wait time for our automated counselor for felonies is currently five minutes.*


Brian Flynn stood in the kitchen of the Café Olé restaurant in Old Dudley with the restaurant's owner, Shirley Mack.

"Background checks came up clean, like I told you," he said to Shirley, "except for the marijuana charge on Freddy."

"That's no big deal." She laughed. "I'm surprised they didn't all—" She stopped and her cheeks flushed pink. "Didn't you use to be a narcotics . . ."

"Not anymore," said Flynn. "Don't give it a thought. Anything you say to me is completely confidential. Anyway, so that's it. The surveillance camera will be up and running by the weekend."

Outside it had started to rain, pinging loudly now on the line of metal trash cans in the alleyway behind.

"I hate being so sneaky," said Shirley, raising her voice over the rain. "Maybe I should just let the staff know I have the surveillance. Wouldn't that be enough?"

"If people know it's there, they can figure out how to get around it," said Flynn patiently. "Look at it this way—you want a successful restaurant or you want to be a nice guy?"

"Both." Then Shirley smiled at him in a way that seemed to mean more than it probably actually did.

"Life is full of tough choices," said Flynn.

"Like to try some of my habañero chili sorbet?" asked Shirley, hopefully.

Flynn looked apologetic. "Sorry. Gotta run."

It was raining hard by the time he got to his black Land Rover down the alleyway, soaking the blue oxford shirt he used to wear to court and now wore to see clients and chilling his skin, even now in early August. His waterproof windbreaker lay on the passenger seat of his vehicle.

He jumped in, started it up, and turned onto Main Street. The rain darkened the brick fronts of the nineteenth-century buildings and sheeted on the tar surface of the street. Various arty types shivered in colorful and as always, in his opinion, inappropriate dress for this occasion or any occasion whatsoever. The tourists handled it a little better, thought Flynn gloomily, in their athletic Eddie Bauer and L. L. Bean outfits.

His office was in Sierra Vista and most of his jobs were there too, but he took jobs in Old Dudley from time to time to keep his hand in. And since he was going to be in Old Dudley anyway, he'd tried to call Chloe earlier, to see if maybe they could get together for coffee at the Dudley Coffee Company, which was just a couple of blocks downtown from Café Olé, or possibly dinner.

They'd stopped seeing each other a few months ago, he'd forgotten the reason—just that she'd gotten mad about something or other, but maybe she'd calmed down by now. Or maybe not, he'd thought as he waited for Chloe to come to the phone, so he'd hung up—it wasn't worth it.

Now he was heading for home, over in the foothills on Highway 90 out of Sierra Vista. It was just as well; with Chloe, he never knew what he was getting into.

Not that he thought of her that much; he was incredibly busy—he'd taken on an office manager who initially came in the three days of the week he was officially open to the public, but that had quickly gone up to five. Lois Hodges was retired from twenty years working dispatch for Sierra Vista PD and she handled calls and billing, and she was so busy he was even thinking about having her come an occasional Saturday—with overtime, of course.

She was good too—had a sense of people, like who to be folksy with and who not.

Plus, with Val his ex floating around town, he hadn't called her and didn't plan to—he didn't need any aggravation from Chloe, didn't need any more aggravation than he already had.

He probably only thought about Chloe once or twice a day, if that. But with the rain coming down so hard, he thought of her now. She had that leak in her roof at home over her desk and he was willing to bet she'd never done a thing about it.

# chapter four

WHEN HER MOM WAS AT WORK, RACHEL
hung out with her friends, Beth who lived down on the Gulch, and
Manny who was the grandson of the neighbors Juan and Lupe.
They used to fill balloons with water and stand on the porch and
throw the balloons at people down on the street, until someone
called the police. The house was on Laundry Hill and you had to
climb a short but steep flight of stairs to get to it. The house was
wood like most all of Dudley houses, with a tin roof and quite a big
front porch. White paint with dark green on the window trim,
paint peeling off some.

Her mom was house-proud enough she would have painted it
if the landlord, Mr. Samuels, had agreed to pay for the paint, but
he owned a bunch of houses in town and he didn't care—he was
waiting for the big housing boom that was supposed to hit Dudley so he could sell all his houses for top dollar—fixing them up
would just eat into the profits.

So the house never did get a fresh coat of paint, but the faded
paint kind of went with the garden her mom had put in, purple
sage and lavender, bronze and yellow marigolds, and pink cos-
mos growing among the gray rocks and rusty objects—an old

birdcage, a water heater with an asparagus fern growing in it, a piece of rusted curvy gate.

Inside were two bedrooms, quite a big living room, and the kitchen. The living room windows looked out over the Gulch and all the beat-up Salvation Army furniture was covered with something bright and third world—Indian or Mexican or Peruvian or Guatemalan—Annie loved loud colors and hand-woven fabrics. And where there wasn't furniture there were plants.

After it happened, Rachel's father Phil Glenn came and took her away and she lived with him in a big house in Tucson, where all the furniture had been bought in a regular store and not a thrift store and her clothes too. The house had beige walls, white carpeting, and Italian leather furniture. It was very, very clean—not that her mother hadn't cleaned, but you could only freshen up old things so much.

In Phil's house, Lourdes came in to clean once a week, and no one worried about money like they did at her mother's, except in an abstract way that had nothing to do with things like food and clothing and coming up with the rent. She and her mother had been poor and the funny thing was Rachel hadn't even known it till she moved in with her father.

Years later she'd asked her father, "How come you never sent child support?"

"I tried to but she wouldn't take it."

Rachel wondered why not. They could certainly have used the help. Later, when she was older and had lived with her father for a while, and had met a few of her father's girlfriends, all doomed to disappointment, she had a better idea why.

Sometimes when she came home from school to her father's house and no one was there, or when she was lying in bed at night, Rachel would close her eyes and go through the house in Dudley, walk through it room by room: here was the kitchen with the fern in the window, and the refrigerator whose door was kept closed with a strip of duct tape, and the sun spiders her mother let live in the upper corners; the bright cloth in the living room and the stereo with the tape cassettes of her mother's favorites. Carly Simon, Emmylou Harris, Gram Parsons. Rachel's bedroom, with its narrow bed and dancing moon and stars painted on the ceiling by her mom.

Walking back through every room except her mother's bedroom.

"Let's go over this again, Rachel," Detective Wishman had said. "Just to make sure we've got it right. Kurt was angry with your mom a lot?"

"He was just arguing," she said. "Not . . . anything else."

"Did you ever see Kurt do anything besides argue when he was mad at your mother?"

"Not really. One time he took a drawer out of a chest of drawers and dumped it in the trash."

"Really? Why did he do that?"

"I think," said Rachel, "because she put everything in that drawer she didn't know what to do with. It was kind of to show her she didn't need it."

"Ah. So anyway, Kurt was angry at your mom. You said that."

"I didn't say it right. He was just an *annoyed* kind of angry. I mean, I got that way too, with my mom."

"But it was different with you, wasn't it? I'm interested in how it was with Kurt. Why was he angry?"

"Because." Ten-year-old Rachel looked right back at him. "Because he loved her; isn't that mostly why people get angry at each other?"


"He loves her a lot," Captain Bert Coleman told Flynn. "And Will, you know, he's my best buddy forever."

Coleman was stationed at Fort Huachuca, a major military installation that anchored Sierra Vista on one end. Not only that, the fort had been there longer than the city. It housed the Army Intelligence Center and Flynn had several clients from there.

In his camouflage fatigues, Coleman sat easy in the client chair, a big blond man with steel-blue eyes, one heavy-booted foot resting on his knee. The boot was well polished, a man for the army to be proud of.

"I can tell you right now," Coleman went on, "in the midst of all the action and danger and fucking *boredom,* Will's heart would break if he found out she . . ." He shrugged.

Flynn nodded. "Got a photograph?"

Coleman pushed across a manila envelope.

Flynn opened it and slid out the photograph. A young woman with slightly buck teeth and lots and lots of ash-blond hair smiled at him. This was his third tail on a marital partner in a month. Marriage was going to hell.

"Goddamn it!" Coleman said suddenly. He leaned over and banged a fist on Flynn's desk. "What the hell is wrong with her— guy's risking his life for his country and she's fucking whoring around. I know she is. I *know* it." He sank back in his chair. "Oh, *man.*"

"Hey." Flynn gave him a look. "Take it easy. I mean, are you sure? You've seen her with some guy in a compromising situation?"

"No. But she's been buying a lot of new clothes. Sexy, they look good on her. Tanya works mornings at the senior center, so what does she need to look good for?"

"New clothes," said Flynn. He remembered when Val had started wearing heels with her *jeans,* no less. Val, who liked to lounge around in sweats.

"It's not like they have that much money. You ask me," Coleman said, "someone's been paying for those clothes, and it's not the government. She's been going to Tucson two or three times a week on a regular basis. At least that's what she says. No one knows if that's where she really goes. You know?"

"I'm on it," Flynn said. "I need just a little more information and I'm good to go."

"The thing is," Coleman said, "guys come back from Iraq and find out their wife's been screwing around, man, you know, they're still in war mode . . ."

Flynn nodded, an especially nasty memory coming back to him—a soldier a couple of years ago who had cut off his wife's head and kept it in a closet.

"This is as much for Tanya as it is for Will."

"I hear you," Flynn said.

The funny thing was, when Val started messing around, in spite of all the signs, in spite of him being an investigator, for Christ's sake, he never put two and two together. He'd trusted her. Well, he wouldn't make that mistake again.

# chapter five

BORED, RACHEL SAT BEHIND A SMALL DESK AT
the Hartman Gallery, where hardly anyone had come in all day.
The theme of the current show was "Critters." From the center of
the high-ceilinged white space a spot highlighted a large insectlike
creation six feet high of wire and papier-mâché. Other, smaller in-
sect creatures stood on display blocks, and in the window three
large bronze-colored scorpions were having what appeared to be a
tea party, their delicate legs holding tiny cups, their stingers curved
gracefully to one side.

"Fun," Roxanne, the owner, had said when they were setting it
up. "This show is such *fun.*"

Rachel noticed that while Roxanne used the word a lot, nothing really seemed that fun to Roxanne, she was a business-
woman through and through. Rachel also knew that Roxanne
had hired her because Rachel looked like the kind of person
who could afford expensive clothes and had taste. Like she
probably looked right now: white capris, white polo shirt, red
ballet flats, and pearls.

Conservative. It was ironic because all the artists looked like
hippies. If Rachel's mom were still around she would look like a
hippie too, probably, still.

"It's the goddess!" someone said. "Roxanne's very own Ice Queen."

Rachel looked up. She hadn't heard anyone come in. But here was one of the artists from a previous show: unkempt curly graying hair, long nose, cut-off jeans, a black T-shirt with the neck ripped, and faded blue flip-flops. He carried a bunch of newspapers under one arm.

"Hi, Ethan," she said.

Ethan set the newspapers on the counter next to Rachel. "Done with these," he said. "You can catch up on your reading." He paused. "You're very pretty," he said.

"Thank you," said Rachel, her voice more polite than grateful.

Ethan began a tour of the show, pausing at various pieces.

"Scorpions are fine as far as it goes," he said, "but really, it's taking the easy way. A scorpion! Eek! Drinking tea. What? Scorpions are Winnie the Pooh now? Double eek. Where's the revelation? The epiphany?"

Rachel wished the phone would ring so she could be engaged with something besides Ethan.

"Where? Where?" Ethan persisted.

Rachel didn't answer.

"She's bored with me," Ethan said to no one, returning to the counter. "You *are* pretty, Rachel, but you don't sizzle. Say hi to Roxanne for me."

Rachel watched him go out the door. He'd left the pile of newspapers. She reached for the ones on top. An old *Tucson Weekly,* last night's *Citizen,* this morning's *Daily Star.* She'd read the *Tucson Weekly* already. The *Star* had a little banner on the top that read "Mystery of Old Dudley Skeleton Thickens. Police seek help from general public. See Metro section."

Suddenly she wanted to see what it said. The article was on the front page right of the Metro section, same headline as the banner.

Below were some photographs, one of what appeared to be a backpack and the other a close-up of a ring. The ring was a silver braid, ends flattened out to form the shape of a marijuana leaf.

For a moment, Rachel couldn't breathe.

Wynn.

That ring belonged to *Wynn*. What was it doing here? She remembered it so clearly because it was a marijuana leaf and Wynn had joked about it with her mom. She'd never seen any other ring like it. She could see Wynn right now, in her mom's kitchen, saying something stupid, making her mom laugh. She could see all of them, Teddy and Billy and Wynn: the band. Teddy played guitar, Billy drums, and Wynn the bass. Wynn was her mom's favorite, she used to call him her best friend.

And Kurt. She hadn't seen him since the trial so long ago—but she'd heard a rumor somewhere that he was living in Tucson. Had he seen the paper? Would he see this too and know it was Wynn's ring?

And Rachel remembered something else. Wynn had gone off not long before her mom was killed. Everyone thought he'd just up and left town without bothering to tell anybody. Flaky. Except for her mom, who always forgave Wynn, everyone else had been mad at him, really mad because they'd had to find some other bass player for the night's gig at the last minute and he'd been lousy.

She called Scottie.


It rained into the afternoon, stopped, started again as I was coming out of court with Patsy Wolhart, whose husband had shot her in the arm, then tried to strangle her after the gun jammed. She'd traveled to court from an undisclosed location to attend the hearing of a motion to modify conditions of release, so she could stand up and explain to the judge why her husband should not be let out of jail.

The motion was denied and Patsy was happy, bubbly almost, as we came out of the courtroom and walked together to the front entrance. Outside the sky was smoky gray behind the dark cypress trees and it was raining, pretty hard.

"Thanks again," Patsy said over her shoulder, as she started down the steps holding the copy of the court calendar I'd given her earlier over her head against the rain. She still looked happy, but sooner or later he was going to get out. At the bottom of the steps she turned and waved: a dark-haired woman, not quite pretty, in a red cotton blouse that washed her out; fragile, in danger.

I wondered again why Flynn had called yesterday.

I stopped in my office briefly to see if he'd called back, more out of curiosity than because I wanted to talk to him. He hadn't. As a twenty-hour person I was done for the day as soon as my work was. I headed for home.

How long had I lived here? I counted up—ten years, more than I would have thought. I might not have stayed but I had inherited the house from my brother's lover, Hal. AIDS had killed my brother James years ago and Hal died not that long after. My other brother Danny was straight as straight could be and for years now had lived in a Buddhist monastery in Vermont.

My parents, oh, my parents—after James's death, Danny and I were both adults and they seemed to decide they were done with parenting. They're academics (Julio-Claudian Building Programs: Eat, Drink and Be Merry) and while I'm sure either of us is welcome to pay a visit at any time, they are never home—always traveling to research some aspect of life in some long-ago Roman time.

There is the occasional postcard.

I drove up the rain-slick hill to my house and pulled into the carport. Orange Mexican sunflowers, planted by a bygone ill-chosen lover, bloomed vividly along the side, freshened by the rains. The house is typical Dudley: old wood, frame, and small—two bedrooms. As I opened the door into the kitchen, Big Foot, my cat, scuttled in, his gray stripy fur soaking wet. From the second bedroom, converted into a home office, I could hear the metallic ping-ping-pinging of rain as it fell from the leak in the ceiling into the large stainless steel pot I'd placed below.

"I checked on Detective Wishman, who was the chief investigator on your mom's case," said Scottie, "just in case you wanted to contact him directly, but he's retired."

Rachel shook her head. "No, I don't want to contact him at all." She made a face. "I mean, why should I? He screwed everything up the first time."

"Sweetheart," said Scottie. He looked at Rachel across the table at the El Macayo Restaurant, then reached over and squeezed her hand. "My little sweetheart. Are you holding up all right?"

"Yes. Fine." She'd taken two Ativans but why mention that? "So what do you think?"

"Well . . ." Scottie picked up a chip and dipped it into the salsa. "The most straightforward thing to do would be to call Dudley PD, tell them you think you know who the body is and why and any other information you might have about this guy Wynn, such as . . . ?"

"My mom's best friend, a bass player—"

"Whatever," Scottie said.

"Then what would Dudley PD *do*?"

"I don't know. They're a small department, not very well funded either. But with new information . . ." Scottie shrugged. "Maybe they'd go all-out, if, ho ho, they weren't already busy with what they have now and brand-new stuff. I guess the worst-case scenario is they open it up and don't do much at all."

"Like they did the first time," said Rachel.

"I didn't say they would," said Scottie. "Just the worse-case. Look, sweetie, as an officer of the court, I urge you to let Dudley PD know what you suspect."

"Please, no," said Rachel. "It can wait a little bit. He must have been there for years, so what does it matter how soon? Maybe . . ." Her mouth trembled slightly. "Maybe someone else will come forward."

"Yes, of course." Scottie reached over again and covered her hand with his. "You're right. You can wait."

"What about a private detective? You said you'd look into that."

"Before we go there, depending on the circumstance, I have to warn you—that kind of thing can be expensive, you know."

Rachel raised her eyebrows. "So? I have money. I have my mom's fifty thousand."

"If that's the kind of thing you want to use it for."

"Of course it is. You said on the phone, Scottie, you *promised,* you'd look into that."

"Okay, okay." Scottie raised his hands defensively. "I did. I checked out investigators here in Tucson, there are several good ones here, but then I thought, no, it would be best if I found someone down there in Cochise County. And I got a name, Brian Flynn—he's a former detective with the Cochise County Sheriff's Department, so he knows the terrain and he comes highly rec-ommended."

# chapter six

AS SOON AS I GOT TO WORK THE NEXT MORN-
ing I ran over to the courthouse across the narrow street that separated it from the county attorney's offices, but there were no
victims waiting for me in the vast marble lobby. I trudged back
across and up the steps that led to my office. Kelly, our secretary,
was at her desk on the phone. Behind her, the screen saver on her
computer said *Jesus Is Coming. Look Busy.* Kelly rolled her eyes
at me in a significant way.

Uh-oh.

Out of the corner of my eye I could see Larry in his office in
front of his computer. He rose as I went by. I had a sudden urge
to just keep going, out the door and into my car and far away, but
I suppressed it.

"Chloe," he said.

"Yes?"

"Now that you're here, I'd like to go over a few things with you.
I've already discussed it with Linda and Kelly. A project we need
to be working on. We really need some *serious change* here."

"Oh?"

"We're not taking full advantage of our computers. There's no
reason why every victim we encounter can't be in a file online so

we can all have access. Starting *now* every victim you're dealing with needs to be entered into the system, I've already set up a form. Then, whenever you have a spare moment, you can enter earlier victims you're still working with."

Data entry. A great cloud of ennui descended over me.

"Why?" I whined. "I already keep track of victims and services for the grant reports."

"I've seen your notes," said Larry. "They look like chicken scratches and no one but you knows what they mean."

"So what? Why would anyone have to know what they mean but me? I do my own reports."

"You could be sick, or hit by a car."

"Killed in plane crash," I said, "or better yet murdered. Murdered would be best, then I could be one of our grant statistics."

Behind me I heard Kelly give a quickly suppressed giggle.

"And worst of all," said Larry as if my impending violent death were a mere trifle, "we could be *audited.*"

"Ah," I said. *Chicken scratches?*

"Linda thinks it's an excellent idea. Kelly too. Right?" He turned and looked at Kelly, who nodded obediently. He turned back to me. "You've been here a long time," he said. "It's natural to resist change. I'd sit down with you right now and go over the whole thing but I've got Rotary."

Well, thank God for that.


Scottie exited the I-10 freeway onto Highway 90 and drove the thirty-some miles past Whetstone and Huachuca City, then turned left onto Fry Boulevard at the light by the entrance to Fort Huachuca. He looked over and smiled at Rachel. "Still doing okay?"

Rachel smiled back. "Yes." He'd taken the day off to come with her to Sierra Vista to meet with the detective.

She had to do this, she knew she had to, but she didn't really want to be here—but at least if she had one of those panic attacks where she couldn't breathe Scottie would be here to take her to the hospital.

Sierra Vista was pretty much the way she remembered—all new and jangly, one of those places that seems to get newer every day. Fry Boulevard, the main street, was jammed with cars, trucks, SUVs, and every fast-food franchise known to man and could have been a street in Tucson. They even had a Target now, she noticed, across from where Scottie had stopped at a light. Her mom would have liked Target.

She had taken an Ativan this morning but it didn't seem to be working as well as before. Maybe she should have taken two. Maybe it was all a scam and the Ativan only worked if you believed it did. What if she stopped believing?

*Another day,* she thought. *How do I get through this one?*

Scott reached over and squeezed her hand. "I just want you to be okay." The light changed to green and he turned right. "That's all I want in the whole world."

For some reason Rachel thought of that movie about the Dixie Chicks—*Shut Up & Sing*—except it was *Shut Up & Be Okay.* That wasn't fair. She looked away from Scottie, out the window at anywhere, USA. She'd come here with her mom, mostly to shop the thrift stores, but it wasn't the kind of place that retained memories. She tried to think of the last time she'd been here.

"*Sears,*" she said suddenly.

"What about Sears?"

"We were in Sears, my mom and I," said Rachel. "They were playing music—to sell stereos, I guess. They were playing Madonna, she was singing 'Express Yourself,' and my mom started to dance."

"Ha," said Scott. He turned left.

"She was a really good dancer. She danced with her whole body like she really meant it. Everyone was staring at her." Suddenly Rachel felt a rush of pride, remembering. "But she didn't care. She—"

"And here we are," said Scott.

He parked and Rachel got out. In front of her was a pink two-story stucco building with wrought-iron stairs going to the second floor. At one end on the first floor was an eye doctor and on the other was a certified public accountant. Somehow that was reassuring, that the private investigator would have an office here between two such bland and ordinary endeavors.

Ordinary. That was it, that was what she wanted—she'd been trying to be ordinary for the last seventeen years. And though she could put up a good front—the exercise classes, the nice all-American upper-middle-class clothes, the pretty friends, even her husband for heaven's sake, she had never really achieved it.

Rachel trailed behind Scott, skirting a giant cactus in a big terra-cotta pot. Ahead was the office, PRIVATE INVESTIGATIONS was all it said, painted on the oak door in neat discreet black letters, then Scott was going in the door and she went in after him.

"Hi!" said a solidly built, ordinary-looking woman at the front desk. She had graying curly hair with a pencil stuck behind her ear. "If you're the Macabees, he's—"

"Rachel and Scott Macabee," said a man's voice, cutting her off. "Am I right?"

Flynn, thought Rachel, and turned. He looked like a Flynn: dark hair cut short, dense black eyes, stubborn jaw. *Black Irish. Bet he drinks too.*


Flynn walked them back to his office, grabbed an extra chair on the way. Rachel and Scott sat. The husband, Scott, had mentioned he was a misdemeanor prosecutor with the Pima County

Attorney's Office. That was interesting. Back behind his desk, Flynn regarded them for a moment, looking for a context. Scott hadn't explained anything when he set up the appointment, except that he was making it for his wife.

Nice-looking couple, the kind that would be right at home on a country club golf course: both blond and good-looking, he in a dark polo and khakis, she in a pink-and-white-striped polo and white capris; one of those thin touch-me-not blue-eyed blondes without a hair out of place, looked like she came from money and never had to work a day in her life. Which meant, nowadays, she could be a doctor or a lawyer.

"So." Flynn steepled his fingers. "What can I do for you?"

"That body they found buried behind a wall in Old Dudley?" said Scott.

Flynn nodded.

"My wife is pretty sure she knows who it is."

"Oh, really?" Flynn tilted forward, his feet hit the ground flat, he grabbed a pen and pulled a legal pad closer. He looked at Rachel with far more interest than he'd felt only a second ago.

"It's Wynn, Wynn Wykoff." She pushed a wing of blond hair back uncertainly.

"Wynn Wykoff," Flynn repeated.

"My mother sang with a band, the Point of No Return. Teddy Radebaugh played lead guitar, Billy Dodds the drums, and Wynn bass and lead guitar."

"When was this?"

"Seventeen years ago. I remember when he disappeared and everyone thought he'd just left town and hadn't told anyone. And all that time I guess he was . . ." She bit her lip.

Flynn looked at her closely. "The body was pretty much decomposed, from what I understand. How—"

"I—I recognized the ring. It was in the paper. It's an unusual one, custom-made—a silver marijuana leaf. My mom and Wynn joked about it. Wynn and my mom were kind of like best friends."

"Aha," said Flynn. "I'm sure Dudley PD will be greatly relieved not to have to spend a fortune figuring out who this person is. But why not just contact them?"

"Because," Rachel said, "well, this is . . . really about my mother. My mother was murdered. Wynn supposedly left town about a week before. Her name was Annie Glenn." She paused and looked at Flynn as if he might recognize the name.

Flynn shook his head. "Doesn't ring any bells. Tough on you, huh? Tell me about it."

"I was ten years old," said Rachel. "My mother and I lived here in Cochise County, in Old Dudley. Twenty-nine Laundry Hill. We were, um, I guess you would say poor. My mom didn't really care about money, she just liked to have fun. Anyway it was summer. Like now. July twenty-sixth. I went to my friend Beth's house, Beth Pearson, to spend the night, and my mom had a date with her boyfriend Kurt. Kurt Dickens. They were going to a Mexican restaurant just across the line. The next morning . . ."

She paused and took a breath. Her face was white.

Scott touched her shoulder. "Want me to take over from here, sweetie?" he said.

*"No."* Flynn saw annoyance flicker briefly in Rachel's eyes, then it was gone.

"It's okay," she said, but she didn't really look okay. "I've only told the story to a million therapists."

There was a pause. Flynn's office had one large window, looking out on the parking lot. He'd closed the shades for privacy, but you could hear traffic faintly: a semi rumbling, the whine of a siren.

"The next morning," Rachel went on, "I left Beth's about eight o'clock and walked home. It wasn't far. Nothing's far from anything else in Old Dudley. My mom worked at the Food Co-op but it didn't open till ten, so when I got home and called out and she didn't answer I thought maybe she'd spent the night at Kurt's."

"Kurt's?"

"Kurt Dickens, like I said. Her boyfriend." Rachel took a deep breath. "Then I thought maybe she was just sleeping in, so I went to her bedroom." Rachel took another breath. "The door was closed. I knocked in case, you know, Kurt was there. But no one answered. So I opened the door." She stopped.

"Sweetie," said Scott. "You okay?"

"*No,*" said Rachel, so fiercely that Scott flinched, "but so what? I opened the door," she went on, looking steadily at Flynn, "and I saw my mom. She was lying in bed wearing her favorite old purple T-shirt she liked to sleep in. Her face, her actual face, looked fine, like she was asleep, and I remember thinking, *Mom got new sheets?* Because they were dark red all around her. It was just unreal, it didn't make any sense, so I went up closer to figure it out and that's when I realized the top, the top," Rachel began to stutter, "the t-t-top of her head was gone."

Tears welled up in her eyes and spilled down her cheeks. "She—she'd been shot. Later on, they told me—it was once, just once. In the head."

Scott reached over and took her hand. She let him. Flynn opened his desk drawer, pulled out a box of Kleenex, and pushed it toward her. Rachel took one and blew her nose. "I'm sorry," she said.

"For what?" said Flynn almost angrily. "You don't have a thing to apologize for." They always said they were sorry, victims, when they cried. Why was that? Flynn preferred they not cry, it hampered the investigation as far as he was concerned, but who the hell could blame them? What really astonished Flynn the most from his days as a cop was how people even managed to survive some of the stuff that happened to them.

Rachel stabbed at her eyes with the wad of Kleenex. "Anyway," she went on, "I ran outside and over to Alice's. Alice Hayes, our neighbor. She called the police."

Flynn nodded.

"After that," Rachel went on, "they asked me about a million questions but it's kind of all a blur. These people from Channel Four and Channel Nine came with cameras—the police wouldn't let the media take pictures of me but they filmed the house. I stayed over at Alice's and someone called my dad and he came from Tucson and got me. I haven't been back to Dudley since then except for the trial. Just the one day." She stopped. No one spoke.

"Annie's boyfriend, Kurt Dickens, was charged," said Scott. "It went to trial and he was found not guilty."

"It's my duty to urge you"—Flynn leaned forward—"to go to Dudley PD. It seems to me to be enough of a connection to re-open the whole case with your mom. You said Wynn was her best friend—boyfriends get jealous of best friends. You know because of double jeopardy they can't try Dickens again for your mom's murder but they could sure as hell try him for Wynn's."

"*No*. It wasn't *like* that." Rachel was almost shouting. Her face reddened. She clenched her fists. "Kurt shouldn't have been charged in the first place. They just decided he did it and they didn't look anywhere else. It was hell for him. Now I'm afraid they'll do it all over again."

"You in touch with Kurt now?" Flynn asked.

She shook her head. "I haven't seen him since the trial. He didn't do it. I know it. I know you have to tell the police, but please can't you investigate a little bit first, find some other suspects?"

Flynn hesitated. The body had been decomposing for seventeen years. A back-burner kind of case. Not some brand-new homicide with a nervous public howling for the solution. He glanced surreptiously at his watch. Eleven-thirty. Today was one of the days Will in Iraq's Tanya went to Tucson, without fail, faithfully, like clock-work, right after she got off work from her part-time job at the se-nior center around noon.

"Tell you what." Flynn spread his fingers wide. "I'll hold off on telling Dudley PD till I run down whatever files are out there. See what it looks like to me."

# chapter seven

ON THE PHONE, BONNIE KAUFMAN WEPT. SHE
wept because the man she'd thought loved her had molested her
daughter, she wept because her daughter had lost a piece of her
childhood and been irretrievably damaged, she wept because the
guy was out on bond—*not even in jail*—and she wept because
everything was *taking so goddamn long.*

"I'm sorry, Chloe," she sobbed. "I know it's not your fault.
Thank you for listening to me."

"Not a problem at all," I said. "Call me anytime."

I made my usual chicken-scratch notes. After Larry had gone to
Rotary, Kelly and I had had a little session where we took turns
tearing Larry to shreds, then I'd taken two calls from victims, the
second being Bonnie Kaufman. I hadn't had time to check my
e-mail for a while and when I did there was the usual long involved
memo from Larry. I read it hurriedly, searching for content, but
found none.

For a moment I felt light-headed and just sat at my computer,
staring off into space. I was angry. I was so angry at Larry and
what he was doing to my job and its consequent effect on my life
that I wanted to take my keyboard and throw it across the room.

I went out to my car and drove downtown to check my mail at

the post office. Main Street was ridiculously crowded as usual, tourists moseying along like cattle crossing the street anytime and anywhere they felt like, not bothering with the crosswalks specifically put there for their use. In my sour mood, I hated them all, self-satisfied, selfish, and on vacation, as if the people who actually lived here didn't have lives and schedules and deadlines to meet, didn't need sidewalks that weren't blocked and clogged up with tourists.

Not only that, I thought as I circled looking for a place to park, what about some of the residents? Those guys who always hung around at the tables outside the Dudley Coffee Company, watching people go in and out of the post office. Middle-aged and old guys who had never grown up, never committed to a life: Peter Pans, tainted forever by the likes of Charles Bukowski and Neal Cassady.

After circling a few times I gave up, parked illegally, and scooted into the building. There was one envelope in my box. Oh, goody, my electric bill.

I drove back and as I was coming in, Marilu, the receptionist, said, "Call for you. Want to take it?"

"Who is it?"

"Brian Flynn."

"Okay." I went back to my desk and picked up the phone. "Hello. This is Chloe."

"Flynn."

There was a brief pause and then we both spoke at once, drowning each other out.

"Sorry," shouted Flynn. In the background I could hear rumbling.

"What's that noise?" I asked. "Where are you?"

"The I-10 approaching Tucson. I'm on a case."

"Ah," I said. "Well, you called. Go ahead."

"I just got hired by a victim to investigate a case and the last time I checked out victims' rights, I understood they're entitled to see the files on their case except for stuff the judge has specifically ordered sealed." He paused. The whole speech sounded sort of stilted, rehearsed. "Is that correct?"

"Yes-that-is-correct," I responded in kind to tease him, but I doubt he noticed.

"How about old cases?"

"How old?"

"Uh, sixteen years, seventeen years. I guess the trial would have been sixteen."

"Sixteen or seventeen *years*?" I made a face. "Then I'd say forget it. Probably been destroyed except for homicides."

Flynn chuckled.

"No kidding," I said. "A homicide."

"A guy named Kurt Dickens was charged." He spelled the name out and I wrote it down. "He was tried and found not guilty. Don't have a case number."

"What sort of homicide was it anyway?" Not because I needed to know to find the file, but out of curiosity.

"Ten-year-old girl found her mother shot to death in the mother's bed."

"Oh, my god," I said, "and that's who's hired you? The little girl grown up?"

"Yes. Rachel Macabee née Glenn."

"Rachel," I said. "Rachel Macabee." God, I thought, ten years old. "Oh, shit, How's she doing, anyway?"

"Maybe a little shaky," Flynn said. "The thing is, the guy was her mother's boyfriend and she doesn't think he did it."

"Let me see what I can turn up," I said.

The red 2002 Toyota driven by Tanya exited at Kolb Road and Flynn followed far enough behind that she wouldn't notice or remember him. Seventeen years ago, thought Flynn. What the hell was he doing taking a case like that, he had plenty of work, private defense attorneys were lined up for his services as well as ordinary citizens like Tanya's husband Will's friend Bert Coleman, with suspicions about this or that. It was hard enough working fresh cases, where you had witnesses who remembered things and actual physical evidence.

Tanya drove sedately down Kolb, not a risky driver. Of course, thought Flynn, the decomposed body of, possibly, Wynn Wykoff, and even that hadn't been proven (he could have given the ring away to someone else for god's sake or had it stolen and the body was some low-life thief), was some kind of evidence. Dead all that time—how come no one came looking for him anyway? Relatives, at least. Run down the other two band members, they might know something. Make that a priority.

Tanya turned left onto Broadway. Damn it, Flynn thought as he followed, he'd meant to ask Rachel if she knew where the rest of the band might be. But hopefully he'd get addresses for them once he got the files, and with any luck one or both of them might still be around. Just for starters, he'd Google Wynn Wykoff.

Tanya reached Park Mall and turned in. She parked, got out. Flynn got out of the Land Rover, and was blasted by the heat—it had to be a hundred and ten degrees. He followed Tanya as she went into Macy's. She was wearing a blousy red tunic, short black pencil skirt, and running shoes. The running shoes were odd, didn't go with the rest of the outfit.

Was she meeting a lover in the food court? Or maybe she *was* just shopping for clothes.

*Seventeen years,* he couldn't even remember what the hell *he* was doing seventeen years ago.

Flynn watched as Tanya methodically went through the racks in the Misses Department. She did it like a pro, a woman born to shop. After a few minutes she carried a pile of clothes back to the fitting rooms. Flynn yawned.

What had he been doing back then?

Still living in Tucson, married to Valentine. They'd moved to Sierra Vista, what? Ten years ago? Moved to Sierra Vista, bought a fixer-upper in the Foothills, cheap. Weekends Flynn had worked like a dog fixing it up for Val, enlarging the bedroom, adding a second bathroom, and building a big deck on the back. He still had the house but not Val—she'd been gone, what? At least five years.

Till now. What the hell was going on? Why had she stopped by anyway, to complain about her marriage? What was it she'd said? Harry gave her a hard time about everything. Well, he didn't want to hear it. But for all he knew she'd left town again, gone back to Portland to the coach by now. He hoped so.

He still wondered sometimes how much of a difference it had made in their lives, that move to Sierra Vista. If they'd stayed in Tucson, Val would never have met Harry Walker. *The football coach*. Flynn's fingers clenched into a fist. *Screw you, Harry Walker*. Tanya came out of the fitting room, taking his mind off Harry Walker, who now lived in Portland, Oregon, with Flynn's exwife. Tanya was empty-handed. All that trying on and she hadn't bought a thing. She headed back out the entrance she'd come in. He followed at a distance. He'd had the impression she was a fairly slim person, but he saw now she was heavier than he'd realized.

Usually if a woman was going to mess around, she got in shape. Val had lost, what? Ten pounds, in a month. An image ran through his mind, he and a newly slim, glamorous Valentine at the grocery store, running into someone Val knew. Must have been Smith's back then, before it got taken over by Food City.

"Harry!" said Valentine. "How are you? Flynn, this is Harry, the *football coach* over at the *high school*."

He remembered that she'd looked really pretty that day at

the grocery store, prettier than he'd seen her in years, her skin had a special glow to it.

"Harry," she'd said, "have you met my husband?"

Tanya reached her car and opened up the trunk. Why, he didn't know, since she hadn't bought anything. She glanced around, fluffed up her hair, and reached under her red tunic. Goddamn it, Flynn suddenly realized—that wasn't extra weight around her middle—she'd been shoplifting.

# chapter eight

*"SEVENTEEN YEARS—A NOT GUILTY VERDICT,"*
I said.

"A not guilty?" Belen, the most experienced of the legal secretaries on the criminal side, snorted through her nose. "Then just forget it. There's no way we've got the file anymore. No way."

"You've never heard the name?"

"No, but you know what, ask Monty. He's been here twenty years."

Monty Festa, a once darkly handsome man now going to seed, was sitting with his feet propped up on his desk, eating cashews out of a can despite the fact that he'd been steadily gaining weight ever since I started working here.

The walls of his office were covered with University of Arizona basketball memorabilia and though he didn't know it, several years ago for a brief while I'd had a crush on him. I couldn't quite remember why.

"Kurt Dickens," I said. "It was a homicide case, seventeen years ago. Belen thought you might remember."

"Yeah, name's familiar." He stared off into space, one hand in the can of cashews. "But why?" he added vaguely.

"A homicide," I prompted, "went to trial. A not guilty?"

*"Kurt Dickens."* Monty sat up straight. "Annie *Glenn,* that was the victim. Oh, man. A heartbreaker. The victim and the case. It was Jim Rasmussen's. It was his first loss and it was a big one." Monty popped another cashew. "To be honest, he probably needed a loss, too much hubris, but to make things worse he knew the victim."

"Really?"

Monty nodded. "What was it?" He snapped his fingers. "Yeah. They both sang in the Dudley chorus."

"Really," I said again. "I don't know Jim Rasmussen. Is he still around? He lives in Dudley?"

"Did then." Monty grinned. "Bet you do know of him, though. He's civil now over in Sierra Vista. Ran for Congress a while back, got some big spread over in the Foothills."

"Jody," I said, "I know a Jody Rasmussen—she took a class from me, oh, eight, nine years ago. Is she his wife?"

He nodded.

"Jody's fantastic," I said.

"Yeah. Wasn't there a child involved in that Dickens case?" Monty said. "Found the mother's body?"

"Yes, Rachel."

He nodded, looked down blankly at his hand in the cashew can, took it out, and put the can on his desk. "Poor Jim was shattered—I think partly not being able to get a conviction for the little girl. Always was big on family, Jim. As you probably figured out, if you knew Jody."

"They had four kids back then," I said.

"Five now," said Monty.

"Rachel's hired Flynn to look into the case."

"Flynn," said Monty. "Heard he's doing pretty well, out on his own. Aren't you two—"

*"No,"* I said.

"What's the point of Rachel having him look into it?" said Monty. "Double jeopardy."

I shrugged. "What do you know about the defendant—Kurt Dickens? I mean, was he an habitual, anything like that?"

"Never heard the name before or since. But aw, Chloe, it was too long ago. If it had been my case it would be different," said Monty. "I could dredge my memory, but you know what? Why not give Rasmussen a call—he'll remember, might even have some files. In fact . . ." He opened a desk drawer, rummaged. "Think I got his card here somewhere."

I went back to my desk and called the number on Jim Rasmussen's card but an efficient-sounding secretary told me Mr. Rasmussen was out of town for a couple of days. For a second I was tempted to call Jody—I had a little picture of her in my head from the class I taught: her red cheeks, fine fair hair falling in her eyes, always laughing at herself, but good to other people.

And another picture of Jody during one of the role-plays— death notification, I think it was, tears in her eyes, breaking down suddenly remembering her own father's death from a heart attack at thirty-seven and how her mother had struggled afterward.

"After that," she said, "all I ever wanted in life when I grew up was to have a complete family—that's why I married a Mormon. Jim is very big on family."

I was tempted again to call her but I didn't. Fishing for information about a case seemed like a bad reason.


Flynn followed Tanya after her stop at Park Mall straight back to Sierra Vista and her house, which was off the army base. Then he went back to his office to write up a report. He wrote it carefully, describing Tanya's actions and appearance but never mentioning the word shoplifting. Give it another shot, there was still the possibility of a boyfriend, a *reason* for wanting the new clothes.

Flynn looked at his watch—time to make it over to Dudley to check in with Dudley PD. He thought he might call Chloe while he was there to see if she'd found any files on Dickens and maybe they could go out to dinner.

Dudley Police had a new station, out past the turnaround on the way to Safeway. A pink and terra-cotta structure of odd angles, it looked like the architect had learned his trade designing convenience stores. Flynn pushed open the door and went up to the glass window and tapped.

He knew the receptionist, Nadia, she used to work dispatch at the county sheriff's. She looked up without interest but when she saw who it was she stood up and came over, a broad smile on her face.

"Brian," she said. Her hair, bunched up on her head in a bizarre sort of bun, was a lot grayer than the last time he'd seen her and she'd acquired a lot more bosom.

"Hey, Nadia. Looking good," he said.

Her eyes wrinkled up with pleasure. "And you—you're doing great in the civilian world, from what I hear," she said. "What can we do for you?"

"You remember a homicide case from seventeen years ago? Kurt Dickens was the perp?"

"A Dudley case?"

"That's why I'm here."

" 'Cause I was over at the sheriff's back then, so I— Wait. *Kurt Dickens?* Killed his girlfriend, Annie Glenn?" Nadia shook her head in disgust. "The jerk got off. That was a darn shame."

"So," said Flynn, "think you might have the file lying around? In storage or something?"

"From that long ago? Plus it was the old station—got flooded, remember, where they kept the closed files—three feet of water. But you should talk to the investigator, that was, yeah, Jerry Wishman. He's retired but I'll give you his number. In fact, I'll call him and let him know you're okay. But it'll cost you."

"Yeah?" said Flynn, suddenly wary.

"You gotta say thanks."

Rachel's dad, Phil Glenn, called while she and Scott were eating dinner, just Chinese takeout, nothing special. "Rachel," he said. "What the hell are you doing?"

"What?" Rachel asked.

"You hired a detective? What's that all about?"

"How do you even know about it?"

Scott stood up abruptly and began to close up the takeout containers. Scottie had told, of course—he and her father, the big protectors, always looking out for her even when she didn't want them to. And from the noise in the background she could tell her father was calling her from a restaurant, rudely yelling into his cell phone, Mr. Big Shot Phil Glenn, not caring about the other diners or for that matter whatever poor hopeful woman was with him. This always annoyed her.

"It's a waste of money and worse," said her father. "Honey, why can't you let things be—it's going to get you all upset again. Have you discussed this with your therapist?"

"Which one?" said Rachel.

"How would I know which one, whichever one you're seeing now."

"I'm not, at the moment," Rachel said.

"See? *See*."

"Dad, I'm tired. Let's do this some other time."

After she got off she sat at the table for a while, her eyes closed. Scottie was in the room that served as a den and his office. She could hear the Discovery Channel. Rachel got up and went into the guest bedroom and closed the door behind her.

It could have been for guests except they never had any, instead it was a dumping ground for things that didn't fit anywhere else and a storage area. She went to the closet and took down a file box from the upper shelf. Then she sat on the bed and took the lid off the box.

Inside was a hodgepodge of items, a white china kitten with blue eyes and a chipped ear Rachel had loved as a child, a dried chayote pod, a devil's claw, a small turquoise-colored pottery jar, broken, and a birthday card from her best friend Beth for her ninth birthday—*Happy Birthday Rachel—Ramona,* it said, because Rachel had always loved the Ramona books.

For a moment Rachel paused—after Annie had been killed she had searched and searched the library in Tucson for books like the Ramona books except with characters whose mothers had been murdered, but had never found any.

Where was Beth, her best friend, now? She hadn't seen her since the murder, as if once that happened the Rachel who had a best friend called Beth no longer existed.

Rachel shuffled through the box and pulled out a manila envelope full of photographs. She opened the flap and took out the pictures, placing them in a line on the bumpy white chenille bedspread. They were all of Annie.

Annie as a little girl, with straight-across bangs in a rubber kiddie pool in a back yard, and as a teenager wearing a long yellow prom dress and pixie bangs, and Annie grown up, with no bangs at all. There was Annie at the Co-op, with a bunch of carrots in one hand, looking surprised, and under a Christmas tree looking red-eyed, then several of Annie with the band, down at the St. Elmo's.

There was Teddy, tall, dark, and skinny. He played lead guitar.

Billy Dodds—drums, the handsome one—and finally Wynn, bass and lead guitar, the funny one with eyes that crinkled when he smiled. The one her mother loved the best. Oh, *Wynn*. But she wasn't going to cry.

Rachel had made herself take out the pictures to find a couple with Wynn and Annie to show Flynn, but she could hardly stand to look at them, especially the ones of Annie with the band, Annie looking so alive, so full of herself, so feisty. Rachel had always been proud of her mom, except when she was totally embarrassed—the way she stood up to people and never took any shit.

Maybe the pictures would help explain that to Flynn so he would understand the important, no, the essential point: he wasn't investigating just another case, but the murder of someone who was different, someone more . . . Rachel didn't know how to say it, Annie had been more truly *in the world* than most people were.

She separated out three: one of Wynn holding his bass and grinning, one of Annie singing, wearing a cowboy hat and a leather vest, and another of her surprised in her kitchen, in a red tank top, pretty face flushed with laughter—*what was so funny?*

"Sweetie?" called Scott.

Rachel jumped. "What?"

"Where are you?"

"In the guest bedroom."

She started to shove the rest of the pictures back in the envelope when Scott appeared in the doorway.

"What are you doing in here?" he asked.

"Nothing," Rachel said. "Looking at pictures of my mom." She hesitated. "To show Flynn. Want to see?"

Scott came in and sat next to her on the bed. She was annoyed that he'd told her father but she had never ever doubted he loved her, from the very beginning he had done everything he could to make her life easier. She hardly had to do a thing for herself, in fact.

She placed the three she had selected on the bed in front of him. "These are nice, don't you think?" she said.

"Umm." He glanced down at them but she could tell he wasn't really looking. "You know, I'll be gone for a couple of days," he said, "at that conference in Atlanta. I'm kind of worried about leaving you alone."

*"Don't,"* Rachel said. "I'll miss you but I'll be fine." The second Ativan she'd taken when they got home was still working, telling her it would be a nice break just being by herself.

"Oh. Sweetie. Bringing all this up again, I don't know if you're doing the right thing."

Funny, but when he said that Rachel knew for sure it *was* the right thing.

Scott took her hand. "I'd hoped you were finally getting over it," he said. His voice rose a little. "This investigating and everything, it could make things worse."

"The worst that could happen has already happened," said Rachel, "a long, long time ago."

# chapter nine

IT WAS RAINING PRETTY HARD OUT ON HIGH-
way 92 as Flynn headed back to Sierra Vista. He noticed he had a
call from Chloe on his cell but decided he'd call her back later. He
grabbed some KFC and at the office found Lois had left him two
messages from potential clients and a note saying, *Val stopped
in to see you. She would like you to give her a call,* and a
number.

*Why?* Why should he give Val a call? Why *had* she stopped in
anyway? Flynn crumpled the note and threw it toward the waste-
basket.

Then he wrote up a report involving a background check on a
young man that he'd done for a suspicious employer two days ago
that he hadn't gotten to yet and reread his report on Tanya. She
should be stopped from shoplifting—that was all Will needed was
for his wife to get arrested—but he hadn't decided on a strategy.

He was definitely regretting taking this Rachel Macabee thing—
it was going to take up a lot of time with probably not much to
show for it and it wasn't like he needed the work.

He forgot all about the call from Chloe until he dashed through
the rain out to the Land Rover and was about to turn onto the
highway and head for his house in the Foothills. It was still raining

like a son of a bitch, sheeting on his windshield and puddling on the road. He checked his phone and found a voice message:

"No file on Dickens at the county attorney's. The prosecutor Jim Rasmussen may have a copy. His Sierra Vista office number is 555-2341, but he's out of town for a couple of days."

Nice, a bit above and beyond the call of duty. He appreciated that.

And he appreciated rain in the desert as much as the next guy but right now it was coming down so hard he could hardly see the road. Up ahead there was a little break in the clouds—looked like the storm might be leaving Sierra Vista and heading for Dudley. Water would be ping-pinging into the big pot by Chloe's computer—her answer to leak control. If it wasn't fixed soon the whole roof could rot out. He was willing to bet she'd done nothing about hiring someone to replace the roof or even to patch it, and besides, with the heavy monsoon this year the good roofers would be all booked up.

*What's it to you?* Chloe would say, but he couldn't help himself.

His father hadn't been able to help himself either. He'd been dead for a few years now, in poor health at the end, but what Flynn remembered most about his father was him always working on the house—working on the house when Flynn was five, when Flynn was ten, fifteen, working on the house even after his heart problems showed up.

The day of his death, in fact, lying dead on the front lawn, man at the door saying to his mother there's a man lying out on your grass. The day of his death, which was the day after he'd finished a last triumphant third remodel of the kitchen.

Monsoon thunder boomed, the wipers on the Land Rover swished, swished. Rachel had struck him as a little shaky but that husband of hers probably wasn't doing her any favors by being so protective. He'd had enough experience with victims of violent crime to know about post-traumatic stress disorder. PTSD. A lot of those guys coming back from Iraq had it too. He wasn't sure how to deal with it.

As a victim advocate, wouldn't Chloe know? He thought of Chloe when he'd first met her in the kitchen of a victim whose husband had just been murdered. How fiercely Chloe had stood up for her victim.


Scott went to bed early—he had to catch a plane for Atlanta the next day for the conference and he hated to travel tired. Rachel stayed up, sitting out by the pool. Where was she? she wondered. Beth Pearson. She and Rachel used to just about fly through Dudley's shabby streets: up and down the steep crumbling cement stairs, feathered on both sides with Chinese elm and cancer trees. Some of the stairs led to houses and some of them led to nowhere at all.

Unkempt, unweeded, unpainted, and full of secrets: Old Dudley. The fig tree in the lot where a house had burned down had fat jammy figs in the years when the monsoons were good, purple morning glories made special gardens of all the yards in town. The Chinese elms had purple fragrant flowers, the fennel that grew in the drainage ditches gave off a strong smell of licorice.

Nothing would dare grow wild at her father's house, including his daughter. It was on the northwest side, in the Foothills, a four-bedroom adobe with a red-tiled roof and a big pool. Unlike at Annie's, everything worked. There was a brand-new big stove in the kitchen, in contrast to the one in Dudley which had been not only old but too small. Annie complained about the stove but she cooked on it almost every night—a little chicken from time to time but primarily vegetarian, curries and stir fries.

Rachel used to joke and tell people the first three months she lived with her father the only vegetable she ate was french fries, but that wasn't really true because a couple of nights a week her father's girlfriend Molly cooked. Molly, blond and blue-eyed and serene, at least when she was with Rachel. She taught Rachel how to make a Moroccan dish with chicken, honey, and grapes that Rachel still cooked from time to time.

Rachel had liked Molly but she never understood Molly and her father. They argued so quietly, voices full of venom; they didn't even seem to like each other. And Molly was fine so far as Rachel could tell, what was it her father wanted? Then one night it was over, though Molly occasionally kept in touch with Rachel, they shopped sometimes or went to a movie, but after that Rachel stayed aloof from her father's girlfriends.

Rachel went to Orange Grove Middle School and later to Catalina Foothills High School. In high school she had good-looking well-dressed friends like herself that she never felt close to.

Her father drove her down for the trial. The courthouse was in Dudley but they stayed at a Quality Inn in Sierra Vista. Her father sat with her in the big marble lobby of the courthouse while she waited to be called to testify. The prosecutor was really nice—he was tall and thin and wore glasses. Mr. Rasmussen. But even nicer was the prosecutor's wife, Jody.

Rachel still thought of her from time to time—her dad was stiff, uncomfortable in the courthouse, a place he had no control over. Jody, in a blue-and-white-striped maternity top, her face was flushed with the exertion of being enormously pregnant, had sat next to Rachel while she waited to be called and talked to her, not about anything really, but the sound of Jody's voice was calming, almost like a . . . a lullaby. Maybe because of her children; Jody already had two and a third on the way, she knew how to comfort and soothe.

Rachel had only had to be there for the first day of the trial. She hardly remembered actually testifying, as though it were someone else on the stand and she was in the audience watching. When she got to the part about finding her mother, one of the jurors, a middle-aged woman, started crying quietly.

"Rachel," asked Mr. Rasmussen, "do you know a man named Kurt Dickens?"

"Yes."

"And who was he in relation to your mom?"

"Her boyfriend."

"Her boyfriend."

"And is he here in the courtroom?"

"Yes."

"Want to point him out?"

Kurt was sitting over to the right in her line of sight, next to his lawyer, Mr. Cooper. His blond hair was much shorter than it used to be and he was wearing a white shirt, a red tie, and a tan sports jacket. The sleeves of the jacket weren't quite long enough. The last time she saw him before her mother's death was when the three of them took a hike into Dixie Canyon to look at the waterfalls made by the monsoons. He'd been funny that day, funny ha-ha.

It was so sad remembering that funny ha-ha day that she could hardly bear it. She pointed to him without really looking at his face.

"We need you to speak out loud for the recorder. What's he wearing, Rachel?"

"A tan jacket, a white shirt, and a red tie."

"Now, Rachel, do you remember at some time Kurt Dickens lending your mother his gun?"

She had tried so hard to remember but a memory wouldn't come. She tried now but it still wouldn't. "No," she said.

"You have no memory of that at all?"

"No," she said. "But that doesn't mean—"

The prosecutor turned away, cutting her off. "Thank you, Rachel."

When it was over she and her father walked out of the courthouse and down the long flight of steps to the street to where they were parked. The courthouse area was well taken care of, there was trimmed grass and a big fountain. Rachel was wearing nicer clothes than she had ever worn in Dudley.

She could see unkempt, shabby Dudley, right there beyond the courthouse, the houses built on the steep hillsides, with the stairs that led up to them and the stairs that led nowhere. She knew who lived in many of the houses, but as she walked slowly down the steps with her father, in her nice clothes, it seemed to her as if she had never lived there at all, had only imagined it.

# chapter ten

RETIRED DETECTIVE JERRY WISHMAN LIVED IN
a solid cinderblock house on a few acres out in the desert near
Palominas, about halfway between Sierra Vista and Dudley. The
house was surrounded by big healthy-looking Modesto ash trees,
full of grackles who screeched raucously at Flynn as he got out of
the Land Rover. Crummy birds, thought Flynn, big and noisy; the
punks and bullies and criminals of the bird world.

Wishman had sounded harried on the phone, maybe not one
of those retired cops who liked to talk all day about old cases.

"Hey there," someone said. "Guess you must be Flynn, huh?"

Flynn looked toward the house. A ramp led down from the
front door to the ground and a man stood just at the bottom: a
big heavy-featured man with more brown hair than a man of his
age deserved, wearing a red and blue plaid western shirt and
jeans.

"Right." Flynn came closer.

"Jerry Wishman. Nadia vouched for you, so I guess it's okay.
Got what you asked for right here." He held up a brown accor-
dion file. "What I could find of it anyway. You got your work cut
out for you—bunch of stuff missing." He shook his head in disgust. "That son of a bitch Dickens. Hope you get him."

That wasn't what Flynn had been hired to do, but he said nothing.

"The prosecutor, Jim Rasmussen, he knew the victim."

"How's that?" asked Flynn.

"They sang in some choir together. Rasmussen tracked down a couple of domestics on Dickens, they're in that file, but the damn judge ruled they weren't admissible."

"Really?" Flynn said. "Why not?"

"Different girlfriend, for one thing."

"Honey?" called a woman's voice from inside the house.

"Hold on just a minute, darlin'," Wishman said. He looked at Flynn apologetically. "Normally I could stand here all day and jaw with you about the case but the wife's not doing too good right now. Got diagnosed with some damn fool disease . . ." His voice trailed off.

Flynn didn't want to ask what disease exactly. "I'm sorry about that," he said.

"Got me doing the housework and all. Never was much good at it."

"I hear you," said Flynn, who always picked up after himself, could hardly finish eating a quiet meal at home before he started in on the dishes.

"Jack Nelson," said Wishman. "You could check in with him. He was the first responding officer."

"I know Jack," said Flynn. "His wife Sukie was friends with Val, my ex, but we've kind of lost touch."

"You know Sukie died? Aneurysm burst in her brain. Gone in seconds."

"Yeah, I heard."

"He's remarried. Damn if he didn't up and marry a hippie woman from Dudley—Frieda, I think her name is."

Frieda.

"Rossi .38," said Wishman.

"What?" said Flynn.

Wishman's lip curled in a sneer. "That's the type gun Dickens used to kill Annie Glenn."

"Cheap son of a bitch," said Flynn. "Dickens or whoever it was."

"Whoever it was? Don't kid yourself, it was Dickens plain and simple."

"Jerry? Honey?" a woman called.

"Hold on just a sec," Wishman said to Flynn. "Let's see if Dixie's up to saying hi."

He vanished into the house and came back a few second later, pushing a wan-looking woman in a wheelchair, maybe pretty once, it was hard to tell. Her skin and her hair were the same pale beige. She had a blanket over her lap though it was warm and wore a western shirt like Wishman's. He wheeled her down the ramp.

"Brian Flynn." She held out her hand. "Dixie. I remember reading about you in the papers when you was Super Narc."

Flynn took her hand—felt the flesh loose on her bones. "Pleased to meet you, Dixie," he said.

"Super Narc." Wishman laughed as if Dixie had said something very witty. He put his hand on her shoulder tenderly.

Flynn looked away embarrassed.

"One thing I didn't give you," Wishman told Flynn.

"What's that?"

"Dickens got the damn Rossi .38 back that he allegedly lent to Annie when they found him not guilty. I knew the sucker did it, so I bought the damn gun off him, figuring if anything new came up we'd still have the gun."

"What?" said Flynn. "You paid money for a Rossi .38?"

"Yep. One hundred seventy-five dollars. Would have paid more but I figured I was too eager he'd back off."

"Jerry?" said Dixie. "I'm a little—"

"Aw, sweetie," Wishman said. "Let's get you back inside. Good luck with whatever, Brian Flynn."

"Thanks for your help," said Brian.

Jerry Wishman pushed his wife's wheelchair up the ramp. At the top he stopped and rearranged the blanket on her lap with that same tenderness as before. Turning away, Flynn saw the gesture, didn't want to, did anyway. The grackles cackled in the ash trees.

Rachel turned at the DEPARTURES sign, drove down to the DELTA sign, and pulled in close to the curb.

Scott got out and reached in back for his carry-on. Then he started around to the driver's side. She watched him in the rearview mirror: a light-haired man, boyish, with regular features. He wore khakis and a navy polo and looked like what he was, a lawyer. He saw her watching and smiled as he came up to her window.

He leaned in and gave her a gentle kiss. He was always gentle, as if she might break. "You'll be okay?"

"Sure."

"I'll be back day after tomorrow."

*Don't go,* Rachel screamed silently. It was hard to believe that only yesterday she had been actually looking forward to him leaving. But today she hadn't taken any Ativan because she'd taken too many the day before and didn't want to turn into an Ativan addict. Of course, he had to go. It was a conference in Atlanta for his job.

*Shape up,* she told herself. *You haven't taken an Ativan yet but it's still an option.*

"You'll call me?" she said out loud.

"Every day. And you can always call me." He looked at his watch. "Gotta go, sweetheart. I love you."

"Love you too." Rachel made her voice light, gossamer.

She watched as he went through the glass door, then she drove away, out of the airport, down Valencia to the I-10. Traffic was light—she scrolled down in her iPod to the Dixie Chicks. Scott didn't especially like them—he always said it was her biggest political statement. Scottie was just a shade Republican.

She sang along, mimicking Natalie Maines's phrasing. She liked to sing along to music when she was alone. Not when Scottie was with her though. He used to tease her. "I've heard you singing in the shower," he said. "Why don't you sing for me?"

It was absurd but when he said that, her first impulse was to say, *Because someone will come up and shoot me.*

But she was singing now and no one was taking aim. As far as she knew. The music gave her a boost, made her feel confident and powerful, as least momentarily, because nothing, nothing at all lasted.

Not only that, she'd hired a detective to find out who had murdered her mother. All those years and no one had ever done that, not her father, not Kurt's lawyer, not the band. Maybe the band had though in a way, with Wynn's body surfacing.

It seemed to her now she had some control over her own life after all, some ability to make things different, better. *I'm not taking the Ativan anymore,* she decided. *I can tough it out, why not?*

She exited at Oracle and thought, maybe hit the Tucson Mall. It wasn't quite eleven, the gallery where she worked was closed that day, summer hours. Do a little shopping, have lunch. She sang along with Natalie about taking the long way around, sang out loud, trying to match her phrasing and, better, learn from it, and suddenly she was sure, positive, that everything was going to be okay. She would sail through today, and this evening and tomorrow, sail through the rest of her life, for that matter. Why not?

# chapter eleven

"*I'VE DONE A LOT OF VERY PRODUCTIVE* thinking lately," said Larry "about ways we can improve our outreach, our networking, our communication skills, and things around here in general. And I think it's time for me to share that with all of you."

*Oh, goody,* I thought.

The Victim Witness staff sat at the long table in the interview room: Kelly the secretary, Cindy the clerk, Linda the misdemeanor advocate, and myself, the felony advocate. I reached for the last doughnut in the box of Krispy Kremes and broke it in half.

"First," said Larry, "we've made great strides in utilizing our computers to their best advantage. We've got an online network going that's accessible to everyone here."

Never mind, I thought, that we were all within speaking distance of each other anyway.

"Chloe?"

I looked over at him, my mouth full of Krispy Kreme.

"I noticed"—his face reddened—"you seem to have entered only *two* victims in the online file."

I swallowed. "I haven't gotten that far on the data entry," I said.

Larry smiled insincerely. "Chloe's a little behind but I'm sure she'll catch up," he said to the others as if I had momentarily left the room. "She's been here longer than anyone else and I understand that change is difficult for some people."

I really wanted to just punch the guy, and I'm not a violent person at all. Instead I tuned out, letting my eyes drift through the window to the parking lot outside. Monty Festa was getting out of his silver SUV, with a big box of files. A black and white cat slunk away under a blue car. It had rained last night, but the sky was clear now, almost the same color as the car.

"What do you think, Chloe?" asked Larry. "Kelly can set it all up."

Set what up? I looked at Kelly in alarm.

"Time sheets," prompted Kelly.

"Modified time sheets," corrected Larry.

"Everyone fills out a tentative schedule for the week," Kelly said, "then they sign in and out on it."

For years, I'd come and gone as I pleased, and I was hours over my twenty a week.

"Ah," I said.

"It's especially useful," Larry pointed out, "for you and Linda, since you guys work twenty and thirty hours respectively."

"It's an excellent idea," brown-nosed Linda.

"Great!" I said.

Larry droned on, speaking of resources and reaching out to providers, networking with community agencies and improving our advocate skills via workshops and conferences around the state. The black and white cat came out from under the blue car and at the far end of the parking lot a couple of finches with red throats dabbled at a mini-pond left by the rain. Monty Festa came out again and took another box of files from the back of his SUV. Then the meeting was over.

I went back to my desk. I couldn't see that victims had it any better now that everything was online. I couldn't see that I had any more time to serve them either, it was more like I had less. I was just a leftover, I thought, from the days before computers, and now the great wheel of technology juiced up by master's degrees in business administration had rolled over me and squished me—a mashed-up relic—a human being.

Though Netflix was awfully convenient.

Rachel came out of Macy's with a Macy's bag containing two Ralph Lauren polo shirts, one in grass green and the other cotton-candy pink. She didn't need them; she even had a pink polo already that was cut a little differently—but it had been a long time since she'd bought something to wear that she actually needed.

The mall was full of high school kids, free for the summer and full of themselves. In the food court she walked past clots of them chilling out and got an Orange Julius hot dog and a raspberry Orange Julius and carried them to a table near a window and out of the mainstream.

Around her rose the din of people eating and talking, noisy and strangely isolating at the same time. Through the window she could see the big parking lot full of cars and trucks. A fat mother pushed a baby in a stroller past the window, headed for the entrance closest to Rachel.

A red truck pulled up and dropped someone off—a woman in her twenties, Rachel's age, dressed all in black and carrying a big black crocheted purse. Her hair was black too except for a stripe of bright red down the middle and suddenly Rachel realized it was Penny, from high school, Penny the Goth. She scooted her chair around so her back was to the room and to Penny coming in through the entrance.

Rachel had never hung with the Goths—they made her nervous

and seeing Penny made her nervous all over again. How could she *still* be a Goth? Some people just never grew up. Needing to look busy, Rachel opened her purse and took out a pen and the notebook she always carried for shopping lists. She opened the notebook.

"Hey, Rach? Is that *you*? Rach?"

*Rach.* Kurt used to call her Rach sometimes. Rachel looked up. There was Penny, of course, standing right in front of her. Her blouse was sleeveless and both her arms had so many tattoos they looked severely bruised. Her eyes were heavily lined with black mascara.

"Hi," Rachel said.

"Looking good," said Penny. She smiled down, as if they were old friends, as if she knew her well, better by far than Rachel's actual friends—as if she saw through Rachel's total sham of a life, clear through to who Rachel really was.

"You too," said Rachel politely.

"Well," said Penny doubtfully. She raised one tattooed arm. "See ya."

"See ya," Rachel echoed faintly, more to herself than to Penny.

Suddenly she had the sense she needed absolute privacy, she wasn't sure why, but she stood up and walked in a way that she hoped would appear utterly natural, to the restroom, went into one of the stalls, locked the door, and sat down. Something flashed then through her mind, quick, a flash of red. Rachel gasped and saw her mother. *Her pretty face, it was still perfect, up to the hairline, her pretty face.* She gasped again, unable to catch her breath thinking of her mother, lying on the bed that was soaked with blood, *her pretty face.*

# chapter twelve

*DROVE TO 101 OCOTILLO STREET IN REFERENCE to a call* blah blah blah. *Female victim* CAMILLE CHARTRAND *stated that suspect* KURT DICKENS *had broken a valuable pitcher which had belonged to her mother and proceeded to show me pieces of blue and white material that appeared to be china. Victim then proceded to cry. I questioned Kurt Dickens who stated the alleged victim had pushed him and he had stumbled back and knocked over the pitcher.*

So much for the domestic violence charge. Who knew what had really happened, everyone lied. God, he'd always hated domestics. Flynn yawned, sitting in his car at the Sonic Drive-in with the file Wishman had given him. He was reading the domestic charges first because they were on top, like an afterthought. He leafed through the second incident report. Same place, same people, different charge.

*Victim* CAMILLE CHARTRAND *stated that suspect* KURT DICKENS *kicked her, pushed her onto the sofa and threatened to strangle her. Dickens stated that he had not kicked her, she had fallen onto the couch and he had indeed threatened to strangle her, but it had been a joke because he was so exasperated with her. He stated she was always complaining no matter what he did for her. I noted that the alleged victim Miss Chartrand did indeed have a red mark on her shin, that was consistent with someone kicking her.* And blah blah blah.

Flynn skimmed the rest. Wishman hadn't mentioned any domestics involving Kurt and Annie, so he assumed there weren't any. And surely, if there had been, Rachel wouldn't be so protective of him.

He pulled the initial report—Jack Nelson, the first response officer, a sergeant now. He and Jack and their wives had socialized together till Flynn's marriage fell apart. Jack remarried now, to a hippie woman. Huh. What would Sukie think about that? Or Val, for that matter. Val had no right to think anything, the way she'd behaved. If she thought for one minute he was going to call her, she was nuts.

Okay, okay, move on.

Coroner's report, report from a gun expert, matching the Rossi .38 found at the scene to the bullet in Annie's brain. Crime scene photos.

Follow-up interviews. An agonizing one with Rachel. A couple with Kurt which he skimmed. Kurt saying he drove around after dropping Annie off. Nobody saw him. The neighbor Alice and another neighbor.

No interviews with the band members. Why the hell not? The file wasn't complete, but Wishman, sure of Dickens's guilt, probably hadn't bothered looking deep at anything. And Wynn Wykoff, the bass player in Annie's band, dead but no one knew that, at least partly because no one had bothered to try to track him down.

According to Wishman, Rasmussen had known the victim. Rasmussen kind of a big shot now—only did civil cases, right here in Sierra Vista; nice cases where you didn't get embroiled in messy low-life stuff like you did on the criminal side.

The waitress came over and hooked up the tray to the Land

Rover's window. Flynn always got a kick out of that old-fashioned drive-in stuff, the main reason probably he went to Sonic.

"Sonic cheeseburger," she said, handing him a bag, "fries, and a Coke." She smiled broadly, an overly thin wiry blonde with dark roots, in her forties. "Anything else I can get you, sir?"

Flynn had a little picture of her life, pregnant right out of high school, three kids, husband with a bunch of domestic violence charges, pled down to nothing, whom she would stick with till the day he almost killed her. "No, thanks," he said. "This looks great."

She walked off and he bit into the cheeseburger.

He wished he knew where the two other band members were. He'd written their names down when he'd met with Rachel but he'd forgotten to ask if she knew their whereabouts. Assumed it would be in the file. After seventeen years? Idiot.

But right now he had an interview about another case with a defense attorney over in Douglas, digging up some dirt on a witness, at two and it would take forty minutes to get there. Why had he taken on a *Douglas* case, for Christ's sake?

He'd eaten that whole cheeseburger and he hadn't even noticed. He reached for a french fry. Wouldn't hurt to give Rachel a call. He punched in the number of her cell.

"Hello?"

She sounded a little off. Surely he hadn't wakened her. "Rachel?"

"Yes?"

"Flynn here."

"Oh, *Flynn.*" A pause. "How are you?"

"Fine, I had a quick question for you. You have any idea where either Teddy Radebaugh or Billy Dodds are now?"

"I . . . I haven't . . ." She took a deep breath. "There was . . ." She began to cry, big gulping sobs. "I'm sorry . . ." she gasped. "I can't think right now. I have to go. Goodbye." And she was gone.

Flynn stared at the cell in his hand, snapped it shut. Was she seriously losing it? *Chloe,* he thought. He punched in the number for the county attorney and asked for her, but she was in court. He left a message for her to call, urgent, and snapped his phone closed again.

Almost immediately it chimed. For a second he stared at it. How did his frigging life get so urgent anyway? No name, and he didn't recognize the number.

"Flynn here."

"Hey. Jack Nelson, you son of a—how the hell did you get so far ahead of me? Wishman says you were over this morning getting a certain file from him."

"Let me guess. You got an ID on that body that was dug up."

"What body?"

"Who was it made the ID?"

"We're not releasing that to the general public at this time."

"C'mon, Jack, I'm not the general public. Tell me." Clearly whoever it was had identified the body as Wynn Wykoff or Jack wouldn't be calling him about the file on Dickens. It couldn't have been Rachel unless she was far, far crazier than he'd thought. Always a possibility.

Jack chuckled. "You got the only file, as far as I know, in existence on a certain case. Hand me that file and I'll tell you."

"It's deal." Flynn could stop in Dudley on his way back from Douglas, but he needed to have Lois copy the file first. He didn't have time to drop it off with her, he'd have to do it himself later. "Look," he said, "this is a bad time. How 'bout tomorrow morning, eight o'clock sharp, at the tourist stop by the pit?"

Flynn looked across the table at me. "I was talking to one of the guys I used to work with at the sheriff's department." He wore a blue denim shirt and a green paisley tie that must have been left over from the days when he spent a lot of time in court. He looked extremely handsome in a dark foreboding kind of way. "He's says county health insurance coverage's gotten so bad, you get sick, you might as well go ahead and die."

"Really?" I said, fiddling with my wineglass and feeling guilty. I hadn't seen a doctor in years, not even for a pap smear or a mammogram.

We were having dinner at Café Olé, the nicest restaurant in Dudley. Not only that but we were being treated like royalty. The owner, Shirley Mack, had actually come over to the table with a special tidbit of something that tasted of chipotles and cream cheese and possibly caviar.

"Just for you, Brian," she said. "Many thanks."

Brian? Many thanks? For what? I looked at Flynn but his face told me nothing.

We had been served a tiny bowl of Parmesan garlic soup, then a tiny salad with raspberry-balsamic vinaigrette dressing, and after that a tiny ball of lemon sorbet, all delicious, and now we were waiting on the entrée. I had ordered shrimp with lime cilantro on a bed of jasmine rice and Flynn was having the prime rib. Flynn didn't care one way or the other about having a bunch of tiny tasty bites and sips leading up to his beef but he knew I liked that kind of thing.

The question running through my mind was, what were we doing here? Why had he asked me to dinner?

Flynn cleared his throat. He seemed a little on edge. "What's the county paying for gas mileage now?" he asked.

"Twenty-nine cents if you can prove you couldn't get a county car. Otherwise you have to take one of theirs," I said. "Why?"

"Gee," said Flynn, "I'd pay thirty."

"Flynn!" I said. "What do you want from me?"

"Well . . . the thing is . . . I'm doing great but," said Flynn, "it's too great. I'm swamped. And I've got this new case I had you look up the file for?"

"Yes," I said, "Kurt Dickens. Murdered his girlfriend, got off, and now her daughter's hired you."

"*Accused* of murdering his girlfriend."

"Aha," I said.

"Um"—he cleared his throat—"did you by any chance get in touch with Jim Rasmussen after that last message you left me?"

"Like I said, his office told me he's out of town. That was yesterday. So maybe tomorrow."

"See?" said Flynn to no one in particular. "See? I didn't ask you to do all that. Above and beyond the call of duty."

"I did it for the victim," I said.

"You're *good* with victims," said Flynn, "and you've got the makings of a good investigator too, especially with the people part. That case we kind of worked together? Terry Barnett? You almost got yourself killed but other than that you were pretty good. Your politics are a little nuts but so what?" He paused. "Come and work for me."

The shrimp arrived, smelling of jasmine and lime and cilantro. Flynn's prime rib hung over the edge of his plate, oozing pink blood. I thought of Larry at the meeting this morning, picked up a succulent pink shrimp by the tail, and suddenly I felt happier than I had in weeks, months.

"If I were to come and work for you," I said carefully, "you would let me think for myself and be a free agent?"

"Of *course*." Flynn looked so sincere, so, well, so in my power. For the moment at least.

"And," I said, "you would match what I make at the county?"

"You only work twenty hours for the county," Flynn pointed out. "You could be working more hours than that for me."

"In reality, I work more hours than that for the county," I said. "If you can guarantee my basic income doesn't go down, we'll take it from there."

"I do." Flynn cleared his throat. "I do promise to guarantee it."

"Then, yes," I said.

"Good." Flynn's mouth twitched as a smile struggled to break out. I watched as he fought it and won. *"Great,"* he said in a businesslike way. He paused. "You're online at home, aren't you?"

"Yes."

"I've got a great system set up on my computer. You can write up reports of everything you do and it becomes part of this network I've created so both of us can see what the other one's doing anytime."

"Aha," I said, trying to look pleased and interested. "Data entry."

"I file reports online and you'd do the same. You can check out everything I have so far on the case, which isn't much. Can you start tomorrow?"

"Sort of. I have to give two weeks' notice, but I'm running a few hours over my twenty, so I don't have to work a full twenty those two weeks."

"I got a case I'm tailing you might be good on, but what I want right now is for you to talk to Rachel. She sounds like she needs some support. Set up a meeting with her and get cozy. She's the best witness we have at this point. I'll give her a call tonight to let her know you're with the team and will be calling her."

"Let me ask you this," I said. "It's an old case. Did something specifically make her decide to hire an investigator? I mean, why now?"

"Oops," said Flynn. "Forgot to mention it."

"What?"

He glanced around. We were at a corner table, an empty table between us and the next one. "That long-ago-buried body they dug up here in Old Dudley?"

I moved to the edge of my seat. "Yes?"

"I talked to Jack Nelson of Dudley PD and it's been identified, don't know yet by who." Flynn's eyes met mine. "But before that, when she hired me, Rachel told me she was sure it was a man named Wynn Wykoff, this guy who played the bass with her mom's band. Everyone thought he'd left town without telling anyone a week or so before her mom was murdered."

He'd forgotten to mention it. Right. I could tell by his overly casual tone he'd been working throughout dinner to set things up just so he could deliver this payoff.

I forgave him instantly.

# chapter thirteen

FLYNN AND SERGEANT JACK NELSON STOOD together, the only people out at this time of day, eight o'clock sharp, in front of the Lavender Pit, the remnant of a copper mining operation, now a vast terraced wasteland where nothing had grown for decades, slowly crumbling in on itself. Even though it was early, it was already hot, the sky an unrelenting blue.

"A woman named Sonora Cloud came in and identified our guy," Jack said, as he took the file from Flynn.

He hadn't seen Jack in, what? Three or four five years. Just after Sukie died. He'd lost some weight back then but he was up to his old weight now and maybe then some, a bulky man with a handsome mustache.

"Sonora Cloud. What kind of name is that?"

Jack shrugged. "Dunno. Buddhist maybe? Teaches yoga."

Flynn started to make some smart remark about the fruits and nuts of Old Dudley, then remembered about Jack's new wife, the hippie. Frieda.

"Sonora's a former girlfriend of Wynn's," Jack said. "It's still tentative, of course, but she recognized a ring and a piece of backpack as well."

"My client recognized the ring too. Rachel. Annie Glenn's daughter."

Jack gave him a look but didn't get into it. "Annie's daughter. Interesting." He cleared his throat. "It's still under wraps as far as the public goes—don't want anybody heartbroke for nothing, in case it's wrong."

Jack had always been a slow careful man, not stupid but methodical. "But we could sure use a relative to ask about broken bones, or dental records. DNA, I guess, if we have to." He winced. "Expensive."

"So," said Flynn, "got a cause of death yet?"

"Still being determined. Look, this is an old, old case." He sighed. "We got a bunch of burglaries over in Warren and a goddamn arsonist in San Jose Estates, so I'm pretty tied up, and now this." He waved the file. "It would sure be good to find a relative for our Wynn," he repeated.

"Hint, hint," said Flynn. "I'll see what I can do."

They shook on it, then headed for their respective vehicles.

As he opened his door, Jack turned. "Hey," he said. "I hear Val's back in Sierra Vista. You guys—"

His voice was cut off by a semi, big Wal-Mart logo on its side, thundering around the curve where they stood.

Flynn cupped his ear, shouted, "Can't hear you!" and got quickly into the Land Rover, started it up, and peeled off.


Rachel woke up that morning with the shadow of a memory she hadn't even realized she'd forgotten.

It had hovered in her mind, and then Chloe Newcombe had called. Flynn had already told her last night about Chloe—a victim advocate who worked with Flynn. Talking to Chloe, the thread of the memory got lost. She'd wanted to meet and since

Rachel was working at the gallery today they'd arranged to meet there. Hardly anyone came in this time of the year, the off-season.

Chloe had said she wanted to talk about the case but Rachel suspected the real reason was because she'd cried on the phone when Flynn called her yesterday and now he was sending someone to check up on her. It would be awful if Flynn ended up treating her just like Scott and her father did.

But she'd made it through the night, last night, hadn't she? Scottie had called her twice and both times she'd told him she was *fine*.

She popped an Ativan before she left for the gallery, just in case.

Sonora Cloud was the name of the woman who'd IDed Wynn's body. Flynn called Chloe to tell her this right before she left for Tucson to meet with Rachel.

"Ask her who Sonora is and see if she knows anything about relatives of Wynn," he said. "Or at least where he came from."

Since he was already in Dudley, Flynn drove the Land Rover down Tombstone Canyon headed for the murder site.

Sonora Cloud sounded like an Indian name and that got him to thinking about buffalo and something his brother-in-law in Wyoming had told him. Buffalo were smart—when a storm came up they walked into it, against the wind, which meant they would eventually get out of it, instead of following along with it like a cow would.

His crazy brother-in-law was raising buffalo, in the hopes that one day very soon Americans would prefer their meat over beef. Flynn had had a few buffalo steaks in his day and he had to admit they were pretty damn good. He'd even cooked some up when Chloe came over one time, but she'd barely tasted it. Where was her sense of adventure?

Flynn turned up Manzanita, headed for 29 Laundry Hill, where Annie Glenn had lived and been murdered seventeen years ago. The distance, as the crow flies, from 29 Laundry Hill to 703 Ocotillo Canyon where Wynn's body had been dug up was about half a mile, longer if you walked because of the twisty streets. Walking it would take maybe eight minutes.

Gentrification had come to Dudley a while back now and many of the houses that lined the narrow winding street were tarted up with fancy colors; some had two, three, even four different colors on the trim, trying for that San Francisco look. Little two-bedroom shacks selling for the same, no, actually more, a lot more than what it would cost to buy a nice cinderblock three-bedroom ranch-style house with a few acres like where Wishman lived.

And, *and* if you bought one of these cute little houses you had to hope it wasn't all just fresh paint—most of them had major structural problems. Look at Chloe's house; she had that bad leak last spring and never fixed it as far as he knew. He needed to ask her if it was leaking again. Not only that, one whole corner of the bedroom probably needed to be jacked up, he'd proven that to her with a marble one day, setting it on the floor so she could watch it roll away. He'd noticed that way back when they first met.

Back when she was a suspect in a homicide case.

Manzanita turned into Laundry Hill a ways down and the street got even narrower, so Flynn parked under a big cottonwood for shade and got out to a serenade of cicadas. It was hot, really hot, damn hot, too hot, and the heavy monsoon season added humidity. Not a breath of a breeze rustled the bird-of-paradise that grew along the side of the street or flickered the leaves of the huge cottonwood. He pulled out a handkerchief and wiped his brow.

Number 29 Laundry Hill was close to street level, just a few steep steps leading up to the house—what Flynn could see of it. There was a wrought-iron fence all around with an arched trellis twined with yellow roses over the wrought-iron gate. Bees buzzed busily around the roses. He walked up, pushed open the gate, and went into the yard. It was spotless, mostly brick with large pots of desert plants and two slatted-wood Adirondack chairs in bright blue that looked as though no one had ever sat in them.

Flynn was willing to bet there was not one trace of Annie Glenn or her daughter Rachel's life left in this place—it had all been gentrified clear out of existence. He went up to the porch—stained-glass transom, lilies and vines, over the door—and knocked. Silence. Everyone out working, paying for those Adirondack chairs; nobody home to answer the door to the nice ex-cop who wanted to come and look around at what was once the scene of a homicide.

The people who lived there, did they know about Annie Glenn? How well did they sleep each night? Did they sleep in the same bedroom that had once had the red sheets?

He went back down to the street. Across the way in front of a yellow wooden house a blond teenage boy with a shovel was digging out small cancer trees and throwing them in a pile on the sidewalk. The air was filled with their dense musty scent.

On this side, next door, Alice Hayes's house—she still lived there according to the phone book—was painted three shades of muted green and had a narrow front porch fronted by a stand of bright red, yellow, and pink zinnias. A bicycle lay on its side by the porch steps. Flynn headed in that direction.

At that moment, a young man with spiky brown hair wearing jeans and a black T-shirt came out the front door, took the porch steps in one leap, righted the bicycle, and swung on a leg over it.

"Hey!" called Flynn.

The young man ignored him.

Flynn walked over into his line of vision and waved his arms. The young man put a leg down to balance the bicycle, removed some earbuds from his ears, and looked at him inquiringly.

"I'm looking for Alice Hayes," Flynn said.

"She's at work."

"And you are . . . ?"

"Max. Her nephew." He paused. "Who are *you*?"

"Brian Flynn. I'm a private investigator."

Max raised his eyebrows. "Wow. I mean, do you have, like, *identification*?"

Flynn pulled out his card and handed it over.

Max took it. *"Awesome."* He examined one side, turned it over and examined the other, then looked up. "My aunt works at Aloe Vera Associates over in Sierra Vista. She's a counselor." He scratched his head. "I don't suppose you're, um, actually *investigating* my aunt?"

Flynn bit off a smile and shook his head. "Just had a couple of questions for her."


The night before when I got home I'd read all Flynn's reports, so I was more or less up to date when I called Rachel first thing in the morning and set up a meeting. I stopped in at work, took a call from Flynn, and then typed up a letter of resignation on my computer and printed it out. Larry was at a workshop in Sierra Vista, so I left it on his desk.

Half the way to Tucson I kept thinking, *Not too late to turn back and retrieve that letter, not too late, not too late.* I could still have a more or less normal job and while I hated Larry, well . . . Flynn and I didn't always get along so well either. Then I was passing Kolb Road, and then the exit for the airport, and it was too late, the freeway looped north around the edge of Tucson, then I turned off on Prince and went east to Oracle and turned again. The gallery was in an upscale plaza way on the northwest side of town.

I walked through paved courtyards, past little adobe shops with red-tiled roofs full of things no one needed, but possibly couldn't live happily without, past a tinkling fountain and lots of spiky greenery, until I came upon the Hartman Gallery.

In the big front window were three bugs. Scorpions, just like the ones that stung me every year or so in Dudley, usually when I was in bed. When I walked in, the first thing I saw was another bug about six feet tall. Bugs were everywhere displayed on little stands: spider-type bugs, kissing-bug-type bugs, beetles, and more scorpions.

Behind a desk at the back was a pretty young woman: blond hair expensively cut in wings that framed her smoothly tanned face and even features. She was dressed all in white: white capris, white polo top, pearls around her neck that looked real, and pearl studs in her earlobes.

She stood up and came around the desk and I saw she was wearing white flip-flops studded with fake turquoise bits.

"Chloe?" Her demeanor was calm, a little aloof.

"Yes," I said, thrown off guard. "Rachel?" Surely this wasn't the woman Flynn had described. I'd imagined someone so different; a victim, sad, anxious, possibly a little disheveled.

She nodded. "That's me, here among the insects. Do you like the show?" As if I were a prospective customer.

"Interesting," I said.

Rachel turned, leaned over the desk, and picked something up. When she turned back her face had changed, she looked almost shy.

"My mom." She handed me a photograph.

Annie Glenn in jeans, fringed purple leather vest, and a cowboy hat, standing in front of a mike. From under the cowboy hat, her bright blond hair was a tangle of curls, her face alive and intent on the music. "She's beautiful," I said.

"Everyone said so." The shy person was gone and the calm young woman was back. She tossed her head as if my remark were a mere bagatelle. And so obvious. She touched a pearl earring lightly. "Sometimes I'd sing with her."

"Do you still sing?" I asked.

She looked away. "No." Back was the vulnerability. As if embarrassed, she took the photograph from my hand. "Here," she said, pointing, "behind my mom you can see Teddy. He played lead guitar. Actually he could play anything, he was the genius."

"And what was your mom?"

"The goddess," she said without hesitation. "Teddy was the genius, she was the goddess, Billy was the nice guy, and Wynn, Wynn was the clown." Her face saddened, then brightened. "I forgot I knew that stuff."

"Wynn was the clown," I said.

"I didn't bring his picture. I don't know why." She made a face. "I guess I should have. My mom, she died without knowing about Wynn. It's so strange. Everyone thought he'd left town for some reason without telling anybody. Teddy and Billy were really mad at him."

"But not your mom?"

"No." She put the photo down on the desk. "She never got mad at Wynn."

"Someone else has identified his body," I said.

"*No. Really?* I was so scared I'd have to." Her voice was eager. "Who was it?"

"Sonora Cloud?"

Her brow wrinkled.

"I guess she was an old girlfriend? She teaches yoga?"

She shook her head. "I've never heard of her. It sounds like an old Dudley person, though, a name like that. If she was one of

Wynn's girlfriends . . ." She shrugged. "The band had lots of girl-friends. I didn't keep track."

"We'd really like to find one of Wynn's relatives. The police will want to be able to nail down the identification."

"Is that, like, DNA?" Rachel asked, for the first time sounding young.

I nodded. "Or dental records, or relatives who would know about bone fractures if he had any. But at least I was hoping you might know where he came from."

"Oh, my goodness," Rachel said. "He was from back East somewhere, but other than that, I have no idea."

"By the way . . ." I handed her my card from work. "You can reach me here for the next two weeks or at Flynn's office, depending. I've added my home and cell number. Flynn said he talked to you yesterday."

"He did," said Rachel. "He wanted to know if I knew how to reach Teddy or Billy, but I don't. I told him that when he called about you."

"He said you seemed upset."

*"Really?"* Rachel raised her eyebrows, backtracking to cool bland blonde again right before my eyes. "I can't imagine what he meant. I'm sorry if you had to come all the way to Tucson to check on me, but I didn't hire Flynn to keep track of my mental health. My mental health is just fine, thank you."

"In that case," I said, "I do have a question for you, about Kurt Dickens."

"What about him?"

"Why are you so sure it wasn't him?" Everyone had asked her that question, probably from the day of the murder, but I wanted to hear for myself what she said.

"Because . . . ," said Rachel. She took a breath. "My mom was just so great, it was always fun being with her, exhilarating, like—like a roller coaster. But when she started seeing Kurt, it was . . . it was different. It wasn't as much fun, but for the first time I felt—I felt *safe*."

There was a little silence. Rachel bit her lip, as if in that moment of candor she'd gone too far and regretted it.

"You know, don't you," I persisted, "he had some charges against him. Domestic violence. One assault and one criminal damage."

"That is so not true." Rachel looked at me pityingly as if she were trying hard to make this work but I just didn't get it. "He never touched my mom."

"Not your mom. From before. Someone called Camille, Camille Chartrand."

*"Her."* Rachel looked scornful. "My mom told me about *her*. She made up bad things to get back at him—she was evil. She got into fights with everyone. Maybe *she* killed my mom. You should talk to her. And one more thing."

"Yes?" I looked at her, all in white with her pearls, her perfect blond hair; but in her blue eyes, something skittered.

"Everyone worked so hard back then asking questions, investigating, putting on a big show for the trial. Like, for what? For nothing. I mean, they asked all the wrong questions." She bent her head, closed her eyes, and put her hands together as if in prayer. "My memory is really bad from that time, whole pieces are gone, but I—I remembered something I never told anyone."

"When—" I began.

"When I woke up this morning."

"Rachel, wow. No kidding. What—"

"But it's not complete." Her voice was apologetic.

"That's okay. Give me whatever you have," I said.

"Someone was with me." She took a breath. "In the house. When I found her."

"You mean Alice Hayes?"

"No. That was later. I ran over to get her. This was in the house, our house."

I'd read the police reports and I hadn't come across any mention of someone being there with Rachel.

"I keep trying to remember more." Her voice rose, distressed. "I just *can't.*"

"Give it some time," I said. "Sometimes it works to let it go instead of trying."

"I'm afraid," she said. "So afraid to let go. I guess I'm afraid if I do, I'll crumble into little pieces."

"Call me anytime, will you? Anytime you want." I could feel myself connecting with her now, all her bland blondness just a show. "When you're feeling crumbly. Sometimes just to talk to someone can help."

She smiled. "You know who you remind me of?" she said. "Just a little bit. Jody Rasmussen."

I was surprised. "I know her," I said. "The prosecutor's wife?"

She nodded. "She sat with me at the trial when I was waiting outside to be called. She was really pregnant. Her third."

"She has five now," I said.

## chapter fourteen

THE RECEPTION AREA AT ALOE VERA ASSOCI-
ates was large and carpeted in wall-to-wall Berber in a soothing
shade of cream. Flynn knew it was Berber carpeting because that
was what Val had wanted—and gotten, of course—for their bedroom. Large green plants stood watch over prints of happy Pueblo
Indians and their pots. Flynn walked up to the desk, where a red-
haired woman sat reading *Guns & Ammo*. When she saw Flynn,
she closed the magazine and smiled.

She was maybe forty-five and her eyes were green and her
skin freckled. "How can I help you?" she asked.

"I'd like to see Alice Hayes."

"Name?"

"Brian Flynn."

She looked at an open book, running her finger down a column.
"I don't see it." She looked up. "Are you sure you made an appointment?"

"I'm not a patient," Flynn said, flinching inwardly at the thought
that anyone might think he would actually have an appointment to
see a therapist. "I just wanted to speak with her."

"I don't know." The redhead looked at him dubiously. "She's
with a client right now. Are you, um, selling something?"

"No," said Flynn. "I'm a private investigator, I just have some minor questions for her concerning a case I'm working on."

To his right was a hall and down that hall, out of the corner of his eye Flynn saw a door open. A youngish woman, very, very thin, in tight jeans and a skimpy orange top, came out and the bells went off in Flynn's head, *meth addict, meth addict.* She was followed by a middle-aged women with tight brown curls and old-fashioned big round glasses. She gave the girl a pat on her bony shoulder and said something Flynn couldn't hear.

"That Alice?" he asked.

The receptionist shook her head.

Flynn didn't buy it. *"Alice?"* he said loudly.

"Yes?"

He turned. It wasn't the woman down the hall, it was a woman who had just walked in: a frizzy haired blond, late forties, wearing tiny red-framed glasses, long craft-fair-beaded earrings.

"Alice Hayes?"

"That's me. How can I help you?"

With a client indeed. But he respected the receptionist's lie—after all, he could have been an irate former patient, unhealed and come back to shoot his unsuccessful therapist. These things happened.

"I'm Brian Flynn." As he came toward her he pulled out his card. "Private investigator."

She took the card, glanced at it, then looked up at him. *"Okay,"* she said. *"Interesting."* Her voice was self-assured and slightly patronizing. "If this is about one of my clients, then you do understand there's confidentiality except in certain very limited circumstances which you might have to get a court order to prove?"

"Well," said Flynn. "I guess I'm lucky it's not about one of your clients."

"Then . . . who?"

"Annie Glenn."

"Annie? Oh, my goodness. *Annie,*" she said, like a real person, instead of a calm therapist. She glanced over at the receptionist. "Mary Beth, how's my schedule?"

"You're free for . . . oh, twenty minutes. Then you have . . ." The receptionist mouthed something Flynn didn't catch.

"Right," said Alice. "Twenty minutes. If I'm not done, they can wait, I guess." She looked at Flynn. "Follow me."

In Alice's large corner office were two green slip-covered easy chairs, a leather couch, and some splashy colorful pictures on the walls. She closed the door. "Sit, sit."

Flynn took the nearest chair and Alice sat across from him on the other.

"I assume you're not investigating Annie Glenn, per se," said Alice. "But her murder. And who are you working for?"

"Her daughter."

"Oh!" Alice put her hand to her throat. "*Rachel.* I haven't seen her since she was ten years old. She was darling . . . a darling girl. I'll do anything I can to help. *God.*" She paused. "I heard the shot that killed Annie. I mean, it was right next door, but it was the monsoon season. Like now." She leaned back in her chair and closed her eyes. "I assumed it was thunder."

"Rachel came over the next morning, *sobbing,* and got me. I went back with her and I looked in where Annie was. I wish I hadn't. I wish to this day I hadn't. The top of her head was blown off, bits of her brain on the wall." She shuddered. "It's taken me years to be able to deal with this; I went to a bunch of counselors; in fact, it's how I became a therapist." She bowed her head and began to weep.

Flynn cleared his throat, looked around the room as Alice wept—there was a desk in one corner with a bowl of yellow roses on it, and the shadow of a tree on a drawn white shade—thinking this was what he hated most about this work, but also why he had to do it in the first place.

"I have something for her," said Alice, between sobs.

"Who? Rachel?"

"Yes. It's a box of stuff that was her mom's."

"Really?" said Flynn with interest. "Like what?"

"It's been a while since I looked at it. Odds and ends. I kept meaning to locate Rachel, but I never— Could you tell her? And also that I'd love to see her, or help in any way that I can possibly can."

"I'll do that," Flynn said. He paused. "Actually, I'd like to take a look at that box myself. You never know."

Alice blew her nose. "She'll have to give me permission herself."

"I can arrange that."

There was a silence.

"Uh, twenty-nine Laundry Hill," Flynn said. "Who lives there now?"

"No one. It's a weekend rental. There have been three or four owners. Annie was just renting and after it happened the original owner sold the place cheap." She glanced at Flynn. "I've got the key, if you'd like to take a look around."

"Thanks. I would at some point." He paused. "The band, Point of No Return? Any of them still around?"

"Teddy is, he still plays in a band, weekends mostly. Still at the St. Elmo's Bar on the Gulch." Alice sighed. "Wynn left town before Annie was murdered, then Billy was so upset he left too, really right away after it happened. I always thought Teddy would leave as well—he's so talented, I thought he might actually make it in the music business. But he stuck around. He lives with a woman, Carol Denny. I remember her from when she first came to Dudley eight, nine years ago. She's had a tough life, lots of abuse. Sad kind of person, but Teddy took her in. Kind of looks after her. She's been a lot happier since then."

"Carol Denny," Flynn said.

She smiled. "He doesn't call her that, he calls her Rosalie."

"Any idea where he lives?"

Alice nodded. "Mule Hill," she said, and gave him directions.

"What about this Dickens guy?"

"Kurt. A nice man but not ambitious, if you know what I mean. He liked working on Annie's house and gardening and he loved Annie. He loved Rachel too." She smiled sadly. "Annie didn't really appreciate him."

"How did you see it?" Flynn asked. "Poor old unappreciated Kurt kills her and gets off?"

"Kurt sure didn't act like he'd killed her. He acted like a man in shock and grief. I guess he could be a sociopath but he never struck me that way. And he was probably a better father to Rachel than her real one. Annie wouldn't even take child support from Phil Glenn."

"Yeah?" said Flynn, suddenly alert. "Why not?"

"That was partly pride," said Alice. "Annie always wanted to be her own independent person. But partly because, well, these were her words, she said he was seriously creepy."

"Seriously creepy?" Flynn perked up. Seriously creepy, and he was down from Tucson picking up Rachel right away? "How so?"

"Well . . . Annie could be cruel, sometimes. She threw out these little expressions. What was it she called him? An emotional basket case. That's all I know. I'd never met him till he picked up Rachel, and that was brief."

There was a pause, then Flynn said, "Dickens had a couple of domestic violence charges in a previous relationship. Did you know that?"

*"No."* Alice looked stunned. "No, I didn't." She put her head in her hands. "I'm shocked. That didn't come up at the trial."

"Just charges, no convictions. Her name was Camille Chartrand."

Alice sat up straight. "Camille Chartrand. That explains it. She really made the rounds back then. She was notorious—she fought with everyone. I didn't know she and Kurt had been together."

"She still around by any chance?"

"Actually, she is. She has a studio on Quarry Canyon—That's just off Tombstone: five-oh-five. Actually I think she was Wynn's girlfriend off and on for a while too, not to mention a few others. She's, um, calmed down a lot. Teaches yoga, in fact. She has a different name now—she goes by Sonora, Sonora Cloud."

Sonora Cloud, thought Flynn. The woman who'd IDed Wynn's body.


I kept thinking about Jody, the prosecutor Jim Rasmussen's wife, all the way home, remembering her from the class I taught. Because she'd lost her own father young, it made sense to me that she would want to comfort Rachel. I'd always thought of Jody as a good person, smart too. I wondered if she'd sat through the whole trial. It would be interesting to get her take on it—especially her opinion as to Kurt's guilt. I pulled into the McDonald's parking lot at the Sierra Vista exit from the I-10, called Kelly at work, and got her to look up Jody Rasmussen's number in the Crisis Intervention Training files. Then I called Jody, mentioned Rachel.

"I'd love to talk," she said, and gave me directions to her house in the Foothills. "I'm fresh out of kids today, thank God, so I'll be out back gardening. Just come around the side."

The house was on a small side road off Turkey Hollow Run, a

rambling kind of place, graying cedar and a lot larger than it looked. I went around the side as Jody had told me and there she was, her back to me, in dirty jeans and a gray man's T-shirt, red bandanna wrapped around her hair, shovel in hand. She was digging a hole in a garden bed. Next to the hole was a rosebush, roots wrapped in burlap.

"Jody?" I said.

She gave a little yelp and turned, the shovel still in her hand.

"Don't shoot," I said.

"Chloe." She giggled like one of her kids might and removed the bandanna. She was a sturdy woman, the muscles of her arms well defined, but her hair as light and gossamer as I remembered it, her face not pretty but pleasant and makeup-free. "Let's go inside, please."

We sat in her roomy kitchen full of sun at a big oak table, drinking hibiscus tea; everywhere children's drawings, stacks of books and papers and kitsch. Little china kittens with balls of yarn, china dogs with tongues hanging out. Over the sink was a framed cross-stitch: NO OTHER SUCCESS CAN COMPENSATE FOR FAILURE IN THE HOME.

"Darling little Rachel," she said sadly. "Sitting so silent and pale—I had to give her some support. Her father was there, but so stiff, no help at all—out of his element, I think." She paused. "I believe Jim had known her mother slightly—through the choir."

I nodded. "Did you sit through the rest of the trial?"

"Yes, and I waited around for the verdict too and it was not guilty. Jim was so . . . so *humiliated,* Chloe." She closed her eyes. "It was awful."

"He lost," I said, "but what did *you* think about the verdict, Jody?"

"It was all over my head," said Jody. "I was just there to support my husband."

"But just between us," I persisted. She wasn't dumb—she had

a master's degree in social work from a good university. "Did you think Kurt Dickens killed Annie Glenn or did you agree with the jury that he wasn't guilty?"

"Oh!" said Jody as if I hadn't spoken. "I am *so* absentminded today. I have to pick up my youngest at the pool in exactly fifteen minutes. I almost forgot. Oh, Chloe, forgive me, I have to run." She stood up. "I'll talk to Jim, have him search through for any files he might have, make sure he contacts you."

I nodded. We walked outside together through the kitchen door.

"It's so good to see you, Chloe," Jody said. "Let's get together again sometime."

Out back next to the shovel, the rosebush lay still wrapped in burlap. We went around the side to my car. A couple of bicycles were propped up on the side of a gray cedar garage near a basketball hoop, a skateboard lay on the grass. I got in my car. She waved as I drove off.

I could see her in the rearview mirror, a sturdy figure, fine hair so gossamer in the heat, and lost, almost lost, in all the paraphernalia of her children.

# chapter fifteen

IT WAS LATE AFTERNOON AND RACHEL SAT
still moored behind the little desk surrounded by metal critters.
Hardly anyone had come in except for Chloe. Why had she said
that to Chloe about crumbling? She'd wanted to show her she
was strong and in control. Her cell chimed.

"Flynn here."

"Yes?" said Rachel.

"I'd like to have Chloe interview your dad."

Rachel's stomach lurched. "Why?"

"We just need to cover all the bases. No big deal. Do you have
a problem with that?"

"No." She felt slightly queasy. "Go ahead if you think it's really
necessary."

"And I spoke with Alice Hayes today where she works in Sierra
Vista. She asked me to tell you she'd love to see you and/or help
in any way she can."

*"Alice."* Rachel blinked. Alice had been probably her mom's
best friend.

"Also she told me she has a box of stuff for you that belonged
to your mom."

"She does?" Rachel was stunned. It was hard to believe that

Alice still existed, that her mom hadn't taken Alice with her, like she'd taken the rest of Rachel's life up to that point. "How *is* Alice?"

"She seems fine," said Flynn.

"I mean, you said work, you saw her at work. What does she do?" The Alice Rachel had known was flighty and had had no clue what to do with her life.

"She's a therapist."

"No. *No.* How can that be?" Rachel said in shock. "She never had any training or—"

"Rachel?"

"What?"

"It's been *seventeen years.* She got training. I'd like your permission for Alice to give me the box so I can go through it. She gave me her cell number, could you call her and tell her it's okay?"

"Alice," Rachel said again. She wrote down the number. "I'll do that," she said.

She should do it right away but she felt reluctant. Instead she watched the second hand on her watch go around and around until it was five, then she closed down the gallery. There was a chance of rain, the weatherman had said, but when Rachel stepped out into the courtyard it was still so hot out that even though she'd parked under a tree and put the big reflector sunshade on the window the seat was too hot to sit on.

And she still felt queasy. Should she take another Ativan? No. The more she took, the less it worked.

*Alice. A therapist.* Did that mean if she called Alice, Alice would do a therapist number on her? Rachel was sick and tired of therapists; she wanted the old Alice, flighty, full of gossip.

She pulled out the old towel from the back, put it on the seat, got in, and turned on the air-conditioning to high. She sat for a moment while the car cooled down. Her cell phone chimed.

"Sweetheart," boomed Phil Glenn.

Rachel closed her eyes and rested her head on the steering wheel. "Hi, Dad."

"Some character called me just now, Brian Flynn? Your investigator."

"Are you going to talk to him?"

"Yes. But not him. Someone called Chloe. Rach—like I said before, why open all that up again?"

"To find out what really happened."

"The guy did it, sweetheart. Kurt Dickens. He just got away with it. Look, honey, I know Scott's out of town. How about dinner tonight? Janos. You love Janos. They have the summer sampler now."

And he would try to talk her out of the investigation. She knew he would. "Thanks, Dad, but I've been at work all day and I'm too tired."

"Oh, well . . . okay. Love you."

"Love you," Rachel echoed.

She drove to AJ's Fine Foods and lingered in the produce section before she hit the deli takeout. She wished Chloe hadn't told her about the domestic violence charges against Kurt. At the deli counter she bought shrimp salad and tabouleh to go. Her cell chimed again.

"Hey, sweetheart."

She smiled. *Sweetheart,* just like her dad, but this time it was Scott. "Hi," she said. "I'm at AJ's."

"Getting shrimp salad."

"Call me when I get home, okay?"

"You're all right?"

"Fine." She paused, wondering if she should mention about Alice, and then said, "But call me later, okay?"

She felt even queasier now, shaky. She didn't want to take

another Ativan and she wished she hadn't thought about her conversation with Chloe. She wished her dad hadn't called. And most of all she wished Alice hadn't turned into a therapist.

Thunder rumbled far away but there was still no rain. Flynn and I were meeting at my house at five-thirty to compare notes, Flynn had promised sandwiches, but it was only four, so I went back to work. Larry wasn't around but Kelly said he'd seen my letter. She said it just like that with a straight face: "Yes, he saw it."

Oh, well, at least I didn't have to worry any more about what Larry thought or waste time disliking him. I entered some old cases into the new program until a little after five and when I got home Flynn's Land Rover was parked down below and he was waiting in my carport, wearing jeans and a navy blue polo shirt and holding a take-out bag from the Prickly Pear Café.

I was the one who'd persuaded him that polos looked better than T-shirts and I was proud of it. He looked great, like Colin Farrell, the movie star, not that I was a particular fan of Farrell.

"Got a meeting with a client at seven over at my office," he said as if he'd read my mind, "a last-minute deal; otherwise"—he half smiled—"I wouldn't be wearing this damn sissy polo shirt."

"I can't believe you're still driving that Land Rover," I parried, disappointed he'd be leaving soon. "What a gas guzzler."

He took it like a man, his face patient, stoic.

I was so glad to see him I cut a wide swath around him on my way to the door, so he wouldn't see me smiling.

"Camille was Dickens's girlfriend and *Wynn's*," Flynn mused as he followed me in. "I wonder if anyone questioned her back then."

He hadn't been in my house since our big fight last spring, the climax of a series of fights in a relationship that was bound to

burn out. For a second I almost imagined a whiff of smoke linger-
ing in the air.

"I need to talk to Stan Cooper," Flynn went on. "He was the defense attorney."

"Uh," I said, "Stan's dead. Heart attack, about a year ago."

"Damn," said Flynn. "Well, at least Jim Rasmussen's still alive
and kicking. You said you talked to his wife, Jody?"

"She's going to make sure he looks for old files and gets in
touch."

"And you can talk to him—you're used to prosecutors."

"Plus he knew Annie from the choir," I said. "Though according
to Jody, only slightly. Coffee?" I offered.

"Sure."

We sat at my dining room table drinking coffee, eating blue
cheese beef and avocado-turkey sandwiches and exchanging information. We'd had a big fight a few months ago. What were we
now? Technically he was my employer, I was his employee.

"So Camille Chartrand and Sonora Cloud are one and the same,"
I said.

"You can talk to Camille too. You're local. But right now let's focus on Daddy. Phil Glenn's a pretty well known developer." Flynn
pushed a file over. "Did a little checking. Nothing really illegal,
but"—he rubbed his chin—"he's a developer and he made a lot of
money off it, so"—he laughed sardonically—"the guy can't be a
saint. Never remarried."

"And Alice said Annie told her he was an emotional basket
case and creepy? I wonder if they even checked out Phil Glenn
back then," I said in exasperation. "Or just rushed to judgment."

"I set you up for an interview with him tomorrow at eleven
forty-five, will that work? See if you get a feel for him, something
off. Did he even have an alibi?" Flynn leaned across the table.
"What I thought was, kind of dress up a little in something you'd

wear to court so Dad won't be telling Rachel we're a fly-by-night organization."

"Come on, Flynn," I said indignantly. I couldn't tell if he meant it or was just trying to rile me. "Have a little faith."

He grinned wickedly. "I'll go find Teddy Radebaugh tomorrow—he's the only band member around, and still playing at the St. Elmo's. Some guys never do grow up."

"You know what," I said, "I know who he is, I just never knew his last name. I've heard him, he's really good. And he's got that strange woman he looks after."

"Carol something, Alice mentioned her. Said Teddy calls her Rosalie."

"Well, I like Rosalie better than Carol," I said. I had a picture of her in my mind, skipping down Main Street like a little girl with a jump rope. And another, darker picture of her, in tears outside the St. Elmo's Bar.

There was a pause.

"Jack Nelson couldn't tell me cause of death yet," said Flynn, "or wouldn't. But I can tell you this—if it's a gunshot wound and it's the same gun as killed Annie . . ." He shrugged. "Wishman bought the damn gun off Dickens after the trial, so it's still around. If it's the same gun, then I think maybe Kurt Dickens is screwed."

"Another railroad job," I said. "Just exactly what Rachel didn't want."

"Rachel has to face the fact that Dickens might be guilty," said Flynn. "But Jack's got a little more sense than Wishman. I hope. You know what gets me? Kurt loaning Annie his gun. I mean if we go with that story. It sucks, you know?" He cracked his knuckles in exasperation. "So now we have a woman, alone in a house, hears a noise, gets the gun, and goes to investigate. Unless she's prepared to shoot and comfortable with it, she's given the intruder a deadly weapon."

I'd heard this riff from Flynn many times, along with the one about people who had inadequate locks on their doors, namely me, until he fixed them. Flynn would be a cop forever, his brain etched with copness.

He stood up. "Gotta run.

"Oh, and by the way," he said, pausing on his way out the door, "how's the roof in your office holding up with all the rain? I bet you never got anyone to fix it, like I said you should."

"It's *fine*," I lied defensively. "Better run, it's late."

The house was so quiet, so empty. Rachel put the shrimp salad and tabouleh on one of the yellow Fiestaware plates, poured out some of the raspberry iced tea she always kept in the fridge, and took it into the living room. She clicked on the TV. Should she call Alice now? Her cell was in her purse. Somehow she couldn't bear to. Maybe tomorrow, or the day after. Just sometime when it felt right. But there might be something in the box that would help Flynn. *Do it.*

She didn't need her cell to call Alice, she could use the regular phone. She went back into the kitchen where the regular phone was and punched in the number. And got Alice's voice mail. In a way she was relieved.

"Alice, this is Rachel. I'm calling to give permission for you to give Flynn the box of my mom's stuff. Okay? 'Bye. See you soon."

See you soon? What did that mean?

Scott always called her on her cell, so she got it out of her purse on the kitchen counter and brought it into the living room, just as the local news came on.

"More bloodshed in the Middle East," said Heather Rowles of Channel Thirteen. "And closer to home . . ."

Not the news, thought Rachel. For a second, she had a flash of Wynn, funny Wynn, curled up in a grave. He looked like a child. She felt a tickle of anxiety.

She changed to the Home & Garden channel, where an expert was telling a woman that her overly quirky bathroom remodel had lowered the value of her home by ten thousand dollars, and made herself eat about half of what was on her plate but she wasn't hungry anymore. She took the plate out to the kitchen, covered what was left with Saran Wrap, and put it in the fridge.

Then she called Scottie but his phone was off. Sometimes at those conferences a bunch of them would all go out to dinner someplace and Scottie always turned off his cell to be polite.

Edgy, she sat down on the couch again and watched back-to-back episodes of *What Not to Wear* but the usually enjoyable sight of Stacy and Clinton transforming plain women into beauties couldn't calm her.

She got an Ativan from the pillbox in her purse, swallowed it with some of the raspberry iced tea, and then went outside and sat by the pool to wait till it kicked in. It was calm tonight here in Tucson; no rain and no wind, the sky so full of stars they put a sheen of silver on the pool. She closed her eyes and felt not the starry sky and silver sheen but a blackness where dark creatures prowled. From inside the house the phone rang in the kitchen. Not her cell.

Alice. Alice was calling her back. Alice was going to offer to be her therapist. But she could handle Alice now, with the Ativan.

She hurried inside. "Hello?"

"Rachel?"

A man's voice, not Scott's, not her father's, not Flynn's. No one she recognized. "Who is this?" she asked.

"Rachel, it's Kurt. Kurt Dickens."

"Kurt," she said. "Oh, Kurt."

# chapter sixteen

DESPITE THE FACT THAT IT WAS WELL OVER A hundred degrees in Tucson, as soon as I walked into the courtyard of the plaza where Phil Glenn had his offices I felt instantly cooler. Red bird-of-paradise edged the Saltillo paving, a big ceramic fountain burbled soothingly. It reminded me of the place where Rachel worked, the same fake world of old-time courtyards and fountains, all the colors time-muted soft Southwest and brand-new. The sign outside said DESERT PROSPECTIVES in simple subdued lettering that hinted at having nothing to prove.

I hadn't needed Flynn's fashion tips to figure out what to wear: a black gauze sundress—you can dress something like that up or down and it's always very hot in Tucson this time of year. Over it I had a black loosely crocheted cotton mini-sweater for the air-conditioning, which hit me full blast as I pushed open the dark carved wood door.

Inside the carpeting was terra-cotta and the walls were hung with blown-up photographs of construction sites framed like expensive art. It was very quiet, as if all the action were someplace else—on dusty desert lots with big Caterpillars noisily gouging the ground and a lot of men in hard hats, yelling at each other.

From Flynn's file I knew that Phil Glenn primarily dealt with commercial properties and had done very well. Flynn had included some newspaper articles with photographs of Rachel's father taken over the years at various charity fund-raisers, a fair-haired man with a big jaw, smiling for the camera, a good-looking woman always beside him, but not always the same good-looking woman.

From behind a big shiny cherrywood desk, a perfect platinum blonde smiled as if she were glad to see me. "Miss Newcombe?"

"Yes," I said.

She pointed to my right. "Through that door."

I went through and as if I had stumbled into a series of Chinese boxes there was another big shiny cherrywood desk and another perfect blonde, this one more ash, a secretary as opposed to a receptionist.

"Chloe?" she said brightly, just as delighted to see me. "You have a lunch date with Phil. He's in his office, just go right in."

I walked where she gestured and opened the door to a spacious room like someone's living room; along one wall were bookcases, half books, half Indian art, and facing me a huge window with a view of beautiful smog-tinged blue mountains in the distance.

The man from the newspaper photos got up from a large untidy oak desk and strode toward me, hand outstretched. He wore a taupe linen sports jacket and was older now, heavier, grown a bit more into the big jaw. His eyes were so bright, so blue they seemed to precede him. "Miss Newcombe?"

I took his hand. "Chloe."

"Great! Chloe. I'm Phil." His hair was well cut, the kind of hair that goes from blond to gray with hardly a difference. You sensed a well-toned body under the expensive jacket. Everything about him seemed worked at, cared for, developed like his projects. "Let's sit down over here."

There was a black leather couch with a stainless steel and glass coffee table in front of it and a couple of wing chairs. I sat on a wing chair covered in red tapestry. He commandeered the couch.

"There's a nice little restaurant close by," Phil went on. "I took the liberty of ordering in a bunch of lunch-type stuff, I thought privacy might be best under the circumstances." He smiled at me, his smile so solicitous for a moment I felt like a client with a million bucks or maybe just someone he needed to lie to. "Of course, if you'd prefer to go out . . ."

It wasn't really a question.

"No, here is great," I said.

"Now"—he relaxed back into the couch and steepled his fingers—"I love my daughter very much, she's my only child, and while I have my doubts about her digging up all this old stuff, I'll do whatever I can to assist you." He raised his eyebrow skeptically. "Whatever the hell that might be, I can't imagine."

"Why don't you give me an idea of your role in all this?" I said. "You came and got Rachel right away," I said, "after Annie was murdered."

"Alice Hayes, Annie's neighbor, called me. I was at work, I drove right down. I was all Rachel had. Annie's parents were still alive but they lived in Washington State and they were elderly, her father was in pretty poor health. I didn't want to further burden Annie's mother."

I nodded.

"And before we go any further . . ." He got up and went over to his desk and picked something up. "Here." He handed me a framed photograph.

A younger Phil Glenn and a woman stood side by side—the woman was so beautiful, gorgeous like some sort of Nordic goddess, I wondered if Phil was showing me this for bragging rights. "And?" I said.

"The woman is Molly Webber, we were together at this shindig to raise money for some kind of cancer, forget which kind now, you can see the banner in the background. It was my first foray into the social scene. Molly was pretty newly divorced and wanted to test out her wings, so we stayed late, two or three in the morning, then I went home with her." He paused. "It was the night Annie was killed."

"Your alibi," I said. And he was right there, ready with it. That was interesting.

"Yes," he said irritably. "It's absurd I should even have to think of an alibi for you. No one asked me for one back when Annie was actually murdered."

"No?" God, what a lame investigation. Kurt Dickens did it, folks, we can all go home.

"Why should they? I was way, way out of the picture by then." He paused. "I hardly had any contact with Annie at all."

"Yes, I understand Annie wouldn't accept any child support—why was that?"

"Ego, plain and simple." Phil shrugged. "Said she wanted to be a free woman." He snorted. "Is that hippie-dippie or what? I wasn't rolling in it yet back then, but I was doing okay, a lot better than she was, and I was perfectly willing to pay. And I still had parental rights whether I paid or not."

There was a knock on the door and then the secretary came in with a tray, which she set on the glass table—some white paper bags, cutlery, and a couple of plates. She took things out of the bags and put them on the plates.

"Go on," said Phil. "Help yourself."

Thirsty from my drive up, I reached for a bottle of water and opened it, took a couple of long swallows.

"You said you still had parental rights whether or not Annie let you pay child support." I bit into a miniature pizza covered with shrimp. I chewed, swallowed. Delicious. "Did you see Rachel a lot?"

"Hardly at all." Phil cleared his throat. "Actually, never. Annie made it so hard, it just wasn't worth it."

"Why would she do that?" I persisted. "Was there some bad blood between you?"

He shrugged. "No more than most couples who divorce, less than amicably. Basically Annie and I were happy together for maybe two years, three if you count before we were married, then sad together for three more before we split."

"How old was Rachel when that happened?"

"Two." He spread his arms, palms up, looking exasperated. "It wasn't *my* idea. Annie and I met in college, she was the star, did drama, art, things like that, I was the faithful friend, rescued her when she went too far, et cetera, et cetera."

"Went too far," I repeated. "Like how?"

His eyes got blank. "Just a figure of speech." He snorted. "I was so damn grateful when she married me. But not for all that long."

"Why's that?"

He looked at me across the perfect white paper bags of delicious food. "She cheated on me. Not just once but many times." For a second his face took on an expression, not angry as I might have guessed, but vulnerable. For a second I could see another side beyond the money and the power, maybe what fueled his drive.

"Now, of course," he went on, "I think, what the hell? People cheat all the time. It's part of life. But back then, well . . . I guess you might say she took away my innocence. To be honest . . ." He paused.

"Yes?" I said

"I figured if she treated that Dickens guy the same way she treated me, he probably did kill her. One reason I didn't want to pay for a further investigation into the whole mess after Dickens got off—I didn't want to turn over that rock. You know, Rachel was always fond of him, I let it go, didn't want her to get hurt any more than she already was."

There was a little silence.

"Besides, back then I thought, the hell with Annie," he said suddenly, vehemently. "She had a child, she could have lived more responsibly than to get herself murdered. Rachel, she's got problems to this day because of it."

"And now she's the one opening up this investigation," I said.

"And I wish to hell she weren't," said Phil. "Listen to me please and listen carefully. I have a lot of concerns for Rachel: she isn't stable. I've sent her to at least half a dozen therapists, some helpful, some idiots. One of the things that's bothered me for years is the sense I've had from the beginning that Rachel knows something." He paused. "Or saw something. Maybe something she doesn't even realize the importance of, but *something*."

I nodded thoughtfully.

"Something that might be threatening to the killer, be it Kurt Dickens or someone else. Another reason why I've never tried opening that can of worms."

"We'll do—"

"No, stop," he interrupted, "and listen." His face had changed again, this wasn't the solicitous Phil Glenn or the vulnerable, this Phil Glenn had power and used it, was maybe even a bully. "If anything bad happens to my little girl as a result of this investigation, then I will personally make sure you and Mr. Flynn will no longer operate out of Cochise County or any other county in Arizona."

Lulled by the excellent food, his pleasant manners, I hadn't seen anything like this coming. I stared across at him, shocked.

He looked a little abashed. "Sorry," he said. "When it concerns my little girl, sometimes I get kind of overwrought."

But menace still hung in the air.

The concrete steps to Teddy Radebaugh's house, high up on Mule Hill, were crumbling, treacherous, and to make matters worse the iron railing was coming loose from its moorings; poured, Flynn noted from a WPA stamp on one step, back in the 1930s. He could hardly see the house, lost behind clumps of cancer trees and a large oleander bush heavy with magenta flowers.

He reached the top and stopped, blocked by a rusted metal gate. He could see the house now, graying wood, potted ferns hanging from the eaves of the porch.

"Hello?" he called. "Hello, Ted?"

No answer.

But on the porch, Flynn noticed a wicker rocking chair, rocking gently back and forth. There was no wind.

Flynn opened the gate. "Hello," he called again.

A woman, very thin, came out onto the porch, wearing a flimsy pink and blue Indian cotton tank top and jeans. Her face was blank, blissful. Carol Denny, a.k.a. Rosalie. A long white cord dangled from her ears. Was she deaf?

No. An iPod. She was listening to music on an iPod, like half the teenagers Flynn saw on the street. That was why no one had answered, he'd been drowned out by whatever she was listening to. An iPod on this weathered gray porch.

Flynn came closer. The woman saw him then and stopped abruptly, removed the earbuds. Her hair was long, loose, and graying but the tank top looked like something a teenager would wear back in 1968 or right now at this moment in some suburban mall.

"Hello?" she said.

"You must be Rosalie," said Flynn. "I'm Brian Flynn. Looking for Teddy."

"Who—"

"Alice sent me. Alice Hayes."

Her face lit up. "Alice. I like Alice. Teddy's at Central School."

# chapter seventeen

CENTRAL SCHOOL WAS A HUNDRED-YEAR-OLD three-story brick building painted cream that long ago had been a school but was now, as the sign outside said, an artists' cooperative. It was a pretty fine building as buildings went, Flynn thought, solid and well made, with a bell tower in the center—he could see the big old bell, still hanging.

He went up three wide steps to the front door and pulled. Nothing budged. The door was half glass and he could see inside to a short flight of stairs that led up to a wide hallway. To his right was a button. He pushed it.

After a while a youngish woman in a loose black dress that only partly concealed a lot of extra weight came down the stairs and opened the door. Her hair was hennaed deep red and matched her mouth. When she saw Flynn she looked annoyed.

"You're not Marissa," she said accusingly.

"No, ma'am, I'm not. I'm looking for Teddy? Plays the guitar? Or used to."

She rolled her eyes. "Still does, along with a lot of other instruments. Up the steps, first door on the left."

The hallway floor was nice, old wood, the kind you used to be able to get that came from trees in virgin forests. There was art hanging on all the walls: paintings, drawings—some of it looked like second-graders had done it. Flynn sniffed alertly. Someone, somewhere, was smoking pot.

He knocked on the first door on the left.

As soon as the door opened into the room, Flynn knew he'd found the origin of the marijuana. A tall, lanky man wearing a red bandanna around his forehead stuck his head out. "Yeah?" He wore jeans and a black T-shirt that said DEE DEE RAMONE LIVES! and his long morose face looked as ravaged by time and drugs as an ancient rock star's.

"Ted Radebaugh?"

"Oh, *shit,* man," he said. "What the fuck? You're a cop, I know it. You got a warrant?"

"No, no," said Flynn. "I used to be a cop but now I don't care what you smoke. I'm a private investigator."

"Yeah?" Teddy's face remained guarded. "A private dick? A gumshoe? A shamus?"

"Take your pick," Flynn said. "Annie Glenn? Remember her?"

Teddy's face collapsed sorrowfully. "Of course I remember Annie. I'll always remember Annie." He sighed. "Come on in."

The room smelled very strongly of pot. Teddy batted the air as Flynn sat down on a sagging old couch covered with an army blanket full of moth holes. There were big dusty windows all along the front of the room and ranged around within it were various instruments: a set of drums, a guitar, a big old bass, even, if Flynn was not mistaken, a saxophone.

After Teddy finished batting the air for a while he sat down too, straddling a small wooden chair across from Flynn, backward, arms across the top.

"Annie loved Gram Parsons," he said.

"Aha," said Flynn. "And who was he?"

"You don't know?" Teddy looked at him with pity. "Practically invented country rock, died in '73. Played with the Byrds for a while, did an album with 'em, *Sweetheart of the Rodeo*? Then played with the Flying Burrito Brothers?"

Flynn shook his head. "Sorry."

"'Sin City,' bet you know that one. Buck Owens covered it, I think, and Dwight Yoakam."

"Dwight Yoakam," said Flynn. "Sure."

Valentine, his ex, had always loved Dwight Yoakam, owned every single one of his CDs, played them constantly, what was that song that was her favorite—"The Heart That You Own." Flynn's eyes drifted past Teddy out a dusty window, saw a piece of tin roof, a patch of blue sky.

"Gram struck out on his own after that, made some great music, and did a whole lot of drugs." Teddy bowed his head. "Dead at twenty-six. His manager burned up his corpse out in the California desert at Joshua Tree. A lot of people were pissed about that but in my opinion Gram would have wanted it that way."

"Live hard, die young, and all that stuff," said Flynn, switching his mind back from Valentine. As for Chloe, the last CD he'd heard her listen to, as far he could remember, was Radiohead, *The Bends*. Along with a deep-sea-diving phenomenon, wasn't the bends a term for heroin addiction? As an ex-narcotics officer he should know but he didn't. He could never figure out why the hell Chloe would listen to something like that, except that it had to do with her being a liberal.

"Anyway," said Teddy, rather loudly, as if he sensed Flynn's attention had strayed. "Annie really liked the songs from *Grievous Angel*—she sang the Emmylou Harris parts, Wynn did the Gram stuff."

Teddy stood up and began to pace the room. "We really were a good band," he said over his shoulder, by the drums. "Had some record company interest but nothing that panned out, and then Wynn split, stupid shit didn't even tell anyone he was leaving." Drumroll. "Then Annie dying pretty much killed us off."

Teddy hit the drums again, the cymbals, then back to the drums. "I'm with a band now called XS Noise. Come hear us play sometime, Friday and Saturday night down on the Gulch." He picked up the guitar and turned the chair the right way this time. "At the St. Elmo's."

"So where are Billy and Wynn now?" Flynn asked.

"No idea where Wynn's at. Haven't heard from him since he left town way back when without even bothering to tell anyone. Billy's in Vermont, got a wife, kids, some kind of general store." For a second, contemplating this, he looked astonished. "Might as well be dead. I'm the only one kept the faith."

He looked over at Flynn. "So what's with this, you being here? Going after old Kurt again? Thought you could only try someone once in this country." He bent over the guitar, strummed it a little. "Oh, wait," he said, looking up. "I forgot. The fascists have almost completely taken over now, haven't they?"

"Rachel hired me."

"*Rachel?* Ten years old? Wow . . . must be in her twenties now. Bet she's good-looking. She sang with the band a few times—a real show-off."

"Really?" said Flynn. Rachel was attractive in a controlled kind of way, but he didn't see her having the chutzpah to sing with a rock band. "So. Did you think Kurt Dickens killed Annie?"

"I think most people did." Teddy played a quick little riff. "It kind of made sense."

"Why's that?"

"Well, basically in Annie's life he was her gofer. Took care of her, beat off the fans, worked on her house. Annie sort of took him for granted the way some good-looking women will do. Maybe he just snapped, couldn't take it anymore, all that home repair and no respect. Or maybe Annie found another boyfriend and he got jealous."

"So did she?"

"Find another boyfriend?" Teddy's eyes shifted to a window. "Annie wasn't committed to Kurt. She was a free spirit."

"Hey," said Flynn, "let's get real here. How old are you anyway? Close to forty, I bet." He paused, looked at Teddy's ravaged face. "Or older."

Teddy looked down at his guitar and plucked a string, lackadaisically, as if he'd lost the energy to play it.

"That free spirit stuff is bull," Flynn went on, relentless. "Society as we know it would collapse if we all went around being free spirits."

"Okay, okay." Teddy held up a hand like a shield. "She saw other guys whenever she felt like it, which actually wasn't as much as you'd think. She was pretty busy between working at the Co-op, singing with the band, being a mother."

"You remember any other guys specifically?"

"No, but Billy said he saw her one night in her car with a guy, oh, a month or so before she was murdered, in what one might call a compromising clench. Wasn't anyone he knew, because he got curious and waited to see who it was."

"Oh, yeah? Did he mention that to law enforcement?"

"No." Teddy sighed. "It's a pretty weird story. When Annie got killed, Billy was so freaked he got in his old junker car and drove away almost immediately. I mean, from one moment to the next Billy was packing his shit and then he was gone. He didn't ever actually talk to that cop, what was his name?"

"Wishman."

"But later the defense—Mr. Cooper?—talked to him on the phone and Billy told him about this mysterious guy, and you know what? Mr. Cooper subpoenaed Billy for the trial. So he gets flown out here, sits outside the courtroom, but he never gets called. I saw him just for a few minutes before he left, he couldn't stand to be here, and you know what he told me? Sitting out there waiting to be called, he got the shock of his life. Well, one of them. The mysterious guy who'd been with Annie in the car was the goddamn *prosecutor*."

Flynn blinked. "Jim Rasmussen?"

Teddy nodded.

"And Billy never told anyone this?" Flynn asked in disbelief.

"Just me. Who's going to believe him, for Christ's sake? And we were all sure Kurt did it anyway. Why muddy the waters?"

"Got any idea how I can reach Billy?"

"Sure. I haven't talked to him for years but his wife sends a Christmas card." Teddy got up and went over to a desk, pulled out a drawer, and rummaged through. Then he came back. "Home address and I think—yeah, an e-mail address."

Flynn copied it all down.

Teddy began to strum the guitar again, softly, the same two chords over and over.

Flynn stood up and took out his card. "If you think of anything that might be useful, give me a call, I'd really appreciate it. And so would Rachel."

Teddy's face softened. "Say hi to her." He paused. "As for Annie—she had her faults, but you know what? When she was around everybody felt happier. She kind of lit up the room and nothing seemed as bad as it did before she showed up."

Flynn thought about that, then headed for the door, opened it. He was still processing that Jim Rasmussen had been seen with Annie in her car.

"In fact," Teddy called after him, "here's a song for Annie." He began to play.

Flynn stopped, listening. He didn't know the name of the song Teddy played, maybe it didn't have a name, but it swooped and sighed and mourned, finding all the sorrow a guitar could find and maybe then some. Flynn stood in the open doorway and thought, *Jesus Christ, the guy really knows his stuff,* and then he thought of Valentine and "The Heart That You Own." And of Chloe. Chloe, the liberal.

Molly, I thought as I headed down Oracle away from Phil Glenn's offices. Molly Webber. The woman in the photograph Phil Glenn claimed to be with all night when Annie was killed. She was in Tucson and so was I. I punched in Rachel's number on my cell.

"Hello," she said.

"This is Chloe," I said. "Molly Webber, do you remember her?"

"Of course. She was my father's girlfriend, years and years ago. I still see her."

"I'm in Tucson—do you have a number for her?"

". . . know it . . ."

"What?" I said. Her cell must have been running down.

". . . can . . ."

That was it, just dead air. Well, maybe I had time to hit the Tucson Mall, I thought wickedly. Ten minutes later when I was nearly there my cell chimed.

"Hello?"

"Chloe?" A woman's voice, unfamiliar.

"Yes. Who's this?"

"Molly Webber. Rachel just gave me your number. Where are you?"

"Just coming up to the Tucson Mall."

"Wonderful. Would you like to meet at the Trader Joes's on Oracle?"


Trader Joe's was doing a thriving business, as usual the parking lot packed, I had to park fairly far away and walk back. A woman in big sunglasses sat on a bench in front near a display of pots of miniature roses and lilies; one of those impossibly slim fortyish women you see in upper-middle-class places.

"Molly?" I said.

She smiled and stood up. "Chloe, *hello*. I'll be happy to talk to you for Rachel. I adore Rachel."

She wore a simple white T-shirt and jeans that fit her like a teenager. Up close you could see her blond hair had been skillfully helped along, but her features were classic and she didn't appear to wear much makeup. She was almost but not quite as pretty as her picture.

"Phil Glenn showed me the photograph of you and him," I said. "The one that was taken the night Annie as killed."

"Ugh." She gave a little shiver. "Do you mind coming along with me? I've only got half an hour before I absolutely have to be somewhere and I really have to get some things. Surely"—she smiled again, though I couldn't see her eyes behind the sunglasses—"you must need something from Trader Joe's."

I grabbed a basket and followed her in and over to the produce.

"I was with Phil that whole night," she said, looking over the produce. "It still seems so unreal that Annie was being murdered at the same time. Phil was devastated and then . . ." She snatched up a bag of organic mixed baby greens.

"Rachel came to live with him. His whole life was turned upside down. I tried to help, I spent time with her, we really did get along and we still do when I can reach her, but—yuck, this lettuce is soupy." She peered at the bag of greens, then tossed it back. "Why does it get that way, I wonder? It's before the expiration date."

I scanned the produce but couldn't remember what I needed, if anything.

Molly glanced over at me. "Rachel's hard to read a lot of the time. Part of her is, I don't know, kind of sealed off. A big part of the time, I think. We got along pretty well, I tried to help her adjust. But then things didn't work out with me and Phil."

"Why was that?" I asked.

"Because"—she tossed her head, her voice weary—"nothing ever works out with Phil and women."

"You said he was devastated by Annie's death," I said. "Of course anyone would be upset under the circumstances but was he even close to Annie anymore? And Rachel—he never saw Rachel while Annie was alive, he hardly knew her. He hadn't seen her in *eight years*."

"I wish," said Molly thoughtfully, "it was still asparagus season. I miss asparagus so much. If you want the truth, Annie was the only woman Phil ever loved and he will love her to his dying day."

I looked at her, stunned.

"Squash," she said. "Yellow squash. *Oh*. This is so upsetting. I didn't realize it would be this upsetting." She pushed her cart away from me.

"I'm sorry," I said.

"It's not your fault but you know, Chloe, I just can't help you anymore. Maybe some other time."

I watched as she hurried off, her cart still empty. She hadn't bought a single vegetable.

# chapter eighteen

RACHEL HAD CHOSEN THE POPPY SEED CAFÉ because she and Scott went there often and she knew some of the staff—they made her feel welcome without being overly friendly, and besides the parking lot was brightly lit—not that she was worried about Kurt, it was the going out at night.

She hadn't told Scott anything about coming to meet Kurt, mainly because he would do his best to talk her out of it. *Wait till I'm home,* he would say. *We'll go together.*

She parked, turned off her cell, and sat for a few moments doing yoga breaths. By the time she got out of the car she was a little late, maybe five, ten minutes. A weeknight during summer, the place was only a quarter full. Ferns, lots of natural wood. There were booths and there were tables. The hostess stepped forward, hair dark and very short, dressed all in black, cool; her hand full of menus. She must be new, Rachel hadn't seen her before.

"One?"

"No. Two. I'm meeting someone. They might be here already."

"Rachel, are you Rachel?"

"Yes, that's me."

The hostess smiled. "He's here."

Rachel followed her to a booth at the back, beside a window.

The light was starting to go and the window cast a shadow on his face until she was right there. Was that really . . . ?

"Kurt?" she said.

He looked startled. "Rachel?" He stood up.

Seeing him, Rachel felt immediately reassured. The last time had been at the defense table at the murder trial, in a white shirt, red tie, and a tan sports jacket and his hair was cut very short. He hadn't looked like himself. Now, in a blue denim shirt and jeans, his blond hair a bit long, snub nose, same pale blue eyes but a bit more faded, he looked like the old Kurt except that his face seemed a little blurred, as if a hand had passed lightly over the features before they had completely set.

She slid into the booth. Kurt sat down again. They looked across at each other. For some reason she was very aware of Kurt's hands on the table in front of him, fingers interlaced. The knuckles were big, the skin on them raw and scarred. Working-man's hands.

"Why now?" she asked. "What made you decide to call me now?"

"I've always kept track of you," he said. "To make sure you were okay. Then they had this story on the news—a body in Dudley—and, I don't know, it brought things back." He paused. "You look so much like her."

"It's what people always used to say."

"It's true," said Kurt, "and it's not. You've changed."

Rachel had to smile. "Of course I've changed. I'm grown up.

"It's not just that. To be honest I thought you'd look like Annie even more—"

"You guys ready to order?" The waitress was standing there. "Hey, Rachel, I didn't recognize you right away. This your dad?"

"No. Old family friend." Rachel smiled up at her. "I'll have the Southwestern chicken salad and some raspberry iced tea."

"Blue cheese steak for me," said Kurt quickly. He glanced at Rachel. "I read the menu maybe three times while I was waiting for you. And the tea," he added to the waitress.

"You were saying?" Rachel asked when she'd gone.

"You look like her and you don't. You're so . . ." Kurt grinned apologetically. "I mean, you look beautiful, but you look so middle-class."

"Oh." It felt like an insult. She looked past him, out the window. Obscurely, she thought of Penny at the mall with her black-rimmed eyes and her red-streaked hair. She wished she could just come right out and tell Kurt she looked just the way she wanted to look, but instead, for some reason, she felt like crying. *I don't know why I do anything,* she thought, *I don't even know who I am.*

"You okay?" Kurt asked worriedly. "Aw, Rach. Did I upset you? I didn't mean it. You look wonderful, you really do. I guess I feel a little awed. Here you are, little Rachel, so beautiful and married and all that. Macabee. Is he nice, good to you?"

His voice was so kind. He'd always been kind, she remembered him telling Annie not to sweep the spiderwebs full of dead flies off the ceilings in the fall. "What will they eat?" he'd said.

"Scott, his name is Scott, and yes, he's nice to me. I'm fine, but Kurt," she said, suddenly paying attention in a way she hadn't before, "how have *you* been? What have you been doing all these years?"

"I moved away from Dudley right after the trial. I got it into my head I wanted to be a Master Gardener, took a bunch of horticulture classes at Pima College."

"You'd be good at that," said Rachel. "Remember all the irises you planted up behind the house?"

His face lit up. "You remember that?"

"Of course. So is that what you are? A Master Gardener?"

"Not exactly." He shrugged, looked down at the tabletop. "I can't seem to ever get off the ground."

"What do you mean?

"Blue cheese steak?" The waitress had returned with the food. Kurt nodded.

After she'd left, Kurt said, "They found me not guilty but no one believed it. They thought it was just wrong, that I really had killed Annie. I couldn't live in Dudley anymore. And I took the horticulture classes but I somehow never got to be a Master Gardener. I do yardwork, home repair, stuff like that. The thing is, I'll start on a job and half the time the people will find a reason to cancel. And I know they've found out about Annie and maybe they've got kids or they're elderly and they don't want to take that chance."

"Oh, *Kurt,*" said Rachel. "It's so unfair. One of the things I'm trying to do is clear your name forever."

"You know about my lawyer—Stan Cooper?"

"What about him?"

"He had a heart attack. Died. Back then, Mr. Cooper said the cops didn't even try to look for any other suspects. He did a lot of research on that, stuff like transients in the neighborhood, or break-ins. There's always the chance she was killed by someone she didn't know. I gave her that gun—"

Kurt put his head in his hands for a moment. From somewhere in the restaurant, a baby wailed, a woman laughed.

"She could have surprised an intruder," said Kurt finally. "If she hadn't had the gun then— God, Rachel, you know that's one of the things I think about the most—that gun. I gave it to her to keep her safe and it killed her."

"Kurt, I was just a child. There was a lot of stuff going on in my mother's life that I didn't know about. I need to know it now, everything. What can you tell me?"

Kurt's face reddened, Rachel was pretty sure, though the

lighting wasn't perfect. He set down the sandwich and wiped his mouth. "Well, she might have had a boyfriend. I mean, another one besides me."

"Like who?"

"I don't know," said Kurt.

"But why would she need another boyfriend when she had you?"

Kurt stared at her for a moment. "Geez," he said, his voice almost contemptuous. "Rachel, grow up."

Rachel was stung. It was as though he were suddenly a different person. Then he changed again. "Jesus Christ. I'm sorry. I didn't mean to take that tone."

"It's okay. I was just being stupid. There's something else too."

"What's that?"

"Camille Chartrand? In the file, Chloe said there were some police reports—"

"Domestic violence," said Kurt. "Christ. Camille was—I don't know—crazy. She lied. You know I wouldn't hurt your mom, Rachel, you saw me with her all the time."

"So what happened?" cried Rachel. "That night. You guys went out to dinner." Her voice rose accusingly. *"Why weren't you with her that night?"*

There was a silence. Rachel heard her own voice ringing in her ears. And the part she hadn't said: *If you'd been with her, she wouldn't have been killed.*

Kurt looked away. "She didn't want me to be there, that's why. We had an argument. It wasn't even about anything. I don't even know—" He spread his fingers. "I don't even know *what* it was about."

Rachel couldn't look at him. She was shaking.

"She told me to just drop her off," Kurt went on, "she insisted. I was so upset, I drove around for a long time afterwards, trying to deal with it. I drove out to the Valley, then over to Tombstone, Sierra Vista."

A tear rolled down Rachel's cheek. She reached into her purse for a tissue.

"Rach, don't be like that," pleaded Kurt. "Don't you know how many times I've thought what you're thinking now? But how could I have known? And there was no way I could have stayed when Annie didn't want me to. You, of all people, know how she was."

Rachel nodded. She blew her nose. "I do."

"I mean, she was almost . . ." Kurt shrugged.

"Scary," said Rachel. "Kurt," she went on, all in a rush, "that body they dug up in Dudley. It was *Wynn*."

"Wynn?" Kurt looked blank for a second. *"Wynn Wykoff?"*

Rachel nodded.

"My God. What happened to him?" asked Kurt. "I mean how—"

"Don't you remember, everyone thought he left town a little before my mom was killed. Instead he was dead. That's why I hired an investigator—there has to be a connection."

"If you say so," said Kurt dispiritedly.

*He's given up,* Rachel thought. He was sitting here in front of her, but he wasn't really there, just going through the motions.


"Jim Rasmussen in a clench with Annie Glenn," I said. My voice rose. "What about *Jody*?"

It was evening, getting to be dusk, and Flynn and I were outside in my yard where everything, the snapdragons, the salvia, the weedy vinca, was overgrown, the side effects of a good monsoon. I had a picture in my mind of Jody, smiling, digging a hole in her garden for a rosebush. She wouldn't have let her garden get away from her like this. What had she ever done to deserve such treatment?

"I mean," I went on, "Jim Rasmussen went ahead after being in a clench with Annie and prosecuted the case? Is that ethical?"

"I guess it depends on whether or not he killed her," said Flynn. He plunked a ladder on the outside wall of the room that was the office and picked up a can of tar and a Mag-Lite.

"Of course," I said, "it sounded to me like Phil Glenn had some kind of fixation on Annie when I talked to him. Like they were divorced but he couldn't let go."

"There's no record of anything like that, phone calls, harassment." Flynn steadied the ladder and climbed to the top. "Want to hand me the brush?"

I climbed partway and handed it up. "Isn't it a little dark to be doing this?"

"Just let me do my job, okay? I know where the leak is and I'm sick of worrying about it."

"It's *my* leak," I said.

Flynn didn't deign to answer.

"Anyway," he said over his shoulder, "Jim Rasmussen called me. He mentioned Jody. He's going to be in Dudley tomorrow and he said he could spare some time to meet. Dudley Coffee Company, two o'clock sharp."

"Great." I slapped at my arm. The no-see-ums were out, pricking at my skin with little tiny jabs, hardly noticeable until tomorrow when they would swell to large itchy bumps.

"Yeah," said Flynn. "Guess Jody has some influence."

"Right," I said, "the power of the innocent over the guilty. I wonder if it was a onetime fling for Jim or if he's an habitual."

I went inside to escape the no-see-ums and Googled Jim Rasmussen, found out mostly what I already knew—he was a successful civil attorney who had run for city council in Sierra Vista once and lost, and was considered a good potential Republican candidate for the House of Representatives seat when the current representative retired in two years.

This wasn't helping. I'd better call Stuart Ross, a Dudley defense attorney and an old friend-adversary of mine. He might know Rasmussen. I picked up the phone.

"Sure," said Stuart. "Worked on a case with him, as a matter of fact."

"Really?" I said. "I didn't know you did civil stuff."

"I'll do anything, but this was a while ago, back when I was in Tucson. After working for the county attorney in Dudley he went into private practice briefly in Tucson, got his chops together before he moved back down to Sierra Vista."

"I can learn about his public life from anyone," I said. "I wondered about, um, his private."

"Gay or straight?"

"*What*—" I said

"Just kidding. Far as I know, he's a straight-arrow family man. Mormon."

"Not even one little unsubstantiated rumor?" I said.

"Actually, in Tucson, there was an office manager—something about sexual harassment but nothing came of it. The story going around was she'd made the initial advances and then got pissed when it didn't work out. But between you and me I think the whole story was horse waggle."


When Rachel got home she lay down on the couch and closed her eyes. The meeting with Kurt had tired her, but oddly, she didn't feel the anxiety. It was as if for a long time she'd had no one in the whole world who knew her and then suddenly there was someone who did.

But Alice knew her too. Alice had left two messages on the

machine; still, Rachel couldn't bring herself to call back. *I should just go and see her,* she thought. *That's what I should do. Another person who knows me.*

Except for Scottie, didn't Scottie know her? Years ago she'd met him—five, to be exact. He was older than she was by a few years, had already done some of the growing up that most of the men she met hadn't done yet. He always had the ideas of what to do, places to go. Everything had just . . . worked out. The phone rang, not her cell.

Alice. Well, it was fate. She picked up without looking at the caller ID.

"Hey," said Scott. "Where were you? I tried to call you earlier but you weren't home. Your cell was off," he added accusingly.

Her cell, she'd turned it off before she went into the Poppy Seed Café and had forgotten to turn it on again. They had a deal where she always kept her cell on so he wouldn't worry.

"I'm sorry," said Rachel. "I screwed up—it was running low and I forgot to charge it up, so I guess it ran all the way down. It's still in my purse."

"I called twice," said Scottie.

"Oh, sweetie, whatever." Rachel took a deep breath. Sometimes Scottie was just a little too concerned about her. One reason why she didn't feel like telling him she'd met with Kurt. Concerned, she thought, but not *interested.* How could that be?

"I wasn't home," she lied, "because I made a run to Trader Joe's."

"So how's it going?"

"All right. I went to work and one person came in the whole afternoon. So how's the conference?"

"Some interesting stuff," said Scott, "concerning the death penalty. Ever since *Blakely* it's gone through a bunch of changes in states where they'd been letting the judges make— Geez, what am I saying? What I really want is to get home to you. You got the flight number and all?"

"Of course I do."

"So what time does my plane get in?"

"Two thirty-eight p.m."

"Good girl."

*Good girl,* thought Rachel after she got off. *Like I'm a dog or a horse.*

# chapter nineteen

FLYNN SAT IN THE FOOD COURT OF THE TUC-
son Mall Nursing a Chick-fil-A sandwich and a large root beer.
Several tables over by the big plate-glass windows sat Tanya in a
tank top and shorts. Like Flynn, she was all by herself. Not meeting any lovers so far, male or female, just drinking an Orange
Julius. Oddly, she wasn't stealing anything either, not in a tank
top and shorts, and her purse was on the small side.

She'd already hit Macy's and Dillard's, trying things on, buying
nothing, except two small items, out of Flynn's range of vision, at
the Lancôme Cosmetics counter. Was it possible she'd driven all
the way to Tucson just to buy cosmetics? Yes, thought Flynn,
thinking of Val, yes, it was. He yawned.

Last night he'd e-mailed Billy Dodds, the drummer, but hadn't
heard anything back. This morning he'd gone over to Aloe Vera
Associates and picked up the box of Annie Glenn's stuff—a
medium-sized cardboard box sealed with duct tape and *Annie*
scrawled on the top with black Magic Marker—and dropped it
off at his office, where Lois stowed it behind her desk for safe-
keeping.

Tanya stood up, dusted the crumbs off the pink tank top, carried her tray over to a trash barrel, and dumped it. Then she

headed to the back of the food court and went into the women's restroom. After a few minutes she came back out.

Flynn stood up and dumped his tray. His cell chimed.

"Flynn here," he said.

"Hey, buddy, Jack Nelson. What's that noise?"

"What noise?"

"Like a murmur."

"The Tucson Mall food court."

Jack laughed for no apparent reason Flynn could see.

"What's up, Jack?" he said as he followed Tanya outside.

"You got a relative for me?"

"Back East somewhere's the best I've done so far."

"We got the medical examiner's report."

"Yeah?"

Tanya was walking briskly to her car.

"Gunshot wound to the head."

"Can we meet later today?" said Flynn.

"What time?"

"I'll call you."

Tanya got into her car. Hopefully she'd head back to Sierra Vista and not at long last be meeting her mysterious lover wearing her new cosmetics. Goddamn, Chloe was working for him now. She could follow Tanya the next time. Hell, she might even enjoy it—get some new clothes while she was working.


The Dudley Coffee Company was in a big high-ceilinged room that, despite the row of windows at the front, always managed to appear murky. I got a latte and sat at a small wood and iron table. Around me were ranged various Coffee Company regulars, mostly male: hairy, unkempt, and loudly opinionated.

I knew it had to be Jim Rasmussen as soon as he walked in,

carrying his briefcase, like an altar boy among the ancients; not that he was that young—late forties, probably—but his haircut was well done and preppy, his face clean-shaven, his light blue suit, well, a suit.

I stood up and gave a little wave. He nodded, held up a finger, went to the counter and ordered. Then he came over and put his briefcase on the floor and his large coffee on the table.

"Jim Rasmussen," he said, leaning over to shake my hand—a good grip—sincerity in the eyes, spoiled for me by the knowledge he'd cheated on Jody not only with Annie but possibly his office manager and who knew who else.

"Chloe Newcombe," I said.

"I'm so very pleased to meet you. Jody thinks the world of you—she loved those crisis intervention classes. I have the greatest respect for the Victim Witness Program."

He sat down, reached in his briefcase and took out a cell phone, and placed it on the table. "Off," he said. "Jody's trained me to turn my cell phone off when I'm in a restaurant with someone. She who must be obeyed."

"Rumpole," I said.

He smiled, as if delighted that I too had watched ancient PBS.

To show good faith I took my own phone out of my purse, turned it off, and placed it on the table next to his.

"So." He rubbed his hands together as if satisfied he'd dispensed with the formalities. "Annie Glenn. Jody said you'd want any files on the case I might have but I searched high and low and"—he shrugged—"zilch. Sorry. But I'm fascinated about this new investigation. Fascinated. I prosecuted the case and now we have this second homicide."

I was surprised. "You know about—" I began.

"Wynn Wykoff? Of course. Jack Nelson called me right away. To be honest"—he leaned across the table and gave me a sincere smile—"if I'd found any files I would have felt more obligated to give them to Sergeant Nelson than to a private investigator." He paused. "Though I suspect Jody might have persuaded me to come up with copies for you."

He removed the lid off his coffee, took a wooden stirrer from a glass on the table, and stirred it. "I knew Annie Glenn, did you know that?"

"Yes," I said.

"You never like to lose in a trial, but in this case it was doubly bad because I'd known her. A beautiful woman. But I don't mean looks, though she was certainly attractive—I mean her spirit, so full of joie de vivre."

"Refresh my memory," I said, even though I knew the answer. "How was it you knew her?"

"Through the Dudley chorus. You live in Dudley?"

"Yes," I said.

"Then you must be familiar with them."

"I went to a Christmas concert they had at the Women's Club last year. I enjoyed it." They had been quite good.

Jim smiled sadly. "I miss them. Haven't had time for that kind of thing in quite a while. Not long after the Dickens verdict we moved to Tucson for a while before we settled in Sierra Vista." He sighed.

I nodded.

He picked up his coffee and stared into it, took a sip. "Annie was with the chorus for six months before she was murdered, never missed a rehearsal. *And* she had a full-time job at the Co-op *and* she sang with a band."

"Oh, to be in one's twenties again," I said.

"Yes. I hadn't been practicing that long and I'd never lost a case. I thought I was invincible. County attorney kept giving me bigger and bigger cases and I kept on winning. Meanwhile, Jody and I had two young children who were running us both ragged. I think the chorus was part of what kept me sane."

Or, I thought, Jody was being run ragged, while he was singing in the chorus and getting to know Annie Glenn.

"Rachel," he said. "She's how old now? Twenty-six?"

"Around that."

"And she contacted Flynn to reopen the case. I gather it had something to do with Wynn Wykoff's body being found."

Fishing for information. I looked as neutral as I could.

"If I remember correctly," he went on, "she was certain Dickens didn't do it. I could never understand that, her certainty."

"She liked him," I said. "Maybe losing her mom was bad enough; if he did it then she lost again."

"So . . . now she's changed her mind?"

"No, not really. She just wants the case reopened and investigated."

"Well, between you and me, that guy did it, we just didn't build a strong enough case." Jim laughed hollowly. He threw his head back and stared up at the ceiling. "If Rachel is still on Kurt Dickens's side, doesn't she realize what this new body can do?"

"If there's the right kind of evidence."

"Maybe you know something I don't." Jim looked at me sharply. "Has Rachel— People mentioned, back then, she might have a repressed memory. You know, don't you, that lots of repressed memory stuff has been debunked." His voice rose. "Don't tell me she went to a hypnotist and recovered a lost memory."

"She hasn't gone to a hypnotist." *Calm down,* I wanted to say to him. *Calm down.* "I know it's been debunked, but not before a lot of people were harmed by it."

"Well, at least we're on the same page here," he said. "And in case you didn't know, things recovered by a hypnotist are inadmissible in a court of law."

I nodded.

Jim sat up straighter in his chair and looked at his watch. "I still think about that case, but I have to remember it's over and done with. I wish Rachel the best of luck. I have to run, but do me a favor, will you?"

"What's that?"

"Annie was so lovely. It was such a tragedy. I really do care. If there's anything I can do, any other questions you think of, give me a call. Give me a call anyway, I'd appreciate it if you kept me updated. In fact, tell that to Rachel, that I'd be glad to talk to her."

He stood up. "Jody tells me she married a prosecutor at the Pima County Attorney's, Scott Macabee."

"Yes," I said.

He looked bemused for a moment, then he smiled. "Well, at least she didn't give up on prosecutors forever."


It took Rachel a long time to find a parking space. They were doing construction at the airport, so there were even fewer places than usual but she finally got lucky when a big gray SUV pulled out fairly close to the Delta baggage claim. The palm trees seemed jagged and hot, the midafternoon sun so strong she felt as if she might float out of her body.

She wore the Ralph Lauren polo in grass green that she'd bought at the mall the day she'd run into Penny the Goth, seafoam-green linen capris, and turquiose flip-flops. She had the little pearls in her ears and the strand of pearls around her neck that looked as though it might have belonged to a grandmother who was the dowager duchess of something had she ever existed. Inside the terminal she ducked into the ladies' room.

The lighting in the restroom was funny, kind of like being underwater, and as she put on fresh lip gloss and fluffed up her hair she saw this woman, herself, in the full-length mirror as if she were floating. Fake, she thought, she's so fake. Then she walked out and joined one of the groups waiting by security.

Scott's plane was due in at 2:38 and it was 2:45, so any minute now. Or not. She went over to the Delta counter and scanned the Arrival screen for the flight from Atlanta. On time. She went back to the group by security and a man got up from one of the couches and offered her his seat. She took it. Now it was 2:50.

Then she saw him, walking toward her, trailing his carry-on. He looked so nice, khakis, a lime-green polo, almost the same color as her grass-green one—he looked so nice and she did too, they looked just like each other. Fake, fake.

He came out through security. "You look so beautiful," he said.

They hugged.

"I missed you," she whispered. She kept her eyes closed. Scott smelled like aftershave and just a whiff of cigarettes though he didn't smoke.

"Not as much as I missed you."

They walked hand in hand out the automatic doors.

"So what'd you do while I was gone?" he asked.

She laughed. "You already know. You talked to me every night."

"Tell me again."

"I went to work, I went to the mall, I bought two polos. I went to AJ's. The next day I went to work and I went to Trader Joe's."

"That's it?"

"That's it."

Outside, it was still hot, hot; why wouldn't it be, and the palm trees just as jagged.

"I always forget how hot it is in Tucson," Scott said, "and the worst thing about these conferences is that I come back to an extra pile of work."

Rachel heard everything he said, though she wasn't listening.

He took out his keys, opened the trunk. He chuckled. "Did you know your carry-on's in the trunk?"

"Yes," said Rachel.

He stowed his bag and slammed the trunk shut.

Rachel waited for him to ask her why her carry-on was in the trunk but he didn't seem curious. She went to the driver's side of the car, even though when they were together Scott usually drove. He looked momentarily confused, then went to the passenger side. She looked across the top of the car at him. She felt a little sad because she knew she was going to upset him but he looked so far away, a man who had been to a conference and had come home to a pile of work.

"Sweetie," she said, "I'm going to drop you off at home, then I'm going to Dudley."

*"What?"* he said.

# chapter twenty

ALMOST THREE IN THE AFTERNOON AND IT
was probably one hundred degrees and the dense humidity from
the monsoon made it worse. Tourists wearing hardly anything
blocked the narrow sidewalks like herds of closely sheared sheep
grazing, ducking in and out of the shops, snacking at the Cornu-
copia Restaurant, browsing at the Atalanta Bookstore.

I'd walked down from my house in spite of the heat and the
fact that I could have gone home and gotten my car to drive to
Sonora Cloud a.k.a. Camille Chartrand's studio, my next stop in
the investigation, but I decided not to—I wasn't one of those
people who had an exercise routine; I had to get it when I could.

The tourist shops on Main Street were full of art and imitation
art, pottery, old clothes, and collectibles. There were frame
shops where you could spend a lot of money framing the art
you'd bought cheap from the portfolios at the galleries. There
were shops full of charming and not-so-charming crafts from India and China, Mexico and Bali. I passed them all, the shops,
passed the bed and breakfasts, reached the High Desert Market
on my right and on my left was the county courthouse, high on a
hill, gloriously Spanish art deco.

I stopped for moment, hot, really hot, sweat dripping down my arms and collecting under my bra strap, missing my air-conditioned car. At the top of the wide steps right in front of the big brass doors, a couple of attorneys argued with their arms waving.

I still had several more days of work—I'd gone in this morning dutifully; talked with a victim; explained some things to Linda, the misdemeanor advocate who would be filling in on the felonies until they found my replacement. But now I imagined being inside the courthouse sitting in the cool marble lobby, waiting for a victim to show up. Watching the courthouse show put on by the attorneys.

I was still technically working there but already feeling the bittersweet pangs of nostalgia. To focus, I thought of Camille/Sonora who'd identified Wynn's body, been Kurt's girlfriend once.

I walked on, past the Circle K, into the residential area where it was greener, leafier, and I could be in the shade of Chinese elms and cottonwoods. The address I had was 505 Quarry Canyon, so I turned left when I reached it. From long ago and far away someone up the canyon was playing the Rolling Stones' "Love in Vain."

Number 505 was a smallish square pink building on my left with a plate-glass window that had probably once been a neighborhood market—the area was dotted with them from back in the days when you walked to the corner store. Painted in strong primary colors, a giant Buddha above the plate-glass window, hands in an attitude of prayer, looked down serenely onto the street while two dark-haired, doe-eyed maidens in saris, one on each side of the window, gazed up at him adoringly.

Well.

By the door was a wooden bench presumably for waiting students, and displayed in the window was a blue and white kimono, some blue and green beads, several pillows printed with goldfish, and a hand-lettered sign with a schedule on it. If the schedule was correct, today was private lessons. The door was shut, with a CLOSED sign hanging on it. From somewhere near the back of the building I heard the vigorous whir of an air conditioner fan working extra-hard in the extreme heat.

I knocked on the door. It was half glass and I peered in, saw a desk to one side, a couple of hard-backed wooden chairs, more pillows, rolls of yoga mats, thin books on a little wooden table, and a closed door at the back. I knocked again.

"She's not there," someone said.

I turned.

A woman stood there, carrying a rolled-up yoga mat under one arm. She was tall and painfully thin, like a stork, and had bright blue eyes in an aging face, wispy orange hair. She was wearing loose black capris and one of those tiny spaghetti-strap tops, also in black, that fit perfectly if you're an A-cup.

I didn't know her name but I recognized her—she had a vintage shop called A Blast from the Past. It was at the mouth of the Gulch and sold mainly stuff from the sixties.

"Hi, I'm Harmony," she said. "Are you waiting for a private session?"

"I'm Chloe, and no, I'm not."

"That's good, because this time is supposed to be set aside for me but I've already knocked several times," Harmony said plaintively, "and she doesn't answer."

"Maybe she's out."

"No, she can't be. I missed her last class and she told me she'd give me a private lesson. That wouldn't be like her at all. I mean"—her voice rose—"how *could* she? We're best friends and she knows I can't function without my yoga class. I just go to pieces. We had dinner together last night and we talked about that very thing."

"The air conditioner's pretty loud," I said. "Maybe she didn't hear you. You could call. Do you have a cell?"

Harmony looked confused. "You mean like a monk," she said.

"A phone," I said. "Do you have the number here?" I reached

in my purse for my cell and saw it, suddenly, back at the Dudley Coffee Company, on the table where I'd placed it to show solidarity with Jim "Cheating Heart" Rasmussen. Damn. "Never mind."

I put my hand on the doorknob, just in case, and tried it. It turned. I pushed open the door and walked in. The air conditioner was even louder inside.

Harmony followed close behind, dithering. "Look, the door to the back is closed," she said. "That means she's meditating. She hates to be disturbed when she's meditating."

I opened that door anyway into a large room: a blast of cold air hit me. Sonora's electricity bill was going to be sky-high this month. There were shelves on one side, windows in the back with bamboo shades. The shades were down, the room was dimly lit, shadowy. The air conditioner blasted away.

"There's no one here," Harmony said, "and she's got the air conditioner going. Not very *green* of her."

I looked for a light switch and found one by the door, flicked it on, saw wide bare floorboards, and in a far corner, someone lying down.

"For heaven's sake," said Harmony. "It looks like she fell asleep while she was meditating or *something*."

"Sonora?" I said loudly.

"Lazy bones, wake up." Harmony walked over and I followed.

Under the fluorescent lighting, things glittered at me, and among those glittery things I saw that the blond hair on the back of the woman's head was dark with blood.

Harmony screamed. She screamed and screamed, but I was a victim advocate, I knew just what I needed to do. I put my hand on her back to steady her.

"Don't touch anything," I said.

\*   \*   \*

*"What?"* Scottie had said. *"What?"*

Rachel could still see the expression on his face. Right before she merged onto the I-10 she reached in her purse for her cell and turned it off.

Traffic was heavy. She accelerated into the left lane, and pushed it to eighty while the Dixie Chicks, Natalie Maines in the lead, spurred her on. She passed three heavy-duty trucks lumbering along at seventy-five. Briefly she thought of Scottie again, back at the house where she'd dropped him off, pouting. No, the word pouting wasn't fair, he would still be a little upset but mostly just deeply worried about her well-being.

She pulled back into the right lane but almost immediately accelerated again into the left to pass an enormous white RV and a big old gray Ford clunker. The traffic was thinning a little now as she passed the exits for Alvernon Way, for Valencia and the airport, for Kolb Road.

Maybe Scottie was right to be worried; for all she knew, she might be experiencing a brief moment of euphoria before moving to a higher stage of anxiety. I don't care, she thought. With my life, I might as well die, why not? Then there was hardly any traffic and she broke away from the pack, speeding deep into the desert.


Tanya had gone straight back to her house in Sierra Vista after leaving the Tucson Mall, giving Flynn enough time left for a meeting with Sergeant Jack Nelson.

Now, in spite of the big chinaberry trees shading the little seating area to one side of the Prickly Pear Café, it was so hot the sergeant and Flynn had to pour some of the expensive bottled water they'd purchased to justify being there onto the wrought-iron chairs to cool them down. The water evaporated so quickly they didn't even have to wipe them off before they sat.

So hot that no one else was out there, which was good. As for the heat, both men were tough, they could take it, sort of.

Jack wiped his sweaty brow with a paper napkin. "To this day," he said, "when it's hot like this I think of Annie Glenn. Same kind of weather, monsoon, real hot, then the storms. It was already hot when I walked into that bedroom and saw her. A beautiful young woman with the top of her head blown off."

"Tough," said Flynn.

Jack looked away past Flynn out to the street, where there was nothing to see, not even, at that moment, a car driving by.

"It's funny," he went on, "but I remember the quilt—green and red velvet squares with kind of colored stitching on them, the part that wasn't covered by the blood. It was my first homicide. Now, best way I know to deal with a homicide is focus on the job. But back then I didn't quite know how to handle it. Talked it over some with Sukie. That helped."

He glanced at Flynn. "Not specifics of the case, just more general."

"Sure," said Flynn.

Val had always hated talking about that kind of stuff—she said it gave her the creeps. Chloe loved to talk about crime. He wondered if Jack talked to his hippie-type wife, Frieda—what had Wishman meant by hippie type anyway? Would he consider Chloe a hippie? Surely not, though she *was* a Democrat.

Flynn swallowed what was left of his water and wished he had more. Jack Nelson finished his bottle too. Water, thought Flynn, and it had cost a dollar seventy-five, *water.*

"Val called me the other night," said Jack. "I kind of got the impression she thinks you're avoiding her."

"Avoiding her? Wait." Flynn felt his face getting red. "Wait a minute. Who's avoiding who? If I remember correctly, she's the one who went off to Oregon with the football coach."

"Aw. You know what, I think she feels real bad about that." Jack stroked his mustache. Flynn wondered why he kept it, it was kind of outdated.

"Jack. Do me a favor, okay?" he said. "Drop it. I thought we were here to talk about Wynn Wykoff."

"We are, we are. You find any relatives?"

"No, I'm working on it, but if I'm going to try to track down relatives, I think I have to let some people know about the tentative ID, okay?"

"I guess so." Jack frowned. "I suppose he's *got* folks. But he wasn't ever reported missing by anyone. That's what I can't figure out. Why the hell he wasn't reported missing. Course, Old Dudley being the way it was back then, hell, maybe his folks never knew he even lived here. Man, can you imagine that? The way some people live their lives."

"Could have been reported missing somewhere else," said Flynn.

"Yeah, of course there's always that."

Flynn could tell Dudley PD hadn't been looking too hard. "So you said cause of death was gunshot wound to the head."

"Yep." Jack crumpled the empty water bottle till it crackled, tossed it at the trash can, and scored.

"Got the bullet?"

Jack nodded. "We do. I'm not saying it is, but it could be from a Rossi .38. Praise the Lord, Wishman's got the gun. Kurt Dickens's damned cheap Rossi .38. We're going to do the test, see if we got a match." Jack rubbed his hands together. "Looks like we might have ourselves a whole 'nother shot at that bastard."

"Rachel doesn't think it was Dickens," said Flynn just as an ambulance, siren going, went past, drowning in him out.

*"What?"* shouted Jack.

"I said, Rachel doesn't think it was Dickens." Shit, thought

Flynn, it was looking more and more like it might be him after all and Rachel needed to understand that. She wasn't all that stable. What would that do to her? Get Chloe on it.

Jack looked alert. "She know where he is?"

Flynn shook his head.

"Look at it this way, his story is he lent Annie the gun to protect herself, so what's he going to say if it turns out Wykoff was killed with the same—" Another siren, this time a police car, zoomed by in a hurry. Jack raised his voice. "The same gun. Rachel might think differently if it *was* the same."

"She might," said Flynn.

"I heard Dickens was living in Tucson," said Jack. "Course, if he did it, he probably left town right after we dug up the body."

Another police car went by with siren and flashing lights. "What the hell is going on?" said Jack. "Guess I better check in."


Rachel took the Sierra Vista exit, forty minutes to there, then another half hour Dudley. She could have gone to Dudley the other, shorter way, through Benson and Tombstone, but if anything happened, Sierra Vista was bigger; its hospital would have a good emergency room. It was always best to be cautious. You could die from a panic attack if it was bad enough—she'd read that online and Scottie had said it was nonsense, but you certainly believed it when you were having one.

She hadn't taken any Ativan yet today and she was feeling really good, *high*. So high that she knew she would be all right, better than all right, she would never need to take Ativan ever again.

Just that kind of feeling could lead to feeling really low later on. She didn't want to think like that but why take chances?

# chapter twenty-one

"SHE WAS MY BEST FRIEND IN THE WHOLE world," said Harmony. "I feel like I'm going to throw up." She made a little gagging noise.

I steered her over to the bench and gently pushed her down. I waited for a moment. "You okay?" I asked.

She nodded.

On impulse I fumbled in my purse, got out one of my cards from work, and handed it to her. As a witness to a heinous crime, or the results of it, I explained, she was eligible to file a claim with my office for counseling. "You'll need to fill out a form," I said. "Call my office tomorrow and I'll send you one."

The first police car had hurtled up the street and skidded to a stop, all hustle and bustle, when there was actually nothing to hurry about—the ambulance had arrived first and Sonora-Camille was already pronounced dead, had probably been dead for hours, so the EMTs had said.

Officer Owen Bagby came out of the pink building, blond and pug-nosed, somewhere in his thirties, and balding rapidly. I knew him from work—in fact he had automatically assumed when he saw me that I'd been called out to the scene as a victim advocate.

"Chloe," he said. "Could we talk privately for a moment, if that's okay with, um—"

"Harmony. You'll be all right?" I said to her.

Her face was white. "Yes," she said vaguely. "Thank you."

Officer Bagby and I walked a few feet away out of earshot.

"This kind of weather," he said, "if it weren't for that air conditioner going, the neighbors would have been retching." He gestured with his head at Harmony. "She a relative of the victim?"

"Friend."

"This isn't official," he said. "Okay? They'll bring in the medical examiner and all. It looks like she suffered a blow to the back of her head that was fatal."

"Caused by . . . ?"

"It appears she hit the back of her head on a mirror that was propped against the wall, smashed it."

The glittery things I'd see on the floor—shards from the broken mirror.

"Now"—Bagby scratched his head—"I guess she could have tripped and fell but usually most people don't trip and fall backwards. And she had to have hit the mirror pretty hard."

"Pushed?"

"I wouldn't rule it out. Maybe a domestic gone ballistic."

"I touched the light switch," I said, "and the phone."

A domestic, I thought, a little giddy, gone ballistic: it rhymed, a poem.

He walked over to Harmony, who was now sitting with her head cradled in her arms. "Ma'am?"

She raised her head.

"What can you tell me about Miss Cloud? Anything going on in her life might make someone angry, want to hurt her?"

"Of course not. *Yoga* is her life. She's my teacher, a very spiritual person, very private."

"She live alone?"

"Yes. In the back of the studio."

"Boyfriend?"

Harmony shook her head. "I've never seen her with a boyfriend, not in the five years I've known her."

"You're close friends?"

"Very. In fact, I had dinner with her last night at Rosa's, they do macrobiotic Mexican."

"Okay," said Officer Bagby. "She worried or disturbed about anything then?"

"She worried about her students. About global warming. The war."

"Ah."

She looked exhausted, her thin orange hair blazing against her pale face. "Could I go home now?" she asked plaintively.

Best friends. I wondered if Harmony knew about Sonora identifying Wynn Wykoff. Old Dudley people weren't that trusting of law enforcement even though Sonora had gone to them. Had she known something, remembered something she hadn't told the cops? Had whoever murdered Wynn and Annie killed Sonora too? If so, then they were still around, listening, keeping track.

Pushing. Domestic violence, which Kurt Dickens had already had a couple of charges against Sonora, way back. We needed to talk to Rachel just in case, warn her to be careful. At least she hadn't stayed in touch with Kurt.

As soon as he left the Prickly Pear, Flynn tried to call Chloe but her cell was off. He drove over to Central School in the hopes of talking to Teddy Radebaugh again. It was time Teddy knew it was Wykoff's body, and besides, Teddy had known him pretty well—maybe he could come up with a relative, or at least a place to look for one a little smaller than "back East."

He parked to one side of the big lot next to a privet hedge in full bloom. The door wasn't locked this time and he climbed the steps to the second floor. No marijuana smell filled the hall and on the door of Teddy's studio was a big sign, OUT.

"Teddy went to Tucson," said a woman's voice, "with Carlos."

Flynn turned and saw the same woman he'd run into before, the one with the extra weight and the hennaed hair. "Carlos?"

"That's the drummer. They do a weekly Tucson run, you know, hit up Trader Joe's, maybe a thrift store or two."

"Ah," said Flynn. "You have any idea when he'll be back?"

"Probably not back here till tomorrow," she said. "If you need to see him today you can always go to his house. He usually gets back around seven."

"Thanks."

There was time to run back to his office, he thought. If he hurried he could check in with Lois, who was getting Chloe's office set up. Chloe needed to settle in. There was the box of Annie's stuff he'd gotten from Alice and he wanted Chloe to go through it. He would probably have enough time to write up the Tanya report and a report, overdue, on a Douglas father living well and way overdue on child support. See if Billy Dodds had answered his e-mail.

Mind racing, Flynn went back outside to find that the privet had dropped masses of tiny white flowers all over the windshield of his Land Rover. The privet was teeming with orange flying insects and he suddenly felt overpowered by its smell, like a woman saturated in cheap perfume. *Goddamn Val, calling up Jack Nelson like that. Why couldn't she leave him alone?*

Flynn brushed the tiny white flowers off the windshield. Sneezed. Sneezed again.

His cell chimed.

For a second he wished everyone would leave him alone.

"Flynn here."

"Chloe . . ."

Rachel drove through Sierra Vista down Fry Boulevard, the long crowded main street with a traffic light almost every block. There was a road that bypassed most of it, but then she'd missed the turn and gone left at the light close to the gate to Fort Huachuca, where she and her mom used to go to the thrift store on the base. Anybody could get onto base back then but maybe not anymore after 9/11. It seemed to her she hit every single red light but that was okay, she wasn't in a hurry.

Waiting at one of them, she drummed her fingers on the steering wheel in time to the Dixie Chicks, watching herself: a regular person listening to music, drumming her fingers. A couple of red lights down farther, she glanced to her left and realized the furniture store on the corner was where the old Sears used to be. Where Annie had danced in the aisles to Madonna singing "Express Yourself."

"Your mom is so cool," one of her friends had said. Which friend? Who knew? Her mom *was* cool. She was out there in the stratosphere being so cool.

Someone honked. Rachel looked up, the light had changed. She drove on, past the park, the car dealerships, the brand-new Target, and the Fry's. Past the county complex of offices on the right and the Sin of Cortez Bar on the left. After that things got sparse and almost immediately it was desert again. She crossed the San Pedro River, huge cottonwoods along its banks, lush from the monsoons. She would be in Dudley in less than half an hour for the first time in seventeen years—well, sixteen if you counted when she went to the trial.

*You'll be fine,* she told herself. Funny, but even though she was telling herself that, the voice sounded like Scottie's, insincere and somehow the tone telling her just the opposite of what was being said.

# part two

RACHEL IN DUDLEY

# chapter twenty-two

WHERE WAS THE CO-OP? RACHEL WONDERED as she drove down Main Street. It had been a kind of town center where everyone stopped in after checking their mail at the post office. Her mother had worked there off and on for as long as Rachel could remember. Now its big plate-glass display windows were full of paintings of roadrunners and blooming cacti, sunsets and cute Indian maidens. And the drugstore was full of antiques and collectibles that spilled out onto the sidewalk.

There was no sign of anything like the co-op anywhere or any kind of store where you could buy the basic necessities, just several restaurants. In spite of this, Main Street was packed with people in pastel tees, khaki shorts, and running shoes, meandering down the narrow sidewalks and even into the street, crossing back and forth, not only on the crosswalks but apparently anywhere they felt like it.

The speed limit sign said fifteen miles an hour, but the SUV in front of her was going five. Rachel gawked at Main Street just like one of the tourists. The town where she had grown up until she was ten was gone and in its place was a replica of the town, similar to, say, Knott's Berry Farm.

For a second she had a gruesome thought—the house where

she and Annie had lived was now preserved just as it had been when she lived there with a sign in front saying MURDER HOUSE and inside a perfect artistically rendered replica of her mother, head half blown away as she lay in bed in a pool of shiny acrylic blood.

Rachel took a deep breath. *Fine, still doing fine.*

She'd checked out accommodations online and had chosen a place called the Oliver House, a bed and breakfast. It had rooms available, though she hadn't actually made reservations. She'd printed up a map of where it was but that could wait. She thought she might get something to eat at a restaurant first and just watch people for a while. She felt a little tired.

She drove up and down Main Street a couple of times until a parking place opened up near the Dudley Coffee Company and she pulled in and parked. The Coffee Company hadn't been there before, but across the street the post office was just the same, except the old miners and young hippies who'd hung out on the benches in front were now just old hippies.

Rachel walked up the sidewalk, past the post office, up Main Street. She could see now that among the tourists were scattered residents: real Old Dudley people, clothes shabbier, artier, more ethnic. They moved through the crowd like ghosts from a former time or maybe just actors hired to lend color.

Rachel blended right in with the tourists, though she was a bit more upscale than the average. The grass-green Ralph Lauren polo, the lime-green capris, the pearls. No one would be hiring Rachel for local color.


Flynn climbed the steep crumbling cement steps to Teddy Radebaugh's house. Below, a pickup truck rumbled by, a motorcycle gunned its engine, but climbing up to Teddy's was like climbing into a different world: quieter. The day was cooling down, not yet sunset, but shadows were lengthening, the sun on the verge of disappearing behind a mountain.

By the stand of cancer trees and the bright pink flowering oleander at the top he paused by the rusted metal gate. The pungent smell of marijuana tickled his nostrils and he heard guitar chords, not really a song but an undercurrent, a croon, a lullaby, and he heard something else. A kind of muted wail—someone weeping.

A little self-conscious, he opened the gate and walked in. The first thing he saw on the wide front porch was Teddy, in the white Mexican guayabera, jeans, and huaraches, sitting on a wicker rocking chair, strumming the guitar. Next to him, on the porch floor, a woman in a long print dress sat with her head resting on her folded arms, weeping softly—he remembered her from his last visit.

"Hello?" he said tentatively.

Teddy looked over. "Why, it's Detective Flynn," he said.

The woman stood up quickly, all in one motion, and vanished into the house.

"Rosalie . . . ?" said Teddy sadly, looking after her.

"I'm sorry if I came at a bad time," said Flynn.

"Not your fault," said Teddy. "Her yoga teacher was murdered—they found her body this afternoon." He reached into a big clamshell on the ground, extricated a remnant of a joint, lit up, and took a long drag.

"Sonora Cloud," he went on. "That was her name. Don't know what happened yet but Rosalie's friends with Harmony, who found her. Harmony says Sonora apparently fell and hit her head on a mirror," he said wonderingly. "That's pretty instant seven years' bad luck, huh? Doesn't seem real, more like a story someone made up. Except Rosalie's very, very upset."

"Sonora Cloud," Flynn said. "Who used to be Camille Chartrand."

"That's right. Back when she was Camille, she was a wild one, slept with everyone in town." Teddy paused, removing a flake of marijuana from his lower lip. "And then she turns into practically a holy woman. Just goes to show—I'm not sure what, but something."

"Remember the body that was recently dug up behind the retaining wall on Ocotillo Canyon?" Flynn said.

The joint had gone out. Teddy relit it. "Yeah?"

Flynn paused for a moment, trying not to breathe in too much marijuana. "It's been tentatively identified."

"No shit. Who was it? Anyone I know?"

"Yes."

"You're kidding me."

"It appears to be Wynn Wykoff."

Teddy Radebaugh dropped the joint he'd been about to take a toke from. "*Wynn?* No way!" He bent, picked it up. "Wynn hasn't been around for seventeen years. Says who?"

"Sonora Cloud, who used to be Camille, as a matter of fact. She recognized a ring and part of a backpack."

"You're saying all that time he was supposed to be gone he was right here—"

"That's what it looks like."

"Wynn," said Teddy, sadly. He looked at the joint, which had gone out, then he looked at Flynn, who was sitting across from him on a white plastic chair. Teddy set the joint down in the clamshell. "Man, I can't believe it. You know, I used to wonder sometimes why we never got so much as a postcard from him."

"To really sew up the ID," said Flynn, "it would be good to find a relative for dental work, DNA, whatever. He must have had relatives somewhere, though no one reported him missing. You got any ideas on that score?"

"Man. I got none. None at all. Pretty amazing, huh?" Teddy raised his eyebrows. "Saw him every day, making music, and we never talked about relatives, hell, not *ever* as far as I can remember. I'm pretty sure, like I think I said before, he was from back East. Oh, man. Who the hell would want to kill Wynn? He was a good bass player, not bad on the guitar either. Give me a moment here, to take it in."

"Sure."

Teddy stood up and began to pace the porch. "We never even suspected. I mean, he just wasn't the kind of person who gets murdered. He was just Wynn playing the bass. He wasn't, like, dealing drugs or making it with anyone else's old lady. Well, I mean, maybe sometimes . . ." He shrugged. "You know how that goes, with a band."

"All those years," said Flynn, "whoever he knew, whoever cared about him, no one wondered . . . ?"

"Well . . ." Teddy paced back to the rocker, sat down. "Even if we *did* wonder, which we didn't—you'd have to go to the cops to report someone missing. Back then Old Dudley was its own little world, you know. If we couldn't solve our problems without outside help, especially *police* help, well, we just didn't solve 'em. You don't have to solve everything, lots of times it just goes away." He lit up the joint again, took a toke, and added, "Besides, like I said, everyone thought he'd just moved on."

"But he must have lived somewhere, left stuff behind," said Flynn.

"He lived in his goddamn vehicle," said Teddy, "a big old Dodge van. Not any color. Maybe blue-gray. He used to park it at the end of the Gulch—" He hit the side of his head. "Shit. Ocotillo Canyon. You said they found him behind a house on Ocotillo Canyon?"

Flynn nodded.

"That's right near where he used to park. I remember he said there was an empty house up there where he used to go to smoke a doobie in the back yard. Oh, *man.*" Teddy sank farther back down in the rocker. "I can just see it, Wynn all stoned and peaceful, and someone comes up and, uh . . ." He paused. "Do they know how he died exactly?"

"Gunshot to the head."

"Wow. Like Annie. You think it was the same killer? Dickens?"

"I'm not saying it was Dickens."

"I guess whoever did it must of got rid of the van."

"Not too hard," said Flynn. "With Mexico five miles south from the Dudley city limits."

Teddy took another long drag on the joint, smoke oozing out of the corners of his mouth. He closed his eyes. *"Jenny,"* he said suddenly. "Or was it Winnie?"

"What?"

"Wynn had a sister named Jenny or Winnie. But he was Wynn— would they name his sister so close?" he mused. "A couple of years older. But, you know, her last name wasn't Wykoff, she had a married name."

Someone wailed inside the house.

"Rosalie!" Teddy stood up. "I'm coming. If I remember Jennie or Winnie's last name," he said to Flynn, "I'll call you. I still got your card." He turned away. "Coming, Rosie-posie. We'll take a walk, maybe, how about that? We can . . ." His voice faded away as he vanished into the house.


Going down the crumbling steps, Flynn was aware of something different, something changed. The light seemed, well, brighter and darker at the same time. Something like that—he couldn't put his finger on it. Halfway down his cell chimed. He stopped and punched it on.

"Flynn here."

"Mr. Flynn, this is Scott Macabee."

Scott Macabee. It took a second to figure out who Scott Macabee was. Suddenly, to his disgust, Flynn realized he was a little stoned, a contact high. "Scott," he said, "how are you?"

"I've been out of town at a conference. Just got back this afternoon."

"And . . ." prompted Flynn, watching a flock of small black birds flying in the luminous sky over the Gulch.

"Well, I'm worried about Rachel. Did she talk to you about coming to Dudley?"

Rachel coming to Dudley—with Camille-Sonora murdered? "Uh, she may have mentioned it to Chloe." But surely Chloe would have told him. He'd just spoken to her this afternoon.

"Chloe?" asked Scott.

Flynn wasn't sure himself what her actual title would be. "My assistant," he said abruptly.

The guy didn't know who Chloe was? He'd seen them as a husband-and-wife team who had hired him but if you split them up it was clearly Rachel he was working for. It didn't sound like Scott and Rachel were communicating too well. In that case, since Rachel was his client, he didn't want to go into the Sonora thing with Scott. He hoped it wasn't Scott paying the bill.

"I don't know if Rachel's coming here is such a good idea right now," Flynn said. "She should probably talk to me first. Could you put her on?"

"*No,* I can't put her on—that's why I'm calling, she left for Dudley this afternoon—in fact, she should be there by now."

"Really?" Flynn said, alarmed but not wanting to show it. "Where's she staying?"

"I don't know—when I asked, she said she wasn't sure." Scott's voice cracked a little. "I haven't been able to reach her on her cell."

"And?"

"She—she's been acting strange lately. She just isn't herself—she seems to have gotten so . . . *independent.*"

"This is a *bad* thing?" Flynn said dubiously. "Her acting independent?"

"I don't mean it the way it sounds," said Scott. "I worry, you know, that she'll start flying too high and crash."

"Tell you what," said Flynn, treading lightly, "I assume she'll be contacting me. I'll have her give you a call."

Scott clicked off. Flynn reached the bottom of the stairs, called Rachel's cell, and got her voice mail. He left a message.

Various scenarios involving Rachel filled his mind. His imagination seemed to be working overtime, not to mention the continuing oddness of the light. Chloe, he needed to see Chloe. He noticed in an oblique kind of way that his fists were clenched.

The Oliver House was located up behind Main Street near St. John's Episcopal Church. It was getting dark as Rachel parked her car in a little parking lot at the church, got out, and opened the trunk. Doing this reminded her of picking up Scott at the airport and the oblivious way he'd put his carry-on in the trunk without seeing any importance in the fact hers was there already.

She felt sad, thinking of Scottie, but irritated at the same time, which made her even sadder.

Though slightly dimmed in the dusk, the Oliver House looked just like the picture online, a big two-story red brick structure with a wide front porch, complete with rocking chairs. A long bridge with metal railings that spanned a drainage ditch led over to it.

Rachel took a deep breath and inhaled the rich pungent smell of licorice. Fennel. Rachel was filled with a deep nostalgic longing—for what, she didn't know. The longing somehow felt a little scary.

Wheeling her carry-on, Rachel began to walk briskly, efficiently; the way one might walk in an airport heading for a departure gate, walking both toward and away from that smell, that nostalgia.

She crossed the narrow bridge, opened a metal gate, and a motion-sensor light came on as she walked down a dirt path and up the steps to the front porch. The three wooden rocking chairs, white with rush seats, sat vacant on the porch. A sign by the front door said OLIVER HOUSE with no further instructions. Inside was a long wide shadowy hall and on the right an office and a middle-aged woman, pretty, blond, at a computer.

"Hi," said the woman brightly. She wore a tie-dye top and long dangling earrings. "Can I help you?"

"Yes," said Rachel. "I'd like a room."

"Sure," said the woman. "We've got plenty of those here." She smiled, with no hurry in her voice.

"I didn't make a reservation."

"Not a problem. I'm Nancy, by the way. I own this place and I run it too. How'd you find out about us?"

"Your Web site," said Rachel.

"It works!" Nancy clapped her hands. "Great. A friend of mine just got that going. Let's get you signed in, then I'll show you around. First time in Dudley?"

"No." Rachel handed her a credit card. "But it's been a while."

"I've lived here thirteen years," said Nancy chattily. "Came here from back East. New York City. I had double bolts on my doors plus a police lock. When I first got here I never even locked my doors. Felt really safe. But you know what?"

"What?"

"I probably wasn't. Just felt that way."

"Maybe," said Rachel, "feeling that way is all that matters."

"Not that I'm trying to be negative," said Nancy. "It is pretty safe here, except when it isn't." She lowered her voice. "There was a murder here this afternoon."

Suddenly Rachel was tired, exhausted, all her reserves gone with this flight to Dudley. She didn't want to talk about a murder. She wished Nancy would shut up and show her a room.

Nancy handed her back the credit card and stood up.

Rachel couldn't resist. "Who was it, that was murdered?"

"A woman," Nancy said. "That's all I know."

My cat Big Foot rubbed against Flynn's legs, looking up at him with eyes of chilly love and purring loudly.

"No real time of death yet on Sonora, I guess," said Flynn. "The air-conditioning being on full blast is going to skew that too. If we had a time of death we could check out some folks, say, Jim Rasmussen, Phil Glenn, and of course Kurt Dickens."

"It's always struck me as funny," I said, "that the people who might be described as lovers are the most likely to kill you."

"Sure," said Flynn, "what's so funny about that?"

"Funny-strange, I mean."

Flynn nodded. "I caught your meaning, but I don't see why it's strange."

"Think about it," I said.

"Of course," said Flynn, instantly changing the subject, "either of the first two guys could have hired someone. As for Dickens, the MO with Sonora-Camille is different than with Annie and Wynn but Dickens has that domestic violence history. And with Sonora-Camille too."

"The cops are already thinking that way, probably. Let them do it so we don't have to."

"Also," said Flynn, "there's Rasmussen's wife."

"What?" I said.

"She could have shot Annie. Had an excellent reason—two kids, husband's out philandering, why not?"

"Sure," I said sarcastically. "That makes sense. And killed Wynn first for practice. Did you get anything useful from Teddy?"

"Some shock and awe," said Flynn, "and a possible first name for a relative of Wykoff. His sister—Jenny or maybe Winnie, he wasn't sure."

"Cute," I said sarcastically. "So we can Google Jenny or maybe Winnie Wykoff, see what we get."

"Teddy says she was married and he doesn't remember her married name. Listen, right now we got bigger worries. Scott called me. Rachel's in Dudley."

"Rachel's in *Dudley*?" I said. "And she doesn't know about Sonora."

"And she's not answering her cell."

Just as he said that, Flynn's chimed. He flipped it open.

*"Rachel,"* he said. His eyes met mine. "Hey, heard you were in Dudley. The Oliver House? Your husband's been worried. Yeah? Good. A murder? You heard about it? Yeah. Hold on." He put his hand over the phone. "She's asking—"

"I know," I said. "I could tell. There is no way you're going to tell her that kind of news over the phone. Tell her I'm coming over to the Oliver house right now."

# chapter twenty-three

RACHEL WAS STANDING ON THE FRONT PORCH about to take a swallow from a bottle of water but stopped when she saw me.

"You didn't have to come all the way over here," she said. She was wearing the same sort of preppy middle-class clothes she'd worn when we met at the gallery—polo, pearls, and capris—but her blond hair was mussed and she had faint blue circles under her eyes.

"I'm really close," I told her.

"I mean, I just wanted to make sure everything was all right, that whoever was murdered wasn't . . ." She let her voice trail off.

It was evening cool on the porch. Crickets chirped in the licorice-scented air and there was even a breeze. A row of empty white wooden rocking chairs rocked gently back and forth as if just vacated.

"Let's sit," I said, standard procedure for bad news, get them sitting.

She sat abruptly. I took the rocker next to her.

"*What?*" she said, with the expression of someone who is used to bad news and therefore always expects the worst.

"Wynn had an old girlfriend," I said. "We talked about her? Camille Chartrand?"

"Yes, I remember."

"Well, she changed her name to Sonora Cloud."

"Sonora Cloud?" she said. "That's who you said identified his body? The yoga teacher?" Her voice trembled. "Is she the one who's . . . who's *dead*?"

"Yes."

*"How?"*

"She fell against a mirror and hit her head."

"Fell?"

"Pushed, more likely."

Rachel blinked. "Not shot, then."

"No."

She shuddered. "You think it's connected, don't you?"

"Yes."

"I had this *feeling* as soon as that woman told me— God. Why is it when I have a feeling and I decide it's okay to ignore it, it's always a mistake? *Why?*"

"Listen, Rachel, Camille was Kurt's girlfriend at one point—"

She cut me off. "No. I don't care. So what?" She looked away from me, out at the streetlight across the bridge. "I don't want to hear anything against Kurt, okay?"

"Okay," I said.

"And I'm not leaving," Rachel said. "I mean, no one knows I'm here anyway. I've avoided it for years, coming back. But nothing could be any harder than what's already happened." She glanced over at me.

"Your choice," I said.

"I'm hoping being here will jog my memory about the murder. I have all these . . ." She sighed. "These blank spots."

"Blank spots?"

"Just stuff I don't remember, I guess. Details. Like I told you in the gallery—someone being there when I found my mom. Listen, I may as well tell you, I met with Kurt the other night."

"What?" I'd been rocking and now I skidded to a stop. I stared at her. "Maybe I misunderstood," I said carefully, "but Flynn gave me the impression that you hadn't seen Kurt for years."

"I hadn't. But he called me and I met with him at a restaurant."

"When was that exactly?" I asked.

"Last night," said Rachel. "He called me the night before that."

"Really?" I said.

"I just forgot is all." She set her water bottle on the ground. Her hand seemed to be shaking ever so slightly. "He's *glad* about my investigation. Things haven't been easy for him. I mean, even if he was acquitted, it still kind of hangs over his head."

"Do you think he'll talk to Flynn and me?"

"I have his number." She reached down for her purse. "It's right in here, I programmed it in. Let me give it to you."

I wrote it down.

"I didn't forget exactly. Things were just going so fast." Rachel's voice was defensive. "And I didn't want Scott to know. He'd get upset the way he always does. I'll call Kurt, tell him it's okay to talk to you guys." She blinked rapidly. "Could you do one more thing for me?" she asked.

"All right," I said.

"Call Scottie. Don't mention the murder. Don't tell him where I'm staying. Say you're not sure. Tell him I'm fine, that—that, I don't know, my cell ran down. That I'll call him in the morning."

"Sure," I said. "You're all right if I go?" I added.

"Fine."

\* \* \*

I'd walked down from my house to the Oliver House and now I trudged back up the hill, worried about murder now suddenly in real time, not seventeen years ago, worried about Rachel.

What if after all it *had* been Kurt who'd murdered Annie Glenn and Wynn too—so off the wall he was murderously jealous even of her friends? Kurt, sneaking down to Dudley to kill Camille-Sonora, his old girlfriend, who he thought knew or suspected something dangerous in him. What made Rachel so trusting of him? She, of all people, had the right to be wary of everyone.

Hired by Rachel, Flynn and I were digging up old stuff—didn't this new murder prove the closer we got to answers, the more in danger Rachel could be? A killer who knew she had blank spots in her memory most certainly wouldn't want her filling any of them in. Didn't she realize this? Was she so used to imaginary terrors she had lost her ability to recognize the real ones?

Back at my house Flynn was gone, leaving a note and a set of keys to his office.

*Call me when you get in,* it said. *Keys are to the office. It's time you moved in. Rachel okay? Let me know.*

I called him.

"Why?" he said when I told him about Rachel meeting Kurt. "She meets with the guy, puts him on high alert, then she doesn't even tell us. *Why?*"

"Because she's not one hundred percent regular straight normal," I said.

Flynn snorted. "Quite a diagnosis. But you know what? It's par for the course. People always have to keep something back, they sure did when I was a cop and now I'm actually hired by them—they're paying me *money* and they're still keeping things back."

"You want Kurt's number?"

"Of course I do. You got the keys to the office?"

"Yes, but first I have to work briefly at my old job."

"Look, once you're set up, have Lois give you the box of Annie's stuff I got from Alice Hayes so you can go through it."

All the time, all the *time,* people asking if she was okay, Rachel thought. Of course she wasn't okay. Her mother had been murdered and she would never, never get over it.

Rachel sat on the bed in the Blue Agave Room. All the rooms had names like that: the Ocotillo, the Pomegranate, the Sego Lily, with a picture of the particular plant hand-painted on the door. The house had been built in the late 1800s and nothing appeared to have been renovated since. Nancy had shown Rachel several rooms that were vacant; in fact, Rachel suspected most of the rooms were vacant. Nancy didn't seem to care if she rented rooms or not.

She closed her eyes. With her eyes closed it was harder to avoid thinking about Camille "Sonora Cloud" Chartrand. Except that wasn't what came to her mind. What came to her mind was Wynn—the same image she'd had of him once before, in a grave, curled up like a child.

Those years, all those years she'd thought of him as this person who'd "screwed the band," as Teddy had put it, all those years he'd been dead, like Annie, lying behind a house in a shallow grave behind a retaining wall, getting more and more covered up as time went by and no one was even looking for his body. That seemed to Rachel to be unutterably lonely, so lonely she could feel that loneliness in her bones.

She started to shake.

She stood up, took a deep breath, and reached for her purse, for the pill bottle, the Ativan. She fumbled through: makeup bag, three pens, address book, Kleenex—where was the pill bottle? She dumped everything out onto the bed. Still no bottle. *Where was it?* Now she felt a little panic rising. Where the *fuck* was the Ativan?

She thought she'd put it in her purse but it must be in her carry-on. She'd unpacked most of it—the carry-on—but the bottle could be in one of the zipper pockets. Except, when she searched, it wasn't. But there was still the car—it could have fallen out of her purse and be on the floor of the car.

She left the room, almost at a run, down the hall, out the door, and over the bridge to the parking lot.

But there was no prescription bottle in the Honda when Rachel looked, not on the seats, under the seats, in the glove compartment, and not in the trunk either. Finally she knew there wouldn't be because at some point in her search she remembered, just before she'd left to pick up Scott, taking the bottle out of her purse to see how many she had left, and with so many things going on in her mind, *not putting it back in.*

She'd forgotten to put it back and now she saw it clearly, sitting on a small white wrought-iron table next to the lounge chair by the pool.

She sat gripping the steering wheel, in the parking lot by the church, staring out the window. It was dark—there wasn't much to see, her back was to the church and down below was the back alley behind Main Street, a streetlight shining on some garbage cans and the NO PARKING sign, and her eyes were closed anyway.

*Call Scottie. He'll bring the bottle to you in the time it takes him to drive here—an hour and a half.*

*No.*

And then, as if it had been waiting for her until she needed it, a memory came to her, of she and Annie and Kurt, hiking in Dixie Canyon. There was a little stretch that was hard to climb and Rachel always had trouble with it. Kurt would stand at the top and look down, she could hear his voice now almost as if he were here in person. "Come, Rach," he would say, "you can do it."

And I can, she thought. *I can do it.*

# chapter twenty-four

I SAT DOWN AT MY DESK AND CALLED PATSY Wolhart, the woman I'd recently gone to a release hearing with for her abusive husband, the motion for release denied. Each day I called some of the victims I was working with and told them I was leaving. Leaving? In most ways it felt as though I'd already left.

New victims were being passed to Linda, the misdemeanor victim advocate, and the last meeting Larry had held was without me. Larry hadn't bugged me at all or even spoken to me since I'd given notice, as if I'd ceased to exist. Even in the break room this morning with the perking coffeepot, the bagels someone had brought from a trip to Tucson, I had the sense I wasn't really there, merely a minor ghost stealing a bagel.

Patsy Wolhart wasn't home. I left a message. Marking off my last days, hours at work, I was twiddling my thumbs until noon, when I planned to drive over to my new office in Sierra Vista, when my phone rang.

"Call for you from, um, Harmony?" said Marilu the receptionist.

"Put her through," I said. Harmony, from the yoga studio, Sonora-Camille's friend. "Harmony, how are you?"

"You mentioned something about your office paying for counseling," she said. "And a claim form?

"Yes," I said.

"I'm stuck at my shop—A Blast from the Past?—I was hoping you could drop one off for me."

"Be right there," I said.

Through the plate-glass window of his office Flynn could see cars and pickups going by on Highway 92. He could see his Land Rover and the green Volkswagen belonging to one of the Realtors. Across the highway was the Sierra Vista Mall, just the parking lots visible. Why couldn't Tanya choose that mall to shoplift in? thought Flynn irritably.

He punched in the number for Kurt that Chloe had given him. He'd been planning to put in some time locating a few witnesses to a car-bashing, a civil case, but the Rachel thing was getting kind of urgent. For a second he was furious at Rachel for meeting with Kurt and not telling him right away. *Furious*. Get a grip.

But it was serious—when Flynn thought about Rachel, centered on her, he kept feeling that something was odd, off, about the whole damn thing. But who knew what finding their mom with her brains splashed against the wall did to someone.

No answer till the voice message kicked in.

"Dickens's Landscaping and Home Repair."

Flynn mentioned Rachel, left his name, office, home, and cell numbers. Damn. Might as well get back to that car-bashing thing. He sat staring at his computer, not feeling all that hyped. *Ping*. An e-mail. Re: Annie Glenn. *Son of a bitch*. Billy Dodds, drummer, had actually responded.

He opened it: *Heard about Wynn from Teddy Radebaugh*

*yesterday morning. This is something I don't want to go into via e-mail. Call me at 802-555-6107.*

Bingo. Flynn felt pretty stoked. He picked up the phone, punched in the number.

"Billy Dodds."

"Hello, Billy. This is Brian Flynn, just got your e-mail."

"Mr. Flynn. Wow. I'm floored about Wynn. Teddy tells me you're working for Annie's little girl."

"Yes."

"I've been thinking, what the hell. I used to see this, um, counselor from time to time. He always bugged me about going back to Dudley. So I'm coming out there."

"You are? When?"

"Say, tomorrow. Yeah, tomorrow, I hope. I gotta drive to Burlington. If not tomorrow, the next day."

"If you let me know for sure when, either me or my assistant can pick you up at the airport," Flynn offered.

"Naw. That's cool. I'll rent a car."

Flynn hung up and called Kurt Dickens's number again just in case, and hung up at the voice mail.

Then he tilted back in his chair, put his hands behind his head, and stared out the plate-glass window. He was feeling optimistic having Billy come out; from what Teddy had said it sounded like he might be a competent person who actually had a life.

His phone rang.

"Hey, I have someone up front who wants to see you," said Lois in an artificial voice. "She was here a few days ago, if I recall. She says she's left you messages but you never respond. Er, Val."

"Val?" said Flynn. "*Val.* She's standing right there?"

"She was till a second ago. Your ex, right?" said Lois. "I said you weren't taking calls and I was going to walk back to check with you but she went to the ladies' room."

Thank God for that back door. Now was as good a time as any to go in search of some car-bashing witnesses.

I parked at the bottom of the Gulch. A Blast from the Past, Harmony's shop, was just a few steps up from Main Street. It was still relatively early, ten o'clock, which was when most Dudley shops opened for business. The dummy in the front window sported a fringed leather vest and patched denim bell bottoms, embroidered with peace signs.

FREE YOUR MIND said a sign on the glass front door. The sign next to it said CLOSED.

I freed my mind enough to try the door. It opened. A bell tinkled. The air was rank with patchouli. Harmony sat on a stool near the back, wearing a long purple granny dress that made her red hair stand out.

"We aren't open," she said. "Didn't you see—"

I came closer.

"Oh, it's you," she said. "Good. I didn't expect you so soon."

I handed her the claim form and the sheet of paper with the explanation.

"Thank you. You're so kind. But it won't—" Her mouth trembled, eyes teared up, and she began to cry, great gasping sobs. "It won't bring—"

I looked for Kleenex, my staple at work, found none. Relaying information about the progress of a case, supplying Kleenex, and listening in a way that elicited emotions rather than facts—these were the tools of my trade.

I lingered, waiting until Harmony had calmed down.

"Sorry," she said finally. "It won't bring her back, was what I was saying."

I nodded.

"I still hear her voice, so clearly, like she's right there. Like the night before last. She had the green corn tamales—Rosa makes them with canola oil instead of lard so they kind of fall apart but—" She stopped abruptly. "What am I talking about?"

"It's okay," I said.

"I have to confess," Harmony said, "I don't care about the claim form, it was just an excuse so I could ask you to do me a favor. When we had dinner Sonora talked about this other person . . ." She hesitated. "If I tell you, is it confidential?"

"Yes. Unless you give me permission to repeat it. I'm assuming it doesn't have anything to do with her murder?"

"I don't think so. She just wanted to find this person before the police did."

"The police," I said.

Harmony nodded. "That's why I asked about the confidential part—Sonora said to me, 'I need to find her and tell her something—the police won't do it right.' Wendy. Her name was Wendy."

"Wendy?" I said.

"The person she needed to find. Wendy Burch, Burch with a *u*. She was pretty sure she lived Colorado. She was going to go search for her online. I don't know what it was she wanted to tell her but maybe Wendy could figure it out—oh, I don't *know*." Harmony's face crumpled. "I'd do it myself, but I don't even have a computer."

Teddy had said Wynn's sister was named Jenny, Winnie. "No problem," I said. "I'll check it out."


Back up here where the tourists didn't penetrate, some of the wood houses still looked as Rachel remembered them: shabby, needing paint, gardens gone amok in the monsoon season. But others were all fixed up, painted with multiple San Francisco colors, hardly recognizable. Rachel paused at the bottom of Laundry Hill next to a stand of ailanthus trees, and the strangest thought came to her—*I'm home, home at last.*

She punched in Kurt's number. It rang until the voice message kicked in. "Kurt," she said, "it's *Rachel,* call me—"

"Rach?"

"*Kurt.* You're there." She felt enormously relieved. "Kurt," she said again. "Camille? You remember her? Camille Chartrand?"

"Of course I do."

"She—she got killed."

"Killed?" said Kurt. "Like how, killed? You mean a car accident or something?"

"No. Not like that. Someone killed her. They pushed her, Chloe said, and she fell against a mirror."

"What?" said Kurt. "That's crazy. Who was it?"

"They don't know."

"Who's Chloe?"

"One of the investigators I hired. Chloe and Flynn. Listen, could you get in touch with Flynn right away? I've got his number—"

"Wait," Kurt cut in. "Flynn. You told me but I forgot his name. I think he called me not that long ago. I mean, earlier this morning."

"Call him back, okay?"

"I will."

"You know what, Kurt? I'm standing at the bottom of Laundry Hill."

"Wow," said Kurt, "that's pretty amazing. You planning on going up?"

"Yes."

"How are you doing, Rach? You all right?"

"Yes, I'm all right." Rachel swallowed. "I'm just going to keep doing this, Kurt, I have to."

"I understand," he said, "I do. I should have been braver myself a long time ago and I wasn't. I'm with you; you get nervous, I'm there holding your hand in spirit and I'll come in person if you need me."

"I know that," said Rachel. "I know that so well. Thank you, Kurt."

Tears welled up in her eyes. Kurt had always been like that, comforting. Once when her mom was out late when she was supposed to be home Kurt had told her some long rambling story about fishing in Minnesota and it wasn't that the story was so good, but Kurt's voice telling it was like a lullaby.

Jody, the prosecutor's wife, had had that kind of voice too. She'd never forgotten Jody. Rachel wondered where she was right now and if she would ever see her again.

"Call Flynn, okay?" she said. "Right now."

"I will. I promise."

She closed her phone and stood there at the bottom of Laundry Hill. Time, her life, she felt as though it were in two segments divided as if with an ax blade by her mother's death.

She took a deep breath, walked up the street, and stopped at the white house a little ways before number 29. The house had sky-blue shutters and a shrine to the Virgin of Guadalupe draped with plastic roses on the tiny lawn in the front yard.

*Juan and Lupe.*

Juan and Lupe, she thought, they were old back then, were they still alive? They must be, their house was still exactly the same. A tiny Chihuahua ran across the lawn at her, yapping.

"Paco!" she called. It couldn't be the Paco she remembered, but Juan and Lupe always gave their dogs the same name. "Paco!" she called again, but the little dog snarled and retreated.

The driveway was empty, they must be out.

Up farther, a few houses past Juan and Lupe's and directly

across from number 29, was a yellow-painted house, who had lived there? Rachel couldn't remember. On the far side was Alice's house but 29 was before that.

When she and Annie lived there, there hadn't been a fence, just a clear view when you sat on the porch, sat on the battered old green couch on the porch, covered with a bedspread from India, a clear view of the yellow house across the street.

Except the house across the street hadn't been yellow back then.

There was a fence now, wrought iron.

Rachel stopped in front of number 29. The house was close to street level, just a few steps leading up to a matching wrought-iron gate with an arched trellis twined with abundant yellow roses. Bees buzzed busily round the roses. She went up the steps, opened the gate, and went into the yard. It was spotless, mostly brick with large pots of desert plants and two slatted-wood Adirondack chairs in bright blue.

Where was the yard with crabgrass that never stayed green very long no matter how much you watered it? Where was the front porch with the battered green couch? She hadn't lived in a house that looked like this. The front door not her front door, but a front door that had a stained-glass transom over it. Should she knock?

*Excuse me,* she would say to whoever answered, *could I look around inside? My mother was murdered here.* She giggled, a little wildly.

"Hello?" said a voice behind her.

Startled, she turned.

A young man in long khaki shorts and a black T-shirt was standing next to the wrought-iron gate. He wore little glasses and his hair was brown and spiky. He was staring at her in the strangest way.

She took a step backward.

*"Rachel?"* he said.

"Yes?"

"It's me, Max."

"So?" she said. "Max who?"

And suddenly she remembered.

# chapter twenty-five

FLYNN'S CELL CHIMED.

"Flynn here," he said, as he made a turn onto Fry Boulevard, on his way to interview one of the car-bashing witnesses who worked at NAPA Auto Parts. "Can I help you?"

"This is Kurt Dickens. Rachel said to call you."

"Kurt!" said Flynn. "Great!"

"I just spoke to her. What's this about Camille getting killed?"

Flynn told him what he knew.

"I hope someone's keeping an eye out for Rachel."

"Listen," said Flynn, avoiding the issue, what the hell was anyone supposed to do—she didn't seem to want protection. "Can we meet?"

"Sure," said Kurt. "But I'm in Tucson."

"I can come to Tucson." Flynn looked at his watch, decided the car-bashing witnesses could wait. "Today?"

"Well," said Kurt, "I'm on a job—I kind of hate to take off too much time 'cause I'm hoping to finish today, have the bill ready when they get back to town tomorrow."

"Yeah?" said Flynn.

"If you could meet me where I'm working—"

"Not a problem. How about, say, two hours, two and a half?" Flynn said. "Tell me where and I'll be there."


The young man with the spiky hair and glasses standing at the gate of the house where Rachel and her mother had once lived had a tiny gold earring in one ear and looked a little nerdy, like a million guys you might see in the mall on a Saturday.

"*Max,*" said Rachel. "Of *course.*"

"You look different," he said, "but I recognized you right away 'cause you look like your mom now"—his face turned a little pink—"really, really pretty."

Rachel had trained herself long ago to deflect compliments. "I'd forgotten all about you till a moment ago," she said coolly. "Alice's nephew."

Max nodded. "Her brother's my dad."

"You used to hang around"—Rachel smiled, she couldn't help herself, there was something so silly and nerdy about him—"getting in the way."

"Hey!"

"How old were you anyway?"

"Eight. Eight and a half, going on nine."

"Flynn told me Alice is a therapist now," Rachel said. "Is that really true?"

"Who's Flynn?"

"I hired him, him and Chloe, they're private detectives—you know about my mom, that she was murdered?"

Max looked puzzled. "Of course."

"I hired them to look into the case."

"I get it!" said Max. "That's the guy who was looking for my aunt the other day. *Awesome!* That is so awesome. Your mom's boyfriend got off—"

"Kurt. He didn't kill my mom."

"My aunt doesn't really think so either."

"Why didn't she say so back then?"

Max shrugged. "Maybe she did and no one listened. Besides, it's not like she actually knew anything or could prove anything."

Rachel glanced at the front door. "Should we be standing here like this? Who lives here now anyway?"

"No one." Max plopped down on one of the Adirondack chairs. "Hot." He pulled up his black T-shirt and wiped his face with the bottom. "It's a short-term rental, but it's not rented now. It's slow this time of year." He stared up at her.

"I remember you so well," he said. "I'll never forget you. It was the first summer I ever came to visit my aunt and the lady next door gets murd—" He stopped and looked stricken. "Jesus Christ, I'm such an asshole. I'm sorry."

"You don't have to be sorry," said Rachel fervently. "It's actually a lot easier if people just say things right out."

It was late in the morning now and it *was* hot, getting hotter. Rachel closed her eyes for a second. She felt a little dizzy. She walked over and sat down on the other chair. It was an attractive piece of furniture but not that comfortable.

"You okay?" asked Max. "You look a little . . ."

Rachel turned her head away. She could see the wrought iron gate and hear the bees buzzing. "I'm *fine*."

"Sorry again." Max paused. "I used to get dizzy lots, not just from heat, but from trying not to remember."

"This house," said Rachel, deciding not to ask him what he was trying not to remember. "My mom never owned it, she just rented it from Mr. Cruz. Does he still . . . ?"

"I think he's dead now," said Max. "But anyway he sold it to some out-of-towners from San Diego. They fixed it up. Mr. Cruz never told them the, um, history but they found out later. It creeped them out, so they sold it to someone else, I don't know who, and then *they* sold it. That's why it's a short-term rental now, the people that buy it don't want to live in it. Actually my aunt manages it. She has the keys. I don't know where they are but I could ask. I mean"—he glanced at Rachel—"if you want to take a look inside sometime."

How could he even ask? There was no way she could ever, ever go into that house again.

Then what was she doing here?

Rachel closed her eyes again and leaned back in the chair. With her eyes closed, it was easier to hear the bees, backed up with the hum of cicadas, easier to smell the roses. The roses hadn't been there before, so even with her eyes closed it still didn't feel like the place she remembered.

"No," she said, "not right now." She sighed. "What is it you're trying not to remember?"

"Your mom getting killed. Seeing her dead."

Rachel opened her eyes and sat up straight. *"What?"*

Behind his glasses, Max blinked. He blinked several times, a nervous tic. "You don't remember, do you? I could tell from the way you were acting before. I saw her. I was right there behind you when you found her."

She stared at him in astonishment. *"That's* what I forgot. Someone else *was* there. I kept trying and trying to remember who it could have been. It was *you.* But how could that be?"

"When you came home from your slumber party, I was in Alice's front yard. I had this big crush on you and you said hi to me and I got so excited I followed you into the house." He paused. "You really don't remember?"

Rachel sighed. "I have these—these *blank* places in my memory." She looked over at Max, noticing his eyes for the first time—they were brown and moist—doggy eyes. In his long khaki shorts and black T-shirt he kind of still looked like a kid. "You *saw her*?" she said.

He nodded. "I was right behind you when you opened her bedroom door. It was just for a second but it, like, *burned* into my brain." The nervous tic came back, blink, blink. "I had nightmares for years. I still do sometimes but not so much."

"No!" said Rachel. "Oh, no. I'm so sorry. You were just a kid."

"So were you. You never had nightmares?"

"I am *so* screwed up," said Rachel fervently. "Sometimes I can hardly function—nightmares, flashbacks, panic attacks."

"Panic attacks?" said Max. "*Me too*."

"Ativan?"

"Xanax."

"You feel like such a freak," said Rachel.

"Yeah."

She looked at him curiously. "Alice has the key? So? What— you've gone back in there?"

Max shook his head. "Uh-uh. Not since it happened. No way."

"Then why would you think I—"

"I kind of . . ." he paused "I've kind of *wanted* to. I mean, I had a therapist once that said it might be helpful. Then"—he laughed— "I had another one that said it wouldn't be. I don't know. What's the worst that could happen?"

"You know how you feel like you're on the edge, about to go over?"

Max nodded. "Xanax time."

"You could go over."

"That's right. You could go right over the edge."

"I wonder what that would be like."

"Ha!" said Max. "Probably they'd put you in a straitjacket, lock you up in this cell with soft padded walls and the rest of your life would be just one long scream."

Rachel giggled.

"Funny?" Max snorted. "You think it's funny?"

She began to laugh. "It is kind of . . . extreme."

"Extreme." Max began to laugh too. "Extreme fear." He laughed some more. *"Gnarly."*


I stopped at my house and picked up a small fern that had been languishing on my front porch to put on my new desk and drove over to Sierra Vista. I had never actually seen Flynn's office before. It was across the street from the new mall in a pink two-story stucco building.

Right in the middle between an eye doctor and a certified public accountant was Flynn, my Flynn. I parked and got out of my car, fond of him for the moment in spite of his lousy disposition.

The glass on the window was painted discreetly in medium-sized black letters, FLYNN INVESTIGATIONS—Flynn and Newcombe Investigations had an even nicer ring, polite, like a stockbroker. I balanced the fern on my knee and started to open the door, but someone inside beat me to it.

"You must be Chloe," said the woman holding the door open. She wore a blue knit pant suit and was maybe sixty, and sixty in the old-fashioned way—undyed, undieted, and unexercised. "I'm Lois. I was going to leave a note if you didn't show up in the next fifteen minutes, I've got a doctor's appointment."

"Nice to meet you, Lois," I said.

"Let me show you your office."

By the front door was an oak desk, with a computer and a spray of artificial pink roses in a blue vase. I followed her past a large room, where, through the open door, I saw a desk and a computer.

"Brian's office," said Lois. "And this is yours."

The room was bare except for a desk, a chair, a phone, and a computer. It had, I noted, a window, thank God. I plunked the fern down the desk.

"Brian got the computer all set up." Lois looked at her watch. "I have to get going. I'll lock the door and put the clock sign up—back at, oh, say, four."

"Fine," I said. "Thanks."

Lois snapped her fingers. "Almost forgot. Brian wanted me to give you Annie's box. It's behind my desk, you can't miss it—a big cardboard box."

I turned on the computer and sat in the chair. It was a good chair, fake black leather, good back support. I gave it a twirl. Then I turned on the computer, tested it out. Googled Wendy Burch, Colorado.

There was the usual stream of listings but Wynn's sister, Wendy Burch, was right up there, if she indeed was the right Wendy. A decorator of some sort, Wendy's Interiors in Denver. An e-mail address and a phone number. E-mail didn't seem quite the right thing for this, so I punched in the number.

"Wendy's Interiors, you fix it up, we make it right," a woman's voice sang out. "This is Jeannie, how may I help you?"

"I'd like to talk to Wendy."

"Wendy's on a buying trip in L.A. She'll be back tomorrow."

"Could you tell me something?" I said. "I'm looking for an old friend. Is Wendy's maiden name Wykoff, by any chance?"

"I don't have a clue, not one clue what her maiden name is. Why don't you call back tomorrow?"

I punched off and went up front for Annie's box. It was shoved against one wall behind Lois's desk, with *Annie's stuff* scrawled on it in Magic Marker. I picked it up, it wasn't too heavy, and carried it back to my office.

Annie's stuff.

What becomes of all our stuff after we die? It lives on and on, burdening the people we leave behind who have loved us and who cannot bear to throw it away. Not the stuff of monetary value that can be sold or the things the relatives squabble over, but the everyday stuff in our closets, our desk drawers, our wallets, our purses. When my brother James died so many years ago now, his stuff was still there, carrying on being his stuff without him.

I kept many things: his art reviews, books, drawings, a journal, photographs. Good things, historical things you pass on, but how to explain the green Izod polo shirt with the frayed collar I kept for so long; a pair of ancient running shoes; some faded striped pajamas? I would open my closet door and there they'd be, whispering to me—*James.*

Someone was knocking on the front door. Lois had said she would put up the clock sign so maybe it was her or Flynn, forgot the key. I walked up front and saw a woman through the glass. She was maybe my age, with blond tousled hair and big sunglasses, wearing tight jeans and a black tank top.

Not so much knocking as tapping. Tap, tap, tap. She looked confident, as if she were sure it was okay for her to tap on the door even when the sign said closed, so I turned the lock and opened it.

"Hi," I said, "can I help you?"

She stared at me, or I think she did. I couldn't see her eyes behind the sunglasses. "Who are you?" she said.

"Chloe, Chloe Newcombe. I work with Flynn. My name's not on the door yet."

"Sure. *Chloe.*" She put out her hand. "Val."

*Val.* Flynn's ex-wife was named Val, short for Valentine. Not that he ever talked about her, it had slipped out maybe twice in the whole time I'd known him. No, it was Shirley, the gossipy secretary over at the county sheriff's, who had told me about Val.

Yak, yak, yak, poor guy didn't suspect a thing, the *coach,* yak.

But Flynn's Val didn't live around here anymore, I knew that. She lived in Portland, Oregon. So maybe it was another Val.

"I'm Brian's ex," she said chattily. "Brian's told me all about you."

*He had?*

"Ah," I said. "Is there anything I can do for you? Fl—Brian isn't here right now."

"Well," said Val, "if he's not around, then I guess I'll take off. Tell him I said hi. Tell him to *call me*." She mouthed the last two words, rather than saying them, as if they were something intimate, just between herself and Flynn.

I closed the door behind her, locked it, went back to my office.

The duct tape was on so thick on Annie's box, I needed a box cutter. Or at least some scissors. I opened my middle desk drawer where that kind of thing might be and found three paper clips. Flynn might have some. So Flynn was back to seeing his ex. So what?

I went into his office, found a batch of pens but no scissors in a metal cup on his desk and a Post-it notepad in the center. I opened the middle drawer. And found a pair of red-handled scissors.

I carried the scissors to my desk. I punched them through the duct tape. Viciously. So *fucking* what?

# chapter twenty-six

KURT WAS WORKING AT A HOUSE IN THE Foothills on the northwest side of town. Flynn turned down the street Kurt had told him, then spotted the smaller street, more like an alley, where Kurt said his truck would be parked. The Foothills was a nice part of town but the houses Flynn was looking at weren't on a par with most of the houses, though they were the same adobe and stucco, same red-tiled roofs—they were smaller, more standardized; built probably before the Foothills become fashionable.

Halfway down the alley, Flynn saw the truck, a blue '92 Ford pickup with a dented back bumper. He parked behind and stepped out of his air-conditioned Land Rover to a wave of blistering heat and a chorus of screeching cicadas. A high adobe fence surrounded the back yard with an open gate in the center. Flynn peered into the yard, which was dominated mostly by a swimming pool. At the far end of the pool was a flower bed, no flowers but dirt freshly turned over, some pony packs of snapdragons, an open bag of bark mulch.

"Hey, Kurt!" he yelled.

No answer.

It was so hot. Flynn wiped his forehead, more a reflex than

anything else, since the heat dried sweat almost instantly. From where he stood he could smell the piney smell of the mulch, hear the hum of the cicadas peak and start again. The swimming pool shimmered like one of those fake sapphires you can buy on home shopping networks.

Then the door of the house opened and a man with longish blond hair in a navy blue T-shirt and jeans came out, a can of beer in his hand.

"Flynn?" he asked.

"Yeah."

"Come on in." He held the beer can aloft. "Want one?"

Flynn shook his head and walked through the gate. Closer to the pool it was a little cooler but not much.

Kurt headed for a ramada at the far end of the pool and Flynn followed. The ramada was made of ocotillo ribs that had dried too much so they'd split. They sat on chrome and aluminum chairs. Kurt set the beer down on a small tile and wrought-iron table. The tiles were painted with bright sunflowers and a couple of them were cracked.

"Not exactly the lap of luxury here," Kurt said. His eyes were very pale blue, as if working in the sun had faded them. "But they pay me okay and they left me a key so I can use the facilities. I appreciate that. The trust, I mean."

Flynn nodded.

"Trust is pretty hard to come by, once you've been accused of a murder—no one cares if you've been acquitted, they just figure it was a technicality or something." Kurt picked up the beer can and turned it around in his hands.

"Course, it beats prison," said Flynn.

Kurt gave him an up-from-under look. "There's all kinds of prisons."

For Christ's sake, Flynn thought, the guy got a raw deal maybe, but he should try to get over it, not let it wreck his life.

"You had a couple of domestics, I understand," said Flynn, "with Camille."

"And?" said Kurt. "If I were going to kill Camille I would have done it back then." He glanced at Flynn. "But it worries me with Rachel being in Dudley."

"Her choice."

"I know."

"I've read the basic police reports," Flynn said. "You and Annie went to dinner, argued, Annie came home early, you drove around all night. Anything you want to add, I need to know?"

"What do you mean?"

"Seventeen years since it happened, that long to think about things—sometimes you remember stuff that never came up at the time."

Kurt shrugged. "Not really." He rubbed his nose where the skin was peeling from too much sun. "I've been thinking, 'cause of this investigation, I might take a trip to Dudley, I mean with Rachel there and all, see if I could remember anything new."

Flynn nodded.

"I always thought I didn't care," Kurt said, "that I was too burnt out, but this has hurt Rachel so bad, made her different, damaged her. I want her to heal."

Kurt's voice was tight with emotion, uncomfortably honest.

Flynn waited a moment out of respect for that before he spoke. "Annie's band," he said, "they must have hung around a lot. You close to the members?"

Kurt shook his head. "I'm not a musician. They were kind of in their own world." He shrugged. "I don't think I really mattered to them one way or the other."

Flynn stared out at the pool. Close to the edge where he and Kurt were sitting a fly struggled not to drown. He looked at Kurt. "Wynn Wykoff," he said. "What about him?"

"Actually, Wynn was an okay guy. Compared with the other two. Teddy went to some fancy music school back East—thought he was better than anyone else. Billy just went along with Teddy. But Wynn, well, like I said, he was okay. I was surprised when he took off—then I guess it turns out he didn't, huh? When Rachel told me they found his body I thought, son of a bitch. *Son of a bitch.* Maybe Annie was killed because of *Wynn.* And I thought, shit, shit, shit, shit. They'd found Wynn's body back then, I might never have been charged. You know that? I had no reason to kill Wynn, no grudge"—his voice broke—"*nothing.*"

Flynn sat quiet, letting Kurt deal with it.

"Annie," Kurt said suddenly, "she was like a bright light, a flame." He paused.

"And?"

"People gathered 'round her. She wasn't always easy to be around, I mean, you could get burned. People loved her but they hated her too. It wasn't until they found Wynn's body that it occurred to me she might not have been killed because of who she was, how she was."

"Rumor has it," said Flynn finally, "that Annie might have had a thing with Jim Rasmussen."

"Rumor?" Kurt shrugged. "I think it was probably true. I always suspected it."

"It didn't bother you?"

"I loved her," said Kurt. "I thought she would get it out of her system. The guy was married, kids. It wasn't going anywhere."

"How come you never mentioned it during the investigation? "

"It wasn't going to get me anywhere."

"But he was trying the case."

"Well, he lost, didn't he?"

I cut the last of the duct tape, set the scissors aside, and opened the box to the smell of patchouli overlaid with must. A pair of jeans lay folded on the top, Guess jeans, size seven, and under that two halter tops, one purple, one fluorescent green. A Gram Parsons tape of *Grievous Angel*. A pair of silver hoop earrings that had gotten tangled up with a silver chain. A black bead and silver necklace from someplace like Guatemala or Mexico.

A folded piece of paper: recipe for Gypsy Soup involving sweet potatoes and chickpeas. A small blue memo pad, all completely blank except for the first page, which said: *milk, Kashi, cantaloupe, toilet paper.* Another folded piece of paper, which unfolded was an announcement for a concert by the Dudley Choir: Midsummer Summer Dreams, July 10. A couple of weeks before she was killed.

An address book: tan faux-suede with ADDRESSES stamped on in gold that had mostly rubbed off. I flipped through. Almost every page full of names, many with just phone numbers. I sighed. Here. Here were the people in Annie's life. At least now I had some work laid out for me, I would call every number in the book. From somewhere my cell chimed. I pulled it out of my purse.

"Hello?"

"It's Flynn. I'm still in Tucson, at a Circle K. I just talked to Kurt Dickens."

"Aha. Anything useful?"

"He's thinking about coming to Dudley."

"Umm," I said without enthusiasm, leafing through the address book.

"And," said Flynn, "the reason I'm calling—Kurt knew Annie had a thing with Rasmussen."

"I wonder," I said, "if Rachel knew."

"Why don't you find out? Get her take on it."

"Right," I said. "Poor Rachel—I wonder how much of that kind of thing she wants to know."

"Do it obliquely. I don't have a take on the guy. He's been a pretty prominent lawyer for years around here. Guys like that, who knows anymore who they are? Probably not even them. What was he like back then? Let's do a little more checking."

"The Dudley choir," I said. "That's where they met."

"Let's get on it, hunt down some of them."

"I opened Annie's box."

"Anything of interest?"

"You like Gypsy Soup?"

"What?"

"Never mind. One thing you will like—an address book." I leafed through some more, going to the C's. "Right here in front of me is a list of three people who were in the Dudley choir back then and their phone numbers."


Rachel's cell chimed as she walked back down Laundry Hill. "Hello?"

"It's Chloe. How are things going?"

"Hi, Chloe." Rachel's voice was warm. "Things are going good." And she meant it.

Talking to that basically nerdy Max had, for some reason, made her feel happy. Up, as if she could walk for a hundred miles without getting tired. She'd been trying to figure out why that was, but here was Chloe on the phone.

"Things are going really really well," Rachel said. "I went back to the house. I met this guy, this kid really, except he's my age. Max. He's Alice's nephew. He was visiting her when my mother was killed and he was *with me* when I found her." Her voice lilted with excitement. "It's what I was trying to remember that day we met at the gallery—that someone was there in the house. It came back! I got the memory back!"

"That's wonderful," said Chloe.

"I'd just blanked it out," said Rachel. It might be fun, she thought, to walk down the Gulch. *Fun.*

"So what was Max doing there in the house with you back then?" Chloe asked.

"He saw me outside, he had a crush on me, so he followed me in. He was only eight and a half."

"I'd like to talk to him," Chloe said. "Do you think he'd mind?"

"No. I'll tell him." This street, whatever it was called, she hadn't seen a street sign, wasn't as pitted as the one on Laundry Hill.

"What I called about," said Chloe. "Jim Rasmussen, the prosecutor? What was your take on him back then?"

Rachel sighed. "He knew my mom, you know, from the choir. He was very nice to me. I had to go into this room at the county attorney's and talk to him about testifying. He said just to tell the truth and if I forgot anything just to say so. He even seemed to understand how hard it was for me to say anything that would hurt Kurt."

"It must have been very hard," said Chloe. "I mean, if you thought Kurt was innocent you must have felt angry at Mr. Rasmussen."

Rachel sighed. She drifted past the Copper Queen Hotel. "Mr. Rasmussen told me we were looking for the truth—if each of us just told the truth, then things would work out the way they were supposed to."

Rachel reached the corner, the beginning of Brewery Gulch.

"It's funny," she said, "but things kind of did. I mean, at least they said not guilty. Except being charged in the first place on top of my mom getting murdered, it wrecked Kurt's life."

There was a silence.

"Besides," Rachel said, "Jody was so nice, I couldn't really be mad at Mr. Rasmussen. I can't see Jody being married to someone awful."

"Right," said Chloe. "Talk to you later, then." And she was gone.

Rachel peered up the Gulch. Why had Chloe called in the first place? And why those questions about Jim Rasmussen? They didn't make sense.

She walked slowly up the Gulch.

The sun glinted off the windows of the cars and trucks parked in the lot across from the St. Elmo's Bar. You could smell the alcoholics from a block away, but the St. Elmo's was where the band played. Her mom's band.

Point of No Return.

St. Elmo's bar was a three-story brick building painted white, a neon beer sign in the window, scratched swinging wooden doors.

Amy Winehouse inside singing about rehab.

"Hey," a man's voice said.

Rachel didn't look.

"Hey," he said again. "Hey, lonely girl."

Rachel felt her face flush. She stepped farther away.

"Rachel. It's you. I know it is."

She turned her head at that and saw a tall man, dark straggly hair and a wrinkled face, an old guy in jeans and a fringed leather vest, nothing underneath the vest.

He held his scrawny arms wide. "It's me," he said. "You don't remember me?"

*"Teddy."* Rachel bit her lip. Tears came to her eyes and she covered her face with her hands. "Oh, *Teddy.*"

"I know I look bad," Teddy said. "That's what happens in life. I'm really sorry."

"No." Rachel put her hands down. She sniffed and reached into her purse for a Kleenex. "Why should you be sorry? It's just the shock."

"Give us a hug," Teddy said.

Rachel moved toward him. She felt his ropy arms around her, smelled patchouli.

"I remember you—skinny and cute," Teddy said. "I heard you were in town or I wouldn't have recognized you, to be honest. But here we are in front of the St. Elmo's."

"Do you still play?"

"Do I still play?" Teddy rolled his eyes. "Gave up my life for music. Gone through a bunch of bands but Radebaugh goes on. I'll be playing this weekend. Come and hear." He paused and looked at her with interest. "You sing?"

"No."

"You used to sing pretty damn good for a kid. Hey, I gotta go, but drop by Central School, will you, that's where we practice."

"Really?" said Rachel. "I'd like that. I remember Central School. You guys practiced there back then. The same room?"

"Same room," said Teddy. "I'm almost always there. Stop by anytime."

He ambled off, heading past the St. Elmo's. Rachel watched till he turned up by the stairs to the park with the bandstand. From the back he looked pretty much the same as she remembered. Just like the St. Elmo's looked the same. Probably she could walk through those doors now and the same morose drunks would be bent over the same cheap alcoholic beverages they had bent over seventeen years ago.

Except now it was Amy Winehouse instead of Waylon Jennings.

Her cell chimed. Scott. Just thinking about talking to Scott right now made her feel tired. He was her husband and she loved him but she didn't want to talk to him right now. She turned it off.

It was quiet in the office, Lois still at the doctor's and Flynn on his way back from Tucson. I was doing my best to avoid thinking about Val and nearly succeeding. There were three numbers listed with first names only under *Choir* in Annie's address book. Peggy, Ryan, Mimi. The first one, Peggy, was disconnected.

"Hello?" said a friendly voice at Ryan's.

"Could I speak to Ryan?" I asked.

"Ryan? My granddad?"

"I think so," I said, clueless.

"He passed. It's three years ago now."

"I'm so sorry."

At Mimi's I got an answering machine. *Hi, leave a name and number.* I left several numbers, then I waited, leafing further through the address book, looking for anything that might jump out at me. Most of the numbers were Dudley numbers, first names only, but confusing because apparently alphabetical under last names.

Under the *D*'s was a Seattle number—I looked up the exchange on the computer. Right. Her parents, dead now, had lived in Seattle. I riffled the pages back to front, front to back: scrawled on an end page was the name *Mel* in big letters and a number, long distance: 801. Salt Lake City, the computer said.

Salt Lake City? I punched it in.

"Sampson and Trueblood!" said a bright cheerful woman's voice.

"Is Mel there?"

"Mel?" The woman laughed. "Mel Witt?"

"Yes," I said, hoping that was the right answer.

"It's not Sampson, Witt, and Trueblood anymore, it's Sampson and Trueblood. Mel retired, honey. What, six, seven years ago. Is this some old case?"

*Case?* That sounded promising. "Yes," I said.

"He loves hearing from old cases."

"What do you mean by old cases exactly?" I asked.

The woman laughed some more. "Honey, why don't you give Mel a call? He can explain whatever. Let me give you his number." And she did.

I punched it in.

"Mel just got out of the hospital," said the woman who answered, "hip replacement. He's stoned out on Vicodin and Oxy-Contin right now but when he gets halfway sober he'll be bored as hell, I'll get him to call you."

I gave her all three numbers.

Sampson and Trueblood sounded like stockbrokers or lawyers. An old distinquished firm full of stuffed shirts. Salt Lake City. Pretty far from the action in this case. Mormons? I was about to look for Sampson and Trueblood online when the office phone rang.

Mimi Garner. "I'm at work now," she said, "but I'd be happy to talk to you this evening. You said it was about the chorus?"

"Mmm, yes."

"Could we meet, say, around six-thirty? My house would be just fine."

We made arrangements, then I went online. Sampson and Trueblood were financial analysts. Strictest confidentiality. Strange. I couldn't see a connection—Annie hadn't had a dime as far as I could tell, or Wynn either.

# chapter twenty-seven

"*TAKEOUT!*" *SAID ALICE BRIGHTLY, COMING IN* the back door. "Takeout from Strictly Takeout." She plunked two bags on the big kitchen table. "Twelve Boy Curry."

Max and Rachel were in the living room among the wicker and the ferns and the local art listening to Max's favorite musician Nick Drake, who had allegedly killed himself with an overdose of antidepressants many, many years ago in England. He was singing "Pink Moon."

"Turn it off, for Christ's sake, Max," Alice called from the kitchen. "I get enough of that at work."

She came into the living room.

Rachel saw a blond woman with frizzy hair wearing little red frame glasses and beaded chandelier earrings. She blinked and saw Alice, older, of course, a little worn but still Alice.

"No!" said Alice. She put her hands over her mouth for a second. "No, I don't believe it. Like Annie but not. Rachel? Is it really *you*?"

"I invited her to dinner," said Max. "If there's not enough, I can just eat some cereal."

"There's plenty. Oh, Rachel. Sweetie pie." Alice held out her arms. "I think about you still, I do. Come and give me a hug."

Rachel got up and came over. It was pleasant, being hugged by Alice, making no demands on her at all.

They ate in the kitchen, a big room with a big table. The Twelve Boy Curry was sweet and spicy all at once. Alice told Rachel all about becoming a counselor. "Your father," she said. "Did he send you to someone?"

"Someone?" Rachel shrugged. "About a million someones. More like everyone."

"Max too," said Alice sadly.

"After dinner," Max announced firmly, "we're going next door to the house. So we'll need the key. I looked but I couldn't find it."

Alice raised her eyebrows. "Who's going next door exactly?"

"Rachel and me."

Rachel couldn't believe she was really going to go next door with Max—it had seemed like something she could never do, but now that she had decided she could, she felt lighter, buoyant.

"It'll be almost dark after dinner," said Alice.

"We're going for extreme fear," Max explained.

Alice looked at Rachel and she looked at Max. "You know the inside of the house looks a lot different now," she said.

Max shrugged. "Whatever."

Rachel waited for Alice to protest, maybe even refuse to give them the key.

"Okay," Alice said.


Mimi Garner's was a neat Craftsman-style house facing the park over in the Warren section of Dudley. When the mines were still in operation, Old Dudley had been more or less considered a slum by the "old money" upper-mining-management folks in Warren. Now, away from the artists and the tourists, with the mines closed down decades ago, almost all of the stores in

Warren had followed suit and it always seemed to me to be in a kind of gentle slumber.

No one had been slumbering at Mimi's house though—they'd been out doing yard work: lawn neatly trimmed, flower beds well weeded and planted with dahlias and marigolds. A sprinkler turned slowly, wetting my shoes ever so slightly as I walked up the sidewalk to the front porch. Once, years ago, I'd had a visitor from New York, where I used to live, and she'd remarked that she'd never seen as many front porches as we had here in Dudley.

"Why, hello," someone said, startling me.

I jumped.

"Chloe, I assume?"

"Yes."

A woman rose from a rocking chair in the deep shade of the porch. She was white-haired, tall, and elegantly gaunt, somewhere in her fifties probably. She had on a blue track suit with a white stripe down the leg and big white running shoes.

"What a beautiful yard," I said.

"Sons," said Mimi. "I have sons and a nephew. Well, come inside, I made some iced tea. Excuse the outfit," she said as I followed her in. "I always hit the gym after work."

"Where do you work?" I asked.

We had reached a kitchen still sunny though the sun was going down: oak table and rush-bottomed chairs, lots of white tile, and pots of african violets in a window over the sink. In the sunny kitchen light, I revised my estimate of Mimi's age up past sixty.

"I'm an accountant for a contractor over in Sierra Vista," she said. "I work out my brain there and my body at the gym afterward—not that it's any use. I'm still getting old."

She opened the refrigerator and took out a big glass jug of tea, got two tall glasses from a cupboard, and filled them. "Straight Lipton's," she said without apology. "Nothing herbal. Sugar?"

I nodded. She added sugar and handed it over, spoon still in the glass.

"There," she said briskly as if dispensing with a boring but necessary chore. "You know, I thought the living room but now I think the porch. Cooler."

Feeling like a little dog, I followed her out again. The large porch was full of white wicker furniture: wicker plant stands, wicker end tables, wicker coffee table, uncomfortable-looking wicker settee, and two wicker chairs. The settee and the chairs had blue chintz flowered cushions on them. We both sat. The cushions had just the right amount of give. I settled back with a sigh, tension I hadn't even realized I was carrying draining away.

"My husband hated all this wicker," Mimi said companionably, "but he died. Heart attack two years ago. Luckily he was quite an irritable man and he drank, so I only miss him occasionally. Now—" She set her glass of tea down firmly on a little end table. "What was it you wanted to talk about?"

A woman like this one deserved all the honesty I could muster and not only deserved, probably wouldn't put up with anything less. "I've been hired by Annie Glenn's daughter to investigate her mother's murder."

"For heaven's sake," said Mimi. "How is that little girl? I always wondered. The choir thought about sending a card, flowers, you know, but she left town pretty fast."

"She's married to an attorney in Tucson," I said. "She's back here now for the first time since the trial."

"In Old Dudley?"

I nodded. "At the Oliver House."

"Ah," said Mimi. "So what would you like to know? Or is this more of a fishing expedition?"

"The choir was part of Annie's life," I said. "Anything that strikes you."

"All right." She thought about this a minute, sipped her tea. "Back then that chorus did more to break down the barriers between the new people and the old-timers than anything else I can think of."

"Was Annie close to anyone in particular in the chorus?"

Mimi snorted. "Other than all the men?"

I blinked.

She held up a finger. "Tell me this—you said the daughter hired you. I assume she's looking for new evidence to reindict the boyfriend?"

I shook my head.

"No? *Really*. She still thinks he's innocent?"

"Yes, she does."

"The defense attorney came 'round asking questions, he was desperately looking for another suspect. He spoke with me among others, wanting to know if Annie was involved with anyone in the chorus."

"And . . . ?"

"Was she involved with anyone in the chorus?" Mimi's voice rose. "That woman was involved with everyone in the chorus! Every man, I mean. Figuratively rather than literally maybe but in some way or another, she liked to make her mark on 'em. With two sons I have excellent antennae for that kind of thing."

"Any one man in particular?" I asked.

"No," she said abruptly. "No one at all in particular." Mimi stirred her iced tea vigorously. "The daughter—what is her name?"

"Rachel."

"Rachel. Poor girl. If she wants to defend the boyfriend—what's his name, Dickens—I don't blame her, in a way, 'cause that's who was looking after her while her mother was running around." She sighed. "I remember him skulking around choir rehearsals, crazy in love with her and miserable most likely. She was the kind that led them all on. And for what? In my opinion what she needed was a real job. Of course he killed her. Of course. It's shame, because he seemed like a good person."

She stopped, took a sip of iced tea.

I didn't know what to say. The sprinkler revolved around on the lawn—in the fading light the wet grass took on a luster.

"Well, he got off," said Mimi. "Maybe that's how it should be. I certainly don't condone murder for any reason, of course, but even getting off, for a person like him, he'll be haunted for the rest of his life." She glanced over at me. "A peculiar kind of justice maybe, but justice all the same."

"How about Jim Rasmussen?" I said. "Was Annie close to him?"

"Jim is a husband and a father," Mimi said. "His wife and children don't need for the man they depend on to be dragged into this and dishonored. For heaven's sake, let people go on with their lives, instead of allowing that woman to hurt anyone else. Let it be."


Flynn had told Chloe about his meeting with Kurt but he hadn't heard from her since then. When he got back to Sierra Vista it was close to six. He made a quick stop at his office but Chloe had left. There was a fern on her new desk.

He had a couple of messages from clients, not urgent, one from a potential client, also not urgent, and one of real interest, an e-mail. *Hey, Mr. Flynn, this is Billy Dodds. I wanted to let you to know I'll be arriving in Tucson at noon tomorrow. I'll contact you when I get to Dudley.*

Fantastic. Flynn picked up the phone and called Chloe at home but got no answer, called her cell and got no answer there either. Flynn put down the phone. For some reason he was deeply disappointed, far more disappointed than the occasion warranted. He got up and left the office, locking the door behind him.

Rachel could smell the roses. It wasn't fully dark yet but the mountains blocked the setting sun so the front yard was dim, the Adirondack chairs just bulky shadows. At the door Max fumbled with the key.

"The electricity's turned on, isn't it?" asked Rachel.

"I told you, it's a rental," said Max, "everything works."

"We *could* wait till morning."

"Hey," chided Max, "we're going for extreme fear, remember?" He got the door open and stepped inside. "The light switch is— ha! Just by the door." He flicked it on. "And tah-dah, here it is! Your childhood home."

But where? Where? wondered Rachel as she stepped inside. There had once been a living room just inside the door, and it was still there, but the wall that had separated it from the kitchen was gone—just a counter there now: a granite counter, like everyone had these days. And the side window where the south sun came in had been taken out and replaced with a bigger window but there was no longer a table in front of it filled with a jumble of plants out of control.

The wooden floor, marred and scuffed, that Annie had covered with a series of fake Persian rugs was now bare and burnished. No old couch covered with a Mexican serape and piled with pillows covered with bright weavings. The couch and two armchairs all looked new, slipcovered like Pottery Barn and just as posed as a Pottery Barn ad.

"Well?" said Max.

"There's nothing here." Rachel turned around twice and held

out her hands. "Nothing." She walked to the counter and peered into the kitchen—all new appliances. "It looks like people from HGTV came and renovated it."

"Yeah," said Max gloomily.

"But you know something? I remember you even better now."

Max brightened. "You do?"

"You were always kind of hanging around and I saw you in your yard that day and I felt—" Rachel gasped. "I felt *sorry* for you, so I said, come over."

"You remember it now, just like that?"

"I guess it was always there but more important stuff was blocking it." More important stuff than Max. She looked at him now—his hair was losing its spike—probably needed more gel or whatever it was he put on it. There were dark circles under his eyes. "Are you scared?" she asked.

"Not exactly." He shrugged. "Come on, we're going to do this, you and me like when we found your mom but this time I'll go first."

He switched on the hall light. Rachel followed him out of the living room and down the hall. Except the hall wasn't the same either.

"My bedroom door," said Rachel. "It's gone. Where did my bedroom go? My little bedroom with the closet with the Indian cotton curtain over it?"

"The door to your mom's bedroom's wide open." Max stopped abruptly. "Jeez. You opened it, that last time."

"I knocked and then I opened it."

"I don't feel anything," said Max. "Do you?"

"No." Rachel giggled. The giggle was breathy, nervous, and went on and on.

"Here goes." Max squared his shoulders, leaned in, found the light switch, and flicked it on. "All right?"

They stepped inside. A large rectangular room, painted taupe with white trim. A whole row of windows on one side that had never been there before.

"Tasteful," Max said.

"Unbelievable." Rachel put her hand over her mouth for a second. "No, no, no. They took my bedroom and tore down the wall and made it part of this one. Not that it *matters*," she added scornfully. "This doesn't look like my mom's room at all—nothing's the same. The bed isn't even in the same place."

Max leaned against the wall, and then slid his back down till he was sitting on the floor.

"Are you okay?" Rachel asked.

"I don't know what I am. I don't remember things that were here, not the way you do. She was lying on the bed and the bed was in the middle of that wall." He pointed.

Rachel went over and slid down beside him. "I screamed. I screamed and screamed really loud so I wouldn't feel anything."

"You scared me. I thought I would be scared now but I don't really feel anything." He looked over at her.

"Do you?"

She shook her head.

"I had this fantasy for a while, that I would come back here and your mom would still be lying the way she was. I'd have a can of gasoline and I'd dump it all over the room and her and then I'd step back, throw in a match, and poof—it would all turn to ashes."

"Well, now you don't have to," Rachel said. "It's all gone anyway."

"Yeah," Max said. "Maybe we should go back to Alice's now and listen to Joy Division. They're fantastic—then their lead singer Ian Curtis hanged himself."

But Rachel wasn't listening. "My mom . . ." she said, and paused.

"Yeah?"

"We used to go for drives out in the desert. She'd go really fast, like ninety miles an hour. She went a hundred once when Kurt was with us. Kurt and I both yelled and screamed for her to stop, we were so scared. She just laughed."

"Are you kidding?" said Max. "That's crazy."

"That was my mom. Wild and crazy."

"I dare you to close your eyes," said Max.

"No."


I drove slowly back from Mimi Garner's, heading into a gorgeous sunset. All the way home I kept imagining Flynn knocking on the door of a house where Val lived. Valentine. What a stupid name. I could even see some of the interior of the house—the living room had a wide-screen TV where you could watch sports all day long on a big leather couch. There was no reason why Flynn should update me on his private life.

I felt weary.


Max walked Rachel back down Laundry Hill and they said goodbye at the street that led to the Copper Queen Hotel. Then Rachel walked alone up by the church and across the bridge that led to the Oliver House while Max watched. Licorice filled the air and the Oliver House looked serene in the evening, a light on here and there, the porch full of shadows. She opened the metal gate. And waved to Max that he could go.

The gate made a metallic click when she closed it behind her. She walked up the path. Down a ways on the porch, near the far end, a man was sitting. She hadn't noticed him before. As she approached he got up from his chair and walked toward her down the wide porch.

"Rachel?" he said.

"Yes?"

She couldn't see him clearly but he struck her as someone she knew. But who? Oddly enough, her first thought was Scottie. He reminded her of Scottie but grown older, forties probably. A nice haircut, good features, the features of a contender.

"I had a meeting here in Dudley tonight," he said. "I heard you were in town so I thought I'd look you up. Do you remember me? I'm the prosecutor from the Dickens murder trial. Jim—Jim Rasmussen."

# chapter twenty-eight

FLYNN STRETCHED OUT ON HIS LONG LEATHER
couch with a beer in his hand, wanting to relax but not sure how
to do it, still hyped from the drive to Tucson and back. He tried
to remember the last time he'd had a full night's sleep. It wasn't
that he didn't try, but his thoughts like tiny ants kept pricking
him awake. Through the window, out past the deck he'd spent so
many hours building, he could see the rising ranks of the mountains, purple. The sun had almost set.

His cell chimed. He leaped up from the couch, glad of a
chance to take a break from relaxing. Chloe, he was sure.

"Flynn here."

"Jack Nelson. I was just driving by and remembered you lived
out in this neck of the woods."

Just driving by, yeah, *right*. But Flynn perked up. "Come on
over. What you got for me?"

"Be there in five. Tell you then. Frieda's with me. We won't stay
long."

Frieda? Ah, Frieda, the hippie woman.

He was standing by the door when he heard Jack's vehicle pull
in. He looked out. Jack was driving what looked like a Volvo. Jack
had never been a Volvo type, had he? Gray, blue, hard to tell in

the fading light. Jack got out the driver's side, closest to Flynn, and a woman got out the other. Belatedly Flynn flicked on the light by the door.

"Frieda, this is Flynn," Jack said, "and likewise."

"Hi, Flynn," said Frieda. The light flickered off her dangling silver earrings, God, she was skinny. Not young either, maybe a little older than Jack even. Long dark graying hair in a braid, red tank top, long skirt from one of those third world countries.

Sukie had been blond, vivacious, normally dressed; a manic talker.

Flynn stifled a half smile. Well, at least Jack hadn't gone for a bimbo. "Come in, come in," he said.

"I can stay out here." Frieda's voice was soft, educated; a little like Chloe's, in fact. "I know you guys need to talk privately."

"But"—Flynn spread his hands—"there's nothing out here."

"There's plenty of dark," said Frieda, "and crickets."

Jack beamed and looked over at Flynn as if she'd said something profound and astonishing.

The guy was nuts about her, Flynn realized. There was no way on earth to predict why one person would love another. But there *were* crickets; in fact the whole night was throbbing with them. Flynn hadn't noticed that till now.

"I got a deck out back," he said to Frieda, "with chairs on it. You can hear crickets and see dark there just as well."

Frieda followed him out there and sat on a white plastic chair with her back to the windows. Jack stayed inside and sat on the black leather couch.

"Beer?" Flynn offered.

Jack shook his head.

"How about Frieda?"

Jack smiled. "Nope. Sit down, for Christ's sake, this won't take long."

Flynn sat.

"I got the gun from Wishman."

Flynn nodded. "The Rossi .38."

"That's the one. Did the test. *Bullet was from the same gun that killed Annie Glenn.* Kurt Dickens's damned cheap Rossi .38." Jack rubbed his hands together. "Looks like we got ourselves a whole 'nother shot at him. Shame, really, if she had to die anyway too bad he couldn't have killed Camille-Sonora Cloud with the same gun. 'Cept of course he didn't have it anymore."

"So you see Kurt for Sonora too?"

"Well, I'm sure as hell not ruling him out. And he's got a history with Sonora back when she was Camille even if it was a long time ago."

Everyone seemed to be out to get Kurt—and Flynn too, if he could just feel more certain that Kurt had done it. But he didn't. To Flynn Wynn's body wasn't a chance to get Kurt again but proof Kurt hadn't done it, because the crime of passion he could see, sure, feel it viscerally—thoughts of the football coach popped up but he would have shot *him* not Val—but Kurt didn't feel right for the Wynn thing or Sonora.

He knew it was dangerous to think that way; by identifying with Kurt he lost objectivity. He had to keep in mind Kurt couldn't be ruled out.

Out the window he could see Frieda standing at the railing, presumably listening intently to the crickets. What did she think about all this, standing out on the deck he'd worked so hard to build? Perfect, it was just about as perfect as he could make it but Val had up and left him anyway.


Jim Rasmussen brushed a hand over his hair, just a hint of vanity there, and smiled at Rachel.

"Of course I remember you," she said. It wasn't cold at all, a hot summer night, the monsoon gone for a day or so, but she felt shivery.

He was wearing khakis, a dark green polo, yes, dressed just like Scottie might dress. She could imagine Scottie, later in life, across the dining room table, smiling just like that. Brushing a hand over his hair.

"Could we talk?" Jim Rasmussen asked.

Rachel looked around. "Here?" she asked.

"Sure." He paused. "I mean, if you're comfortable."

Rachel sat in a rocker, then Jim sat too.

"You're very pretty," he said. "Like your mother."

"Thank you," Rachel said politely.

"The trial," he said. "I know it was an ordeal for you. And I failed. I'm sorry."

Failed? It would have been worse if he hadn't and Kurt had been found guilty but Rachel said nothing. She didn't know what he was doing here. There was a silence. Crickets chirped. A couple went by on the road that led to the Copper Queen, their voices loud, argumentative.

"Rachel." His voice thickened. "Your mother was so beautiful. I—I loved her," he blurted out.

"What?"

"I loved your mother, we sang in the choir together—she was so *vibrant*. I treasure her memory, I treasure the small period of time that I knew her. It was a rough time for me otherwise."

"Oh?" said Rachel. He was so involved in what he was saying, she didn't want to hurt his feelings.

"I was just starting out, two small children at home, my wife, she—she was always busy with them. Annie and I, well, we enjoyed each other so much."

Chloe had just asked her about this man and Rachel hadn't

known what she was getting at, but now she did. But Jody, what about Jody? *Jody* was the wife he was talking about. Jody, who sat with her outside the courtroom, with the two small children and the next one on the way, who was so nice?

"My mother and you," Rachel said carefully, "you were lovers, is that what you're telling me?"

"Yes, *yes,*" said Jim fervently. "It's so good to say it to you. Her daughter. I think she'd want you to know."

*She wouldn't,* Rachel wanted to scream, *she wouldn't have wanted me to know at all.*

". . . just between the two of us," he was saying. "Anne wouldn't have wanted the whole world in on it, with their narrow minds. It can be our secret."

Our secret? She didn't want the secret. The man sitting there was telling her he'd neglected his wife, his children, the same way Annie had come home late, all the time, just Rachel and Kurt there waiting for her, worrying. And now he was telling her how in love he was with her mother, but he'd hardly known Annie at all. Not known her like Kurt had.

*Why,* thought Rachel, *Mr. Rasmussen is just like my father, just like Phil, loving someone they couldn't have, so much easier than being there for a person, being there like Kurt always was.*

Rachel stood up. "Thank you," she said. "Thank you for sharing that with me. I'm really tired now. I need to go to bed."

# chapter twenty-nine

THE PLANE CAME IN LOW OVER THE SANTA Catalina Mountains. Billy Dodds, former drummer for Point of No Return and a nervous flyer, had a window seat, though he'd wanted an aisle, easier access to the exits. The mountains looked so close he could imagine clipping the top of a peak and coming down onto the rocks, just a few badly wounded survivors and they wouldn't last long. He missed his wife, his seven-year-old daughter already.

Then the mountains were gone and Tucson was below and even though he felt as though he'd been traveling for days, because of the time difference in Arizona, it was only noon.

It seemed incredible. He'd had to get up at four in the morning to drive from the small town in Vermont where he lived to the airport in Burlington to catch a six-fifteen flight, had had to change planes twice, once in New York and once in Atlanta. All that hustling from one place to another only to sit and wait in an airport. Sit and wait and think about Annie. Sit and wait and think about Wynn.

He just had a carry-on, so when the plane landed and he got off he strode directly to the rental car booth and got a silver Toyota.

"Here on business?" asked the kid behind the counter, all dressed up like a little monkey. His tone of voice was perfunctory and he didn't actually look at Billy as he handed him the keys.

"Going to Dudley," Billy said.

The kid grinned then and met Billy's eye. "Cool place!"

As soon as he hit the parking lot Billy was almost overcome by a heat that surpassed any heat they ever had in Vermont even on record-breaking days. He'd forgotten, totally forgotten this heat. He unlocked the rental, got in, and turned on the air conditioner. Waiting for the car to cool down, he noted the palm trees, the relentlessly blue sky. It would be cooler in Dudley.

Just like the kid said. "Cool!"

Billy rested his head on the steering wheel and closed his eyes. He thought about Annie and he thought about Wynn. He thought about Dudley too, what a great place he'd thought it was back then, what a good time he'd had there and then it all blew up. For a second he felt sick to his stomach—all he'd eaten all day were some granola bars. He could remember the old days when airlines served you actual food and people complained about it.

He opened the car door in case he did throw up and the heat overwhelmed him again. The palm trees shimmered like a mirage, not real. No wonder he'd chosen to live in cool green Vermont.

But the heat was appropriate—going back to Dudley after what had happened there was like going back to hell.

Flynn—he should call that guy Flynn, let him know he was in town. But the person on his mind most was Teddy. When had he talked to Teddy last? It had to be five, six years anyway.

Max and Rachel stood in front of Central School looking up at the bell tower. The cream-colored paint was dingy. Wasps had built a nest on an overhang near the entry and they were going and coming and humming. A beer can was lodged midway up the privet hedge that grew on one side.

"God," said Rachel. "It looks the same *exactly*. It even feels the same."

"You remember it that well?" Max said.

"This I do. Mom rehearsed here all the time. Some nights when it was hot, me and my best friend Beth would come over and sit outside where it was cool and listen to them play. Oh!" Rachel closed her eyes.

"I remember Beth," said Max.

"You do?"

"She had short kind of red-brown hair and she was pretty but not as pretty as you. Whenever she came over to see you, you guys would start laughing about nothing. It always felt like you were laughing at me."

"She took Jinx," said Rachel sadly, "'cause my dad didn't want me to have a cat. Do you know what happened to Beth after I left?"

Max shook his head. "She moved, that's all I know."

For a moment she and Beth—Beth, where was she now? gone forever?—she and Beth were lying on the ground, staring up at the lighted window on the first floor. The music was loud, raucous— they all smoked pot while they practiced—it was so obvious; her mom and Teddy and Billy and Wynn all red-eyed and giggling.

"Oh!"

"What?" said Max.

"Remembering, is all. Let's go in."

The front door was propped open with a brick; they went inside and climbed the short flight of steps. Art was hanging on the walls.

"Wow." Rachel laughed. "It looks like exactly the same stuff that was hanging here fifteen years ago. Teddy's room is over here."

"Someone's smoking pot right now," Max said.

"That'll be Teddy, I bet. Come on."

Flynn met me at my house right after lunch. He parked his Land Rover outside and we walked over to the house where they'd found Wynn. It was at the peak of a gentle slope, near the end of the Gulch. It hadn't rained in a couple of days and what had once been a torrent of water flowing down the street had been reduced to a trickle.

We climbed the hill and stopped in front of the house. There was a FOR SALE sign in the front yard.

"Didn't know it was for sale," said Flynn. "Jack never mentioned it."

"Maybe it wasn't for sale," I said, "until they found the body."

"Down there?" Flynn pointed where the hill went down again. The paved road ended a couple of houses farther along and turned to dirt. The dirt road meandered through the canyon and then vanished into the desert. "From what Teddy said I figure that's where Wynn parked his van—where he lived, in other words. Peed in the bushes and showered at friends' houses."

"Ah, the golden days," I said.

"Wynn used to come here to smoke a number in the back yard, Teddy said. The house was just an old miner's shack, vacant, probably falling to pieces."

It wasn't falling to pieces anymore—painted rose-pink with cobalt-blue touches, it looked as if it had been completely remodeled or at least, I thought, knowing something about Dudley renovations, artfully painted and trimmed out.

An older man in khaki shorts and a light blue polo came out the front door. "You folks here about the house?"

"Sure," lied Flynn glibly.

The man came down the porch steps, a man in his sixties, white close-cut hair and a benevolent face. He held out his hand. "Don Barnett," he said.

We introduced ourselves and we all shook on it.

"Come in, come in," said Don. "I'll give you a look around."

We went into a pleasant room, minimally furnished, with sanded wood floors the color of honey and French doors at the back.

"Wife's up in Phoenix with our daughter," Don said. "She was a little shook up—no point in hiding things, since it was on the news and in the papers—guess you know about the body they found."

"We do," said Flynn.

"Well," said the old man, "huh-huh, take it or leave it. Realtor lady said it shouldn't be that much of a problem since it was out behind that retaining wall and not in the house or even in the yard. Where you're standing, of course that's the living room. Stained-glass window over there?" He pointed. "Local artist. Nice Saltillo tile in the kitchen."

"Two bedrooms." Don led us back to the back, opening doors and closing them. Flynn and I followed dutifully, husband and wife looking at a house.

"Talavera-type tile in the bathroom," Don went on.

"Wife couldn't take it, huh?" said Flynn. "The body."

"No, she could not. I think she was getting a little disillusioned anyway, the whole Dudley thing. Had some kind of idea about art, artists, wasn't realistic, you know."

"How so?" I asked.

We were back in the living room.

"All sweetness-and-light-type stuff. But I've read up on artists, a whole lot of them had awful lives. Drinking, drugs, lots of mental illness."

"Yard in back looks nice," said Flynn, looking through the French doors.

Don opened the door and we stepped outside.

It *was* nice—a little tiled patio with pots of flowers and a concrete retaining wall studded with handmade tiles and draped with bright yellow crime scene tape.

"Oops," said Don. "Now, that's no way to sell a house, is it?" He walked over and pulled down the tape. There was a big mound of dirt at one end of the wall. "They're done with this part of the investigation. The guys from the Verhelst House are coming back tomorrow to finish digging out behind it. Rain brought down a lot more dirt, put more pressure on the wall."

We peered behind.

"Nothing's left," Don said. "They took everything away in little bags like *CSI*. If it hadn't been for the heavy rains, body would still be there. Sergeant Nelson told me it had probably been there years and years. Nobody missed the guy or something. Think of that!"

"Sad," I said.

"And now," said Don, "after all those years, someone out there, whoever did it, is not going to be sleeping quite so peacefully."

"Excuse us a minute," Flynn said. "I'd like to consult with the missus."

"Missus," I said when Don had left. Normally I would have laughed but I kept thinking about Val and her big-screen sports TV.

Flynn's eyes veered off mine. "Give me a break, it's the first word that came to mind." He put one hand on top of the retaining wall. "You know what? I have a picture of Wynn, like Teddy said, smoking a joint back here. It wouldn't have been a nice patio like now. My guess is he'd be sitting on the wall."

"So all someone had to do," I said, "is shoot him and push him

over the edge, shovel some dirt on top of him. No messy trans-
porting of the body."

"Could've been a woman," Flynn said, "as easy as a man."

"What are you getting at?" I said.

"Just that it's good to stay flexible."

Billy Dodds called Flynn and they arranged to meet at Café Olé
that evening, Flynn buying. Arrangements made, now it was time
for Teddy. He assumed he'd still be living in the same place. He'd
bought it for ten thousand dollars, which wasn't much at all even
back then, but no one else in the band had even had that kind of
money or anything close. Not that Teddy did either, but his parents had come through.

Billy parked the rental down below and climbed the long flight
of concrete steps, even worse than they'd been back years ago
when Teddy first bought the house. Back then Billy had run up
these same steps like a billy goat, ha ha, but he'd played football
in high school and now his knees were starting to give him trouble.
The oleander at the top had grown really tall—you couldn't even
see that side of the house anymore.

"Teddy!" he called on his way up. "Hey, Teddy!"

At the rusted metal gate, Billy stopped, uncertain. "Teddy?"
he called again.

Did he still live here? It didn't look like he'd ever even painted
the house—it was just graying wood, but the porch was still
there, ferns hanging down that hadn't been there back then.
What a great porch. The band or sometimes just Billy and Teddy
had sat out there for hours in the evening making music, the
sound echoing up and down the canyons. Or sat quietly, smoking
dope and listening to the owls and the javelinas.

But thinking about it, remembering, brought up darker

undertones. Billy felt cheated; it should have been such a good memory. He opened the gate and went in, down the short path and up the steps to the porch. The screen door was closed, but the main door was open. Billy peered in. Someone was in there, he could see a shadowy form, dancing.

He knocked on the wood at the edge of the screen. Knocked again, harder.

A woman in a black tank top and long red and black printed India cotton skirt came to the front door, white cord dangling, an iPod. Her face looked tired, her hair nondescript, pinned on top of her head in a kind of braid. Was this Teddy's *girlfriend*?

She removed the earbuds.

Billy composed a face suitable for meeting Teddy's girlfriend, if that was who she was. "I'm Billy Dodds," he said, "I'm looking for Teddy Radebaugh. Does he still . . . ?

She nodded. For the first time he noticed how puffy her eyelids were, as though she'd been crying.

He felt guilty, intruding on her privacy. "But he's not here now?" He made his voice soft, gentle.

She shook her head.

"You live here too?"

She nodded again. She didn't seem to really be there, as if she were only an image, a hologram projected from someplace far away.

Billy gave up. "Could you tell me where he is?"

"Central School," she said.

"We're old friends—" Billy began, but she had already replaced the earbuds.


Kurt packed up his tools in his truck. The job was done. It was kind of a bummer because the people weren't back from their vacation to pay him the rest of what was owed but it was okay, he had enough money to manage. He'd only worked half a day today to finish up but he felt as tired as if he'd worked eight hours. Lately, he'd been noticing, with all this Annie stuff coming up again, he tired more easily. And he had a funny kind of ringing in his ears—it woke him up frequently during the night and then he couldn't get back to sleep.

It would never end. Funny, Annie had been so beautiful, so full of life, he'd thought how lucky he was that she'd paid any attention to him, much less that they were actually a couple. And then it had turned out to be the worst thing that had ever happened to him and the worst thing that probably ever would happen.

*Shut up.*

I'm so used to feeling sorry for myself, he thought, it just comes automatically. It was disgusting. And Rachel. If anyone should feel self-pity it should be her. Did she? He wasn't sure. She was screwed up a little: scared, he could see that, but not too scared to start this investigation. She was in Dudley now. That worried him.

It worried him so much the only way to stop worrying, to maybe be able to sleep through the night again, was to go to Dudley himself, check it out, and keep an eye on her.


It looked the same, Central School looked exactly the same as he remembered when they had practiced there. Billy was still driving the rental, which was like a big albatross in Dudley's narrow streets, and he was always having to find a place to park it. If he'd been thinking clearly he would have already checked into the Copper Queen where he planned to stay, and found a place to park near there till he left. But at least at the Central School there was plenty of parking, same big empty lot, just an old beat-up white van and an old blue Chevy pickup parked there now.

Teddy would probably put him up but then he'd be climbing those steps over and over and trying to have a conversation with the iPod woman. She was obviously upset about something and Billy would feel as though he were intruding. What was Teddy doing with *her*? He'd always been such a good musician he could have any woman he wanted once they heard him play.

Billy got out of the rental and stood in the lot for a moment, gazing up at the building. Unbelievably he could actually hear Teddy playing right now. His style had always been so distinctive.

Even though it was cooler in Dudley—much cooler than Tucson—it was still pretty hot. Billy felt the sweat under his cotton shirt. Oddly the sweat felt not cool, but cold.

*Get it over with.*

He went up to the door, which luckily had been propped open with a brick, and bounded up the short flight of steps. The smell, that old smell of blackboards and chalk and mold, probably, if you were honest, that smell was still here. Even the pot smell was still there, getting stronger as he approached the door to Teddy's studio.

He knocked. The guitar kept on playing, so he knocked again harder. The guitar stopped and the door opened. Not Teddy but a young man, early twenties, nerdy with little wire-rimmed glasses.

"Teddy here?"

The young man opened the door wider and the first thing Billy saw inside was not Teddy. The first thing Billy saw inside was not Teddy but someone else, and seeing that person, for a moment the whole nightmare stopped and went into reverse like a videotape played backward to get to a scene you'd missed, a scene you'd particularly loved.

The whole nightmare played backward—it had only been a nightmare after all, a bad dream, because, thank god, here was Annie, not dead, not dead, but completely alive and not a day older than the day she was when he'd dreamed she had been murdered.

# chapter thirty

"I THOUGHT I'D COME DOWN AFTER WORK tomorrow," Scott said. "I'm really worried about you."

"Scottie." Rachel was sitting in the common room of the Oliver House, on a big couch upholstered in a green-and-blue-striped fabric. On the far wall was a large abstract painting, kind of Jackson Pollocky by Nancy's son Bailey, who was an artist in Tucson. Next to Rachel on the couch was the box of her mom's stuff Chloe had just dropped off. "I'm *fine*."

"You're sure?"

"Yes," said Rachel impatiently. "Yes, yes, yes."

"Are we *fighting*?" Scott's voice was wounded.

"No." Of course they were but if she said yes they would keep fighting some more. "When are you coming exactly?"

"I'm not sure, it might be pretty late."

"Scottie, listen, I went to see Teddy today, he's going to be playing tomorrow at the St. Elmo's, this bar on the Gulch. That's where I'll be probably, okay? 'Bye."

"But—" said Scottie.

Rachel closed her cell, put it down, and opened the box. Shut her eyes for a moment; couldn't look because of the smell, the smell alone, identifiably patchouli, but more, perhaps it was her mother's sweat, the dust in the air at 29 Laundry Hill, hint of cat, oh, the cat, Jinx, forgotten for so long, given away to her friend Beth now who knew where.

Rachel took a deep breath.

Her mom's Guess jeans, halter tops, one purple, one fluorescent green. Annie never wore the green one, it had been an unfortunate gift from Kurt, obvious it wouldn't work the minute Annie unwrapped it. A silver and black bead necklace. A pair of large silver hoop earrings tangled up with a silver chain. Rachel gently took apart the tangles and put on the earrings though she usually didn't wear hoops, especially ones this big.

Gram Parsons tape of *Grievous Angel,* recipe for Gypsy Soup. Gypsy Soup—Annie had been so enamored of the recipe for a while they'd had it twice a week, till Rachel was sick of it. A small blue memo pad, completely blank except for the first page, which said: *milk, Kashi, cantaloupe, toilet paper.* An announcement for a concert by the Dudley Choir: Midsummer Summer Dreams, July 10.


We got a good table at the Café Olé, near the big front window: Billy Dodds, Brian Flynn, and me. It was evening, finally cooling down, and through the window out on Main Street we could see the tourists ambling by, sometimes peering in at us—languid as cattle, finally making their way slowly back to the barn at sunset. Actually it probably wasn't like that at all, weren't cattle speeded along by dogs or cowboys?

Billy was a handsome man, clear blue eyes, even features. Well built, but balding, softening at the edges with a little extra weight. In photographs I'd seen of the band he'd had a beard but now he was clean-shaven, sandy-colored hair cut in a longish preppy style.

"We were wondering if you knew how to reach any of Wynn's relatives," said Flynn. "Names, numbers, addresses?"

"No." Billy looked surprised. He was nervous, anyway. I could feel it. "No, not really. We didn't talk that much about our families, you know? He mentioned a sister once. Wendy."

"Wendy Burch," I said. "I'm working on that. Have you seen Teddy yet?"

"I have," he said, "and I saw Rachel too, over at Central School. And Max."

"Max?" said Flynn.

"Alice Hayes's nephew," I told him.

Billy scratched his head. "I'm going to be jamming with Teddy tomorrow at the St. Elmo's, for old times' sake. Come and listen."

"We might very well do that." Flynn emptied his glass of beer. "That place you live in, in Vermont, small town like here?"

"Small town but a little different." Billy took a final swallow of his beer too.

We'd already ordered and Billy was on his second beer, as was Flynn. Was there some subtle competing here? I didn't know, I was out of the running, drinking herbal iced tea.

"Me and Megan, that's my wife," Billy said, "we run a little general store, sell old-time stuff like general stores used to. You know, like that catalog, *Vermont Country Store*?"

"Yes," I said. "I know it. My brother Danny lives in Vermont."

"Another beer?" Flynn said to Billy. "I'm having one. Or maybe some wine?"

"Sure. Make it beer, not wine." Billy looked at me. "Where in Vermont?"

I suddenly realized that Flynn was deliberately trying to get Billy a little drunk, loosen him up. I guessed, as the sober one, I was supposed to take notes. "Karmê Chöling," I said. "My brother Danny lives at Karmê Chöling."

Billy brightened. "The Buddhist colony. He's a Buddhist?"

"Yes. He has been for years now."

"Fantastic," said Billy.

"What?" Flynn looked at me in alarm. "Your brother's a Buddhist? You never told me that."

The food arrived. Prime rib for Flynn, shrimp scampi for *moi*, and pasta with wild mushrooms for Billy. I bet he was a vegetarian.

"I did a lot of meditating for a while," Billy told me after the waitress had left. "I did a lot of things, actually, tai chi, yoga, after Annie was murdered—looking for a quiet mind."

"It must have been really hard," I said. "Devastating. You all right talking about it?"

Billy shrugged. "Talking about it's not a problem. The worst thing for me was sitting outside the courtroom waiting to be called to the stand."

"But you never were," I said

"Yeah. I was incredibly relieved. Did Teddy tell you what happened? That I was supposed to answer questions about seeing Annie with this guy and then it turned out to be the prosecutor?"

"Yes," I said.

"It would have been really embarrassing." Billy's face flushed pink. *"The prosecutor's wife was in the courtroom."*

"Jody," I said.

"I knew who she was because I saw Mr. Rasmussen introduce her to someone out in the hall when I was waiting. She was really, really pregnant, like she might give birth any minute. When I realized who she was, was when I started praying I wouldn't have to testify."

I could smell the alcohol on his breath.

"Seeing Rachel today, God." He shook his head. "It just made me remember so much. She looks like Annie, but she's not like her. Thank God for that, I guess."

"What do you mean?"

"You can't be like Annie and stay out of trouble. I have to ask myself, if she wanted to live the way she did, why bother having a boyfriend? I mean, in the end, Kurt couldn't take it anymore, he lost it and murdered her. I don't say he was right, but I can see how it happened."

"Hold on," Flynn said. "Aren't you forgetting something? Wynn was killed too. You can see how that happened?"

"No," said Billy. "No, I can't. That's what really gets me, that he probably killed Wynn too. That's what brought me back here. Finding out about Wynn."

"But why?" I asked. "Why would Kurt kill Wynn? Didn't Kurt understand that they were just friends, not lovers?"

"Yeah, he did understand that they were friends," said Billy. "Wynn hung out with her a lot and Kurt never seemed to mind. What I think is that Wynn must have seen it."

"Seen what?" I said.

"Kurt shooting Annie."

"But how could he? He went missing a couple of weeks earlier," Flynn pointed out. "He was already dead."

There was a little pause.

"No, he wasn't," said Billy. "I saw him the night Annie was killed."

"What?" Flynn and I said in unison.

"Yeah," said Billy. "It was at the Circle K, the one out of town, I can't remember what I was doing there—but anyway, he told me he was on his way through town to pick up a few things—that he'd just come back from a little side trip and he didn't want to live in Dudley anymore."

"You never told anyone this before?" asked Flynn.

"Why should I have? When they found Annie, I just wanted to get out of town fast, and besides, later, no one asked me about Wynn. Wynn was the last thing on anyone's mind at that point."

"Wynn told you he'd just come back from a side trip?" I said. "Where was this trip?"

"It was totally bizarre, actually. He said he'd gone to Mormon Town."

"Mormon Town?" I said.

"You know, Salt Lake City."

"*Really?* Annie had a phone number in her address book for Salt Lake City. Does the name Mel mean anything to you? Mel Witt?"

He shook his head.

"How about Sampson and Trueblood? No, Sampson, *Witt*, Trueblood?"

"I give up," said Billy.

Time to get back fast to Mel, Mel Witt, formerly of Sampson, Witt, and Trueblood. Mention Wynn's name, maybe that would get me somewhere.

But other things were running through my mind—if Wynn and Annie were murdered the same night, maybe Wynn knew something, had seen something, and that was why he was murdered too. Maybe someone had followed him back to the vacant house, with the wall in back, where he liked to smoke the doobies.

And it could have been anyone—it didn't take any strength to shoot someone and shove him over a wall. Anyone, even a woman. I was ashamed, embarrassed like Billy, but the first person who came to my mind was Jody, Jody Rasmussen, telling her story about losing her father when she was a girl at the training class I taught. Jody, defending her home and hearth by any means possible. What had stopped me from suspecting Jody was Wynn was already missing, but now it was plausible.

# chapter thirty-one

ALICE WAS INSIDE IN HER KITCHEN MAKING
a cake for her receptionist's birthday and Max and Rachel were
out in her garden. Alice's garden was a secret garden, at the back
of the house. You couldn't see it from the street. It was planted
with pink snapdragons and yellow columbines and deep red
marigolds. Max and Rachel sat in matching resin wicker rockers.

Music was playing, a guitar, Max's choice.

It was evening, getting dark. Rachel could feel and smell the
flowers but she couldn't see them very well, their bright colors.
The guitar was soft; the voice of the guitarist soft as well and exhausted, but beautiful and to Rachel against all hope.

"What's that song?" Rachel asked.

"'Angeles,'" said Max. "One of my favorites. You like it?" His
voice was hopeful.

"It's sad. Who's singing?"

"Elliott Smith. You know him?"

"No." Rachel closed her eyes and listened. The next song was
sad too. "Max," she said after a while. "Is Elliott Smith still alive?"

"Um, no," said Max.

"What happened to him?"

"He died when he was thirty-four."

"Of what?"

"Two stab wounds to the chest."

"Murdered?"

"No one's too sure. Self-inflicted, they think."

"Oh, Max." Rachel began to laugh.

"Hey, what's so funny?" Max's voice was hurt.

"Nothing," Rachel sputtered. "Nothing at . . . all."

Max began to laugh too.

They laughed and laughed in Alice's garden, laughed with the smell of the flowers; laughed so hard they even drowned out Elliott Smith and his sad fatal songs.

Rachel's cell chimed. It lay on the kitchen table.

"Rachel!" Alice called.

Alice thought they probably couldn't hear her over the music so she wiped her hands on a dish towel, picked up the cell, and went to the door leading to the garden. Max and Rachel looked flushed and full of mischief in their wicker chairs. It was good, thought Alice, to see Rachel like that, she needed more mischief in her, and Max too.

"Phone call," she mouthed to Rachel, holding up the cell.

"It'll be *Scott*," Rachel said. "Tell him I'm *asleep*." She bent her head on her hands to one side and pantomimed sleep.

Alice hit the OK button as she walked back to the kitchen. "Hello?" she said.

"Hello?" said a man's voice. "I'm looking for Rachel? Do I have a wrong number?"

"No. Rachel's asleep. I'm answering the phone for her." Alice put on a mitt and opened the oven. You weren't supposed to look in the oven when you were baking a cake but she always did and it never made any difference. "Is this Scott?"

The cake looked okay, but not quite ready to come out.

"No, it's not, it's a friend," said the man. "Who's this?'

"This is Alice Hayes."

"Alice. No kidding. *Alice*. This is Kurt."

"Kurt." Alice sat down on a kitchen chair. Suddenly she had a memory of Kurt, quite a pleasant one, of him digging up her garden in back and putting in snapdragons. "Well, for heaven's sake. It's been such a long time," she said to that Kurt, then the memory went away and she said, this time in her therapist's voice, she couldn't help herself it just came out automatically, "Kurt, how *are* you?"

"I'm . . . I'm okay." He laughed emptily. "You know—keeping on, keeping on."

Not okay. Alice instantly regretted having asked the way she had—as if she sincerely wanted to know. Well, she did want to know in a way but this was hardly the time for a session. "Good," she said, like a dope. "Well, keep it up."

"What about you, Alice. How are you doing? Still in the same house?"

"Same house. I'm just great. I'm a therapist now and I've got my nephew visiting, Max, do you remember him?"

"I do. Just a little kid. Listen, Alice, I'm coming to Dudley tomorrow. I wanted to ask Rachel where she's staying."

Why? Why did he want to know? For a small moment Alice froze, staring at the oven where the cake was baking, not sure what to say. But why shouldn't he want to know? They had been close. In fact, Rachel had mentioned they'd met for dinner quite recently. It was a reasonable question.

"With me," she lied. Better safe than sorry.

"Fantastic," Kurt said. "Then I don't have to worry, she's in good hands with someone who can be trusted. She can call me back if she wants or just tell her I'm coming there tomorrow, okay?"

# chapter thirty-two

RACHEL HAD SLEPT AT THE OLIVER HOUSE, THEN
had come right over to Alice's the next morning and she and Max
ate some cereal.

"Let me show you something," Max said afterward.

They'd gone into Alice's guest room, which was where Max
slept in a bed you blew up and where Alice kept the sewing machine she hadn't used in fifteen years. Max pulled something out
of his backpack and showed it to her.

"What is it? It looks kind of like magic markers, or lip gloss,"
Rachel said now.

"But it's neither," Max said.

"Then what is it?" Rachel asked.

"Streekers."

"Right. I know just what Streekers are. Thanks a lot."

"I'll show you." Max pulled off the top and ran the tip on a
strand of his hair. It turned a muddy pink.

"Yuck," said Rachel.

"It's better on blond," he said apologetically.

"Does it wash off?"

"Of course."

"Where on earth did you get these?" Rachel exclaimed. She paused. "And *why*?"

"Just because. I got 'em online, but I think they have them in stores too."

"But why?" Rachel persisted.

"You say it so disdainfully. What do you mean, why? You haven't noticed?"

"Noticed what?"

"That I'm just a little bit punk."

Rachel looked dubious. "Maybe."

"I can be more so," said Max earnestly. "I can be very, very punk. I used to have matte-black hair and a pierced eyebrow. The eyebrow was a big pain," he added.

"Really? You really were a punk?"

"Sure. There's lots of punks of Seattle. I gave it up because it got old."

"There's punks in Tucson too."

"But Miss Rachel doesn't hang out with punks, they're so . . ." Max shuddered. "So . . . *poor*-looking. Miss Rachel likes to look rich."

"Shut up! And it's *Mrs.*"

"The pink's okay but the ultraviolet's my favorite," Max said. "It'll go with that purple halter top of your mom's. Just right for whoever's singing with Teddy's band tonight."


"Morning, Chloe!" Lois said brightly, all dressed up in a red pantsuit. "Pot of coffee's going." She gestured with her head to the reception area. "And Brian brought in some Krispy Kremes."

"Where is, um, Brian?"

"Running down some car-bashing witnesses. Every time he's started to do that, something comes up, so he's got his cell turned off."

Lois would know about Val. Did she stop in all the time to schmooze with Flynn? I'd never seen Flynn schmooze. So probably not.

I poured myself a cup and took a jelly doughnut and went back to my office. The doughnut had red jelly. Raspberry maybe or cherry. I took a bite but I still couldn't tell. I wanted to run down Mel in Salt Lake City right away, but I called Wendy Burch first, I hadn't gotten to it yesterday when she was supposed to be back.

"Wendy's Interiors, you fix it up, we make it right," the same voice sang out. "This is Jeannie, how may I help you?"

"I'd like to talk to Wendy."

"Wendy's out with a client now."

"What does that mean?" I said. "That she's actually there and you're screening her calls?"

"It means," said the woman, "that she's out with a client. Maybe I can help you. Give it a try."

"You can't," I said, "because this is personal. It concerns her brother."

The woman laughed. "I've never heard her mention a brother."

"Give this a try," I said. "Tell her a Chloe Newcombe in Dudley, Arizona, would like to talk to her about her brother Wynn." I gave her my office, home, and cell numbers. "If she calls back in the next hour or so, I'm at my office," I added.

I finished the doughnut, went to the restroom to wash my hands, and came back. Called the number for Mel Witt and it was busy.

My phone rang.

"It's a Wendy Burch," Lois said.

"Great. Put her through." That was fast. "Hello? This is Chloe. Wendy Burch?"

"Yes, it is." Her voice was eager. "I understand you know my brother Wynn?"

Not knew, know. The eager voice. Seventeen years and she was still hoping. I hadn't really considered that possibility because surely after seventeen years at least resignation would have set in. Who was I kidding? How many years had I been working with victims? Lots of times resignation never sets in.

In essence I was about to deliver a death notification over the phone. It wouldn't be confirmed without a DNA match but of course it was Wynn. As a victim advocate I knew you don't deliver death notifications over the phone. I was an idiot.

I should have talked to someone, found some victim's group in Colorado to send someone to be with her. I should have called Jack Nelson and told him—then he could contact law enforcement in Denver and let them handle it.

But it was too late.

"Hello?" said Wendy.

"I'm sorry, no, I don't know your brother," I said, soldiering on. "I just have a couple of questions I wanted to ask you. But first, Wendy, where are you now? Are you on a cell phone? Driving?"

"I'm home," Wendy said, "about to have a late breakfast with my husband. You're going to tell me bad news, aren't you?"

Straight out was the way for death notifications. "I'm here in Dudley, Arizona," I said, "and they've found a man's body—he's been buried for a long time," I said, careful to refer to the body as he and not an it. "He's been tentatively identified as Wynn."

"Dudley?" said Wendy. She laughed. "He can't be in Dudley. I mean, he left Dudley. He went to Mexico and something—I don't know—something could have happened to him there."

I waited, letting her get through those initial moments of denial.

"You're *sure*?" she said.

"All I know," I said carefully, "is what I've just told you. An old friend"—no point in going into the Sonora thing—"identified him from a ring and pieces of a backpack."

"That just can't be," she said. "They told me Wynn had gone to Mexico. That he'd be out of touch for a while."

"Who told you?" I said.

"I don't know." Her voice rose. "You're talking seventeen years ago."

"Wendy," I said urgently, "this is important. What are we talking about here exactly? You called someone, looking for Wynn? Who was it that you called?"

"I told you." Her voice wobbled. "I don't know. It was just a number I called that Wynn had given me for emergencies. I can't even remember if it was a man or a woman. They never told me who they were. Oh, Noah," she cried. "Noah! Noah, come here. It's Wynn. They found . . ." her voice faded out.

I heard weeping. The weeping went on and on.

After a while a man came on the line. "She's pretty upset," he said. "We'll get back to you later."

It was afternoon and the sun shone brightly on the Gulch, strong sun that obliterated subtleties, rendering all the colors flat. The bright clothes of the tourists, the faded richness of the vintage fifties clothes at Va Va Voom, the rude in-your-face art at the Subway Gallery.

A couple of regulars were sitting at the bar, bent over their drinks and morose, hardly affected at all by the light of day; the interior of the St. Elmo's Bar was as dim as ever except where the darkness was pierced by neon and a little faint sunlight coming in one window.

"Teddy! Hey, man," said Ben the bartender, a balding guy with a big mustache. "You ready to set up?"

"Hey, Ben," said Teddy. "You remember Billy, don't you?"

Ben looked at the guy with Teddy. "Billy? Billy?" He broke into a smile. "Billy Dodds. Son of a bitch. Course I remember. You played with the Point of No Return, back when Dudley was still real."

He came around the bar and slapped Billy on the back. "Hey, man, good to see you. You playing with Teddy tonight?"

"Yeah," said Billy. "I am."

"Jeez," said Ben. "The Point of No Return. Good band. But unlucky. Yeah. I'd say that was about the unluckiest band ever played here at the St. Elmo's."


I finished a second jelly doughnut. I felt bad about the way I'd handled Wendy, and the doughnut had had no taste at all. I figured it was up to Dudley PD now that I'd contacted a relative, so I called them and left a message for Jack Nelson to call me. I went out to the front, got another cup of coffee, came back to my desk, and called the number for Mel Witt.

A woman answered, the same woman as before, I was pretty sure.

"What was your name again?" asked the woman.

"Chloe. Chloe Newcombe. But he wouldn't know me. It's in regards to a Wynn Wykoff."

"I'm monitoring Mel's calls," said the woman. "I'm his wife too but that's incidental. It's his third day home and he's feeling okay but he's asleep right now. When he wakes up I'll tell him you called and he can decide if he's up to talking to you. Are you sure I can't help you?"

"It's about an old case," I said.

"How old?"

"Seventeen years."

"Back when it was Sampson and Witt," said the woman.

"Yes," I said.

"Derek Trueblood was Sampson's brother-in law," said the

woman chattily. "It was Sampson, Witt, and Trueblood for a while, but you know they wanted Mel out. Trueblood was upscale, Sampson was going that way. They wanted to be strictly white-collar kind of stuff, Mel dragged down the tone. And he didn't give a damn if he did either."

"How's that?"

"Well, Mel started out in law enforcement. Criminal was what he liked, not your white-collar criminal, your blood and guts."

"You tell Mel," I said, "I'm conducting a murder investigation and his name came up."

There was a pause.

"A murder investigation?"

"Yes. Actually two murders."

"Two of 'em? Like a serial? That's something." The woman's voice warmed up considerably. "I'm Marsha, by the way. You got names for the deceased?"

"Annie Glenn and Wynn Wykoff."

"And Mel fits in how?"

"They were both killed around the same time. Wynn Wykoff was supposedly in Salt Lake just before that and Annie Glenn had Mel's name and the Sampson and Witt number in her address book."

"Annie Glenn. Wynn Wykoff. You know, honey, he just woke up. Let me run those names by him."

I sat and waited.

The woman came back finally. "Annie Glenn he's never heard of. Wynn Wykoff rings a bell. He'll talk to you but he says not on the phone. Where did you say you were calling from?"

"Arizona," I said. "Dudley, Arizona."

"Guess that's too far to drive over, then."

"Yes," I said, "but I can fly."

# chapter thirty-three

THE EVENING BEFORE I WAS FLYING TO SALT
Lake, Teddy's band was playing at the St. Elmo's. Flynn and I had
shrimp and chicken fajitas at a newish Mexican restaurant just at
the entrance to the Gulch. Through the big plate-glass windows
we could see tourists going by, different from the usual lot wan-
dering down Main Street like lost sheep—these tourists were dat-
ing couples, younger and hipper, here for the bars and the music.

It was still relatively early but already there was a quality to the
evening—a kind of tuning up, as if the night itself were a band,
getting ready to play.

And Flynn and I, we might have been one of those couples—
Flynn looked like a tourist, neat and clean-shaven, in a navy polo
shirt—actually the only polo shirt I'd ever seen him in was navy.
I suspected he owned just one, which he wore for me. The fact
that Flynn might consider me when he put on a shirt—tough, no-
nonsense, practical Flynn—for some reason struck me as close
to heartbreaking.

I smiled at Flynn. He looked away, glancing at his watch as if
time were of the essence. Which it wasn't at all, we had hours of
unconstructed evening ahead of us.

"Dessert?" asked the waiter, brandishing a couple of menus.

"Not for me," Flynn said.

I shook my head.

"Coffee?"

Flynn looked at me and I shook my head again. "Just the check," he said.

Afterward we strolled up the Gulch heading for the St. Elmo's. The farther up the Gulch you went the seedier it became and also the most like Dudley had been in the old days, before it took off as a tourist town. The parking lot by the bar was full of hulking SUVs and new cars, with just a scattering of old pickups. A group of noisy kids hung out on the street blocking traffic and, from the smell, smoking weed. The marijuana mingled with a strong waft of alcohol, creating a literally intoxicating air.

I'd quit my job, which was quite likely a big mistake, I was working with a man who wasn't always easy to get along with, and I wasn't prepared for any unforeseen financial disasters that might be coming my way. I hadn't done any of the usual things I'd imagined I might have done by now—husband, family, kids; in fact, my whole life seemed to be the results of a series of unplanned accidents. But at that moment, walking up the Gulch in the evening with Flynn, I was as happy as I had ever been and probably ever would be.

We passed the tattoo parlor, passed a smoking cowboy, and went through the door into the St. Elmo's Bar. The jukebox was playing Amy Winehouse's "Me & Mr. Jones." The tables along the side were half full, the bar mostly full. We went to the back and turned a corner to the big room where the bands played.

I recognized Teddy, whom I'd heard play a few times—he was onstage tinkering with an amplifier. A young man I didn't know was joking with him and Billy Dodds was in a far corner with the drums, talking to a blonde with purple streaks in her hair whose back was to me.

He hadn't known how he was going to feel coming back, but Kurt certainly hadn't expected to feel good. It wasn't just the fact of Annie being murdered here, which was bad enough and tainted all his memories of better days right here on the Gulch, as a matter of fact, strolling over to hear her sing, proud to be the chosen boyfriend of someone like her, *chosen.* He hated Annie, he now realized, had actually hated her in a way before she was even killed, because she made him suffer so much. He'd been too young and too besotted to understand.

Then there was the entire aftermath, his arrest and charge, when his only glimpses of the Gulch were from the jail van on its way to the courthouse.

He'd spent months in the county jail, waiting for trial, being driven in the van with the other orange jumpsuited defendants in from the jail to the courthouse for the endless hearings and motions. Seeing people he knew in the courtroom, come to watch, maybe some even on his side but he couldn't be sure, and he wasn't allowed to talk to anyone. Just shuffled past them, hobbling in his chains.

And now here he was, walking down the Gulch again a free man, sure, but damaged. Damaged forever. Walking down the Gulch again. Downtown Main Street had changed, not the buildings but the street, full of people in the evening. Back then the streets were empty after five. But not the Gulch, the Gulch had always been jumping.

He took a deep breath, tried to bring his mind fully to the

present. Hopefully not looking too bad—in jeans that weren't new but not old either, just casual, and a blue plaid shirt—sort of cowboyish. He would be seeing Rachel. She looked like Annie, but she was a good soul, she had a heart. And Annie, who had considered herself to be a good mother, had damaged her, too.

It was so ironic that in this whole rotten mess the person who had it the worst was the only one in the whole affair who was blameless. Because he wasn't blameless himself, he could have done more for Rachel, he could have saved her.

At the mouth of the Gulch he'd passed a Mexican restaurant that hadn't been there before; a Chinese restaurant that had been on the right side at the mouth of the Gulch was gone. And there was a park with ash trees where the old garage had been. Thunder rumbled overheard. It smelled like rain. But now, almost to the bar, he heard the sound of musicians tuning up.

He eased inside, it was packed, and made his way to the room where the band played and wedged himself in between a young woman in a sequined tank top and a cowboy. From here he had a glimpse, just a glimpse of, was it? Teddy? Yes. He looked old. Kurt wondered if he looked as old as Teddy did.

The microphone buzzed, then Teddy's voice came on.

"Welcome, all you guys, welcome one and all. Couple of big surprises tonight, first one is, Billy's back. Billy Dodds, used to play right here with my old band Point of No Return. He's going to be sitting in tonight. Let's have a big hand for Billy."

Billy and Teddy, God, how he'd hated them.

"Now," said Teddy, "surprise number two. All the way from Tucson, Arizona, a former Dudley resident, come on, sweetheart, stand up."

The blond woman with the purple streaks in her hair stood up. "She's going to be singing for us, so give her a big hand."

The last time Scott had been to Dudley was before he met Rachel when he was a senior at the University of Arizona. He'd come down with some other students to drink in the bars. Because they all frankly planned to get drunk, someone in the group had worked it out with a friend of a friend where they could all sleep over in an old house. The house had hardly any furniture—whoever it was who lived there was more or less camping out. Scott had no recollection of actually meeting the host.

Actually he had very little recollection of anything about that trip except he'd gotten very very drunk.

This time he didn't arrive in Dudley till a little past eight, after dark. He found the Gulch with no problem but parking was something else. He drove up the street pretty far, found nothing, turned around, and drove back down, all this to the conflicting beats of rock music coming from not only the St. Elmo's but another bar closer to the entrance of the street, plus there was an impromptu group of drummers in City Park.

Couples and groups of people hung out on the sidewalks, in the alleyways and right on the street with no regard for traffic at all. Some of them were dancing, some making out, some standing quietly drinking beer. Hard to imagine Rachel here. Not her kind of scene at all, he thought as he gave up on the Gulch and drove up by the Copper Queen Hotel, the terrace packed with animated people, then a full parking lot, until he finally found a spot halfway up the hill near a church.

It was cool here in Dudley, so much cooler than Tucson. Scott enjoyed this feeling of being cool as he walked down the hill. Overhead, clouds covered the sky, blotting out the moon and stars. It smelled like it might rain but you never really knew, this time of year.

It seemed to him even though it hadn't been monsoon season the last time he was here that it had rained, a brief cloudburst, then it was gone.

Bits and pieces of memory from that trip came back to him now—he'd been a conscientious student—he'd already known he was headed for law school. He had rarely partied in fact, but that weekend, just before he graduated, he'd let everything go. It had been in the spring, just after finals. The Gulch had been as noisy, raucous then as it was noisy and raucous now.

Probably Rachel wouldn't even be in the bar; she would have fled for safety back to the Oliver House. Sweet nervous Rachel. He'd tried her cell when he first drove in but it was off. It had been off a lot lately, that wasn't like her. He'd always thought this investigation, her getting involved like this, was psychically dangerous—he worried it would push her over the edge, which she was always so close to anyway.

Now the St. Elmo's was ahead and the band playing, a woman singing. He pushed open the door. Inside it was uncomfortably crowded. He eased himself into the mass of people. Couldn't see anything. Heard the woman singing. She was quite good. He didn't know the song, something about wild geese and dance floors.

He shoved his way farther in, dodged some dancing couples, turned a corner, and found an empty seat at a table where a couple was already sitting, looking pretty wasted, too wasted to object to him joining them. From here he could see pretty well. The woman singing wore a purple halter top with purple-streaked hair to match. But of course. This was Old Dudley. She looked familiar, like someone he knew, someone from high school or maybe the U of A. So familiar. Then he realized:

*The woman singing was Rachel.*

No. It couldn't be Rachel. Could Rachel even sing? Yes, of course she could. He'd heard her sing in the shower. Not only could she sing, he saw now, but she had a sense for the audience, she was in fact pretty spectacular. She was beautiful too, in a different kind of way than he'd ever seen her.

Scottie thought of all the things they'd done together since they met, thought of her story: a sad story, to him romantic in a weird way, so out of the realm of what he had known of life. How beautiful she had been and still was, and how in need of protection.

She was his wife.

But seeing her now on a stage, singing, she didn't seem fragile anymore, but what? She seemed strong. It was just an illusion, that strength, and he knew it, but there was still the sense, like a smell almost: he could smell his marriage burning.


Teddy caught her eye, dear kind wonderful old Teddy. If it hadn't been for him so strongly encouraging her, working with her, Rachel would never have imagined she could actually do this. She'd rehearsed with Teddy and Billy and they'd told her she was great, but it wasn't till she stood up and starting singing that it happened the way it used to when she was just a girl, ten years old and allowed to sing with her mother's band—she lost her self and the song took over, the song sang itself, but it wasn't even that—everyone in the bar helped to sing the song though not a sound came from their lips.

*I want to do this more,* she thought. *I'm not scared when I do this.*

Then again, maybe she hadn't sung at all, maybe Annie had come back and taken over. She had to fix the Annie thing, had to fix things for her mom, then she could begin her life. About then was when she spotted Scottie at a table near the middle. He was standing up and clapping, and though she would have bet the last thing he'd have wanted her to do was sing in a bar with ultraviolet hair, he looked pleased, happy for her. Seeing him so pleased, so happy, made her really sad. *I'm sorry, Scottie,* she thought, *I'm so so sorry.*


*Why,* thought Kurt, *she's back, my little Rachel.*

# chapter thirty-four

A STEWARDESS LURCHED DOWN THE AISLE, holding a trash collector, as the plane bumped and dipped. Out the window were the mountains surrounding Salt Lake: white-capped even now, pristine. Then they vanished into thick cloud cover. I looked away. Out of the corner of my eye I could see the hand of the woman next to me, white-knuckled as it gripped the arm of the seat. I sensed the other passengers all around me, politely gripping their armrests in terrified desperation.

Then the plane went bumpity, bumpity, bumpity, hard to imagine air being so palpable. I closed my eyes. I was going to die, bits of my flesh strewn over the mountains, identifiable only with DNA testing. I thought of *Lost,* thought of the aptness of the words *final descent.* I thought of Flynn.

Then, like that, the ride smoothed out. I opened my eyes. We'd broken through the cloud cover and below were tiny houses, tiny toy cars on thin gray strips. They got bigger and bigger, we reached the runway, there was a bump, and we hit the ground.

The morning was overcast, though it hadn't actually rained the night before. Rachel, in her white capris and sunglasses, followed

Scottie as he walked over the bridge from the Oliver House and out to his car. He opened the back door and threw in his carry-on. Scottie had been so nice last night, waiting around without complaint until the bar closed, shaking hands with the band, and Max and Alice and Kurt.

"Rachel's such a fine person," Kurt had said to Scottie. "She's always stood by me."

It was after one by the time they walked together back up to the Oliver House. For a while, too wired to go to bed, they'd sat out on the front porch and talked, until Scottie fell asleep in his chair and she had to wake him long enough to get him to their room.

Now they stood outside together in the morning sunshine.

Scottie smiled. "Your purple hair," he said.

"It'll wash out."

"I know, you said."

They grinned at each other for a moment like two people on a first date.

"Well," said Scottie. "I have to go. Take care of yourself, you promise?"

"I promise."

"I love you," he said.

Behind the sunglasses, Rachel's eyes glanced away, observing the peeling white paint of the little house next to St. John's Episcopal Church, the feathery fennel in the drainage ditch. She could smell the licorice of the fennel. She and Max were going to Central School later to jam with Teddy and Billy. She'd invited Kurt to come too. Chloe was on her way to Salt Lake City.

"Love you too," she said politely.


Going to see Mel Witt, formerly of Sampson, Witt, and Trueblood, I turned the rental car down a little side street into an aging middle-class development, red brick two- and three-bedroom houses once probably all alike but now individualized by the owners' endeavors: here a stand of pink roses, there a cement yard with a flagpole. Mel Witt's house was almost obscured by a variety of hedges, shrubs, and what must have once been two little saplings but were now big leafy trees. There was a two-car garage attached but the driveway was filled with a silver SUV.

I parked on the street in front and got out. It was warm, a summer's day in Utah but nothing like the desert. I could see the mountains, white-capped and sunlit in the distance. Then it was shady as I walked up the driveway, under the trees. At the window by the front door I saw a beige curtain flicker.

By the time I reached the door it was already open. A red-headed woman, late fifties, in jeans and a red and green print blouse stood in the doorway, backed by a powerful whiff of tobacco smoke.

"Marsha?"

She smiled a big welcoming smile. "You're Chloe. Come in, come in. Mel's tapering off that OxyContin they prescribed for him, so he's actually making sense."

I followed her down a short hall to a living room, big for the house.

"Here she is!" Marsha sang out.

Two green leather couches faced each other, a wide-screen TV was on, with the sound off. A man sat on one of the couches, with a walker on one side and an overflowing ashtray on the other. A big man with a gray crewcut, lined face, bushy eyebrows. He was wearing a white T-shirt and striped pajama bottoms.

"Chloe," said the man. "I'm Mel. Pleased to meet you."

"Sit down, sit down," Marsha said. "Coffee?"

"That would be great," I said. "With everything if possible, please."

"You with law enforcement or what?" Mel asked.

I explained my situation, gave him the details of the crimes I was investigating and who I was working for.

"Wynn Wykoff, yes, but the rest of it rings no bells," Mel said. "Annie Glenn?" He shrugged. "Never heard of her. But a kid, that's tough. Finding her mom."

"Yes," I said.

"What'd you say her name was?"

"Rachel."

"Rachel," he repeated. "Tell you what I did after you called yesterday. Got my old files arranged kind of chronologically now, so I had Marsha go through the ones from eighteen to sixteen years ago, 'cause, to tell you the truth, the name rang a bell but it was kind of fuzzy. Plus I figure I lost a few brain cells with the damn surgery—the minute they put you under, it's bye-bye gray matter."

"Of course," said Marsha coming back with the coffee, "you got extra of that."

"Atta gal." Mel winked at me. "Anyway," he said. "Nothing came up."

"Oh." I took a sip of coffee, rich and strong. And another.

Mel held up a hand. " 'Cause I was focusing on *your* murders. Once I started thinking outside the box, to *my* murders, it came to me. Marsha, I said, let's pull the file on Sara Aikman."

"That's right," Marsha said. "And I told him, we don't have that file anymore."

"Oh," I said again.

"But—but," said Marsha, "I did find some of Mel's notes and there it was. Wynn Wykoff. Wynn Wykoff came to see Mel in regards to the Sara Aikman case." She looked at me expectantly.

"Who is Sara Aikman?" I asked.

"You don't know?"

I shook my head.

"Well, rats to that," said Mel. "Sara Aikman was murdered back in the eighties by her boyfriend Chad Sommers."

"It was a big deal here," said Marsha. "TV and the newspapers covered it for months, even when there wasn't anything new to report. You know how they do, act like there is."

"But what did that have to do with Wynn?" I asked.

"Wynn didn't say. He looked through my files, I had a bunch back then, but he didn't really comment. All he said was his interest was in something connected but peripheral to the case. I wrote that down in my notes, quoted him exactly."

"That's it?"

"That's it."

I stared at Mel. Connected but peripheral? What the hell did that mean? No one was smoking but the smell of tobacco suddenly seemed overwhelming. "So what happened to Chad Sommers?" I asked. "Did he get convicted?"

"He vanished," Marsha said.

"So the Aikman family hired me to track him down. The cops weren't doing shit, not really. Chad's family had some money and it turned out Chad had hightailed it over to Australia. Once he was there, he disappeared into the bush."

"Wow." I drained my cup and set it down.

"Yeah. As far as real details about the case go, at this point I say go talk to Sara's sister Emily. She lives right here in Salt Lake and she's the one took back almost all the files. Stormed in one day and got 'em before I even had a chance to make copies."

Early afternoon and thunder rumbled outside Central School. They were supposed to be playing music but the amps were all unplugged because of the storm.

"The Thirteenth Floor Elevators," Teddy said to Max. "You ever heard of them?"

Max shook his head.

"They created the term psychedelic rock," said Teddy. "Roky Erickson."

"He's dead?"

"No, he's alive I'm pretty sure, but you don't want to be too precise about these things. What we're talking about is a kind of existential letting go—opening up to the full horror of life. He got shut up—"

"Jeez, Teddy," Billy interrupted. "Give the kid a break."

"No," said Max, "I want to hear. Go on."

"He got shut up in a mental hospital with a bunch of murderers for possessing marijuana. I don't say he wasn't already unstable but after that—over the edge. Wrote songs about the devil and having his arms torn off. 'Night of the Vampire,' 'Don't Shake Me Lucifer,' 'Two-Headed Dog.' "

"Cool!" said Max.

Out the window thunder boomed loud, right there, followed by a flash of lightning.

"See, *see?*" said Teddy. "He's listening to us as we speak."

"Who, Erickson?" said Billy.

"No, Lucifer."

It began to rain in earnest, hammering on the roof; one of those monsoon cloudbursts that came and went in a matter of minutes. Rachel could see water gushing down the street outside. Luckily they were all high up on the second floor of Central School: Max, Rachel, Teddy, Billy, Kurt. And there was someone called Eddie, who'd been the bass player last night.

Rosalie too, though you could hardly tell she was there. She sat in a corner with her iPod looking out the corner window and had never once, as far as Rachel could tell, turned her head to the inside of the room.

Eddie did a drumroll.

Rachel sat on a battered couch with Kurt.

"How's it going with Chloe and Flynn?" asked Teddy over the sound of the rain. "Any leads?"

Rachel shook her head.

"I thought Chloe flew to Salt Lake City on a lead this morning," Max said to Rachel, just as the rain let up, so Salt Lake City came out extra loud.

Kurt got up and went over to the window.

Rachel glared at Max. She wasn't supposed to tell anyone just in case, but she'd told Max.

"Mormons?" Teddy raised his eyebrows. "Annie was maybe murdered by Mormons?"

Rachel smiled, she couldn't help herself.

"Hey!" said Billy. "Wasn't the prosecutor a Mormon? That Rasmussen guy?"

*He was?* thought Rachel. Did Chloe know that? Did Flynn?

Rosalie stood up suddenly, and walked away from the window, past Kurt, past Max, past Teddy and Eddie and Billy and Rachel, out the door.

"Listen," said Teddy. "No more talk, we're playing music. By the way, you're all invited to my house tonight for dinner."

Eddie did another drumroll.

"You know, what would be interesting," said Teddy. "Why don't I invite that prosecutor for dinner too?"

"You think he'd come?" Billy said.

Suddenly Rachel was tired, as if the excitement from last night and saying goodbye to Scottie this morning and even coming up here and hanging out, which they'd been doing for the last hour, which had been fun, were suddenly too much for her. But that wasn't it either. More like something had entered the room and drained it of energy. Which made no sense at all.


I called the number Mel had given me for Emily Aikman, now Emily Christiansen.

A man answered, young by his voice. "That's my mom," he said, "but she's in L.A."

Great. "When is she coming back?"

"Tonight, actually. Dad's going to pick her up at the airport tonight at eight."

My flight out was at eight-thirty. It looked like I'd be changing it and spending the night in exotic Salt Lake City.

# chapter thirty-five

JIM RASMUSSEN, THE PROSECUTOR, DIDN'T
show up for Teddy's dinner party, even though Teddy had called
over to his office in Sierra Vista and invited him. The dinner, a
green chili, squash, and corn stew with couscous and a green salad,
was set up as a buffet, with everything spread out on a big table in
the kitchen. People filled their plates and carried them outside to
the porch, sitting on the rocking chairs and the porch steps.

Billy was there and Alice, Rachel, Max, and Eddie the drummer, Kurt. Rosalie could be seen occasionally flitting around in
various rooms and once Rachel saw her way down on the street.

"I wonder why Mr. Rasmussen didn't show," Max said.

Billy snorted. "Are you kidding? I can think of maybe a million
reasons. For one thing, he's a Mormon."

"Oh, Billy," Alice said, "what does that have to do with anything?"

"Don't they stick to their own kind?"

"It all depends," Alice said. "And besides, I'm not even sure he
is one. How do you know?"

Billy shrugged. "I don't, I guess."

"Everyone shut up," Rachel said. "Scottie's a Mormon on his
mother's side."

*"No,"* said Alice.

"He's not a *practicing* one."

"What's his family like?" Alice asked. "Do you get along with them?"

"It's really sad," Rachel said. "He doesn't have any family at all really. His parents were killed by a drunk driver when he was eighteen. He's got an uncle in Sacramento and an aunt in Utah someplace but he isn't really close to any of them. But his parents being killed like that is one reason he became a prosecutor."

There was a little silence, out of respect for Scottie's parents.

"Where the *hell* is Teddy?" said Billy. "He has this dinner party and he doesn't even show up?"

He hadn't shown up and no one knew where he was. Even Rosalie had just shrugged, as if to say, *Teddy and his whims.*


I called Flynn from the Motel 6.

"Sara Aikman," he said. "I don't know the case but I'll look into it. I wonder what that Mel guy meant, peripheral but connected."

"Mel didn't know either," I said. "I think they were Wynn's words."

"Might mean nothing," said Flynn. "A thing to say to Mel so he wouldn't get too interested in exactly why Wynn was there."

"You know something? That makes sense."

"Call me back again tomorrow after you've seen the sister," he said.

"Sure."

"Hey, Chloe?"

"What?"

"Good work."

"I hope so anyway," I said, unable to easily take a compliment from Flynn.

I waited till nine-fifteen to call Emily again and she was there. I explained why I was calling.

"I'll be happy to see you." Her voice was sad. "I still miss Sara and I always will." She gave me her address. "Come over in the morning, ten or so."

Teddy never did show up for his own dinner party. Things broke up around eleven and people started to trickle away. Alice, Kurt, Max, and Rachel walked down the steps from Teddy's together. Earlier, when he found out that Kurt was sleeping in his van, Teddy had offered to let him sleep in his room at Central School, so the others walked him there. Billy headed for the Copper Queen.

At the house on Laundry Hill, Alice gave Rachel a hug. "Are you sure you don't want to sleep over here tonight?" she asked.

"I'll be fine," said Rachel. "And Max is going to walk me back to the Oliver House."

They walked down Laundry Hill, went the long way past the Copper Queen Hotel just to look at the night people.

"You should come to Seattle," Max said. "I've got loads of friends in bands that would love to have a singer like you."

"Right," said Rachel. "Just abandon my whole life."

"You could be a teenager again."

"I guess I never was," said Rachel. She began to sing softly: "Never really got to be a teenager."

"Never got to do stupid things!" Max sang back. "Never got one body part pierced! Or tattooed!"

"I had to be good," said Rachel, suddenly sobered. "*I had to,* so no one would kill me."

"It didn't affect me like that at all," said Max. "It got me interested in the dark side."

They meandered down the steps in front of the Copper Queen, sat on a bench in the Grassy Park under a light. People sat on the other benches too, some couples, but mostly punks, or meth people, sitting in the dark, away from the lights.

"Listen," Rachel said. "It's strange but while we at Teddy's I remembered something else."

"Remembered something else?" said Max. "Like from where?"

"One of my blank spots."

"No kidding."

"You know, I spent the night at Beth's?"

"Yeah?"

"Well, I promised her this book, actually I think it was the first Harry Potter, and I had forgotten to bring it, so I ran back home. It was raining and thundering, so I had this big umbrella that was Beth's mom's. Then, just before I got there I remembered— I'd left it in my locker at school. So I turned around and went back."

"Wow," said Max. "What if whoever killed your mom was there—"

"Someone *was* there," said Rachel. "I saw them leaving. They had something over their head for the rain, so I couldn't really see exactly who it was and I don't know who it was now but I have this strong feeling it was someone I knew."

"Of course," said Max, "could have been someone just stopping by."

"I can almost see whoever it was right now," said Rachel. "It kind of scares me that I *will* see them." She shivered. "Let's go."

They stopped by the bridge. Max said, "Want me to stick around?"

"No. It's okay."

On the front porch the lights were on. By herself, Rachel

crossed the bridge, smelled the licorice. She wasn't really afraid. She opened the iron gate, it creaked.

A man was sitting on a plastic chair by the side of the house in the shadows. Oh, no, she thought, Jim Rasmussen *again*? He got up just like before and came toward her into the light.

"Scottie," she said. "Oh, Scottie."

# chapter thirty-six

EMILY CHRISTIANSEN LIVED IN A NICE THREE-
story whitewashed brick house with green trim in an upper-
middle-class section of Salt Lake. There were dusky lavender
roses in the side yard, and a red front door with a brass knocker
shaped like a genteel lady's hand, but the door opened before I
had a chance to try it out.

The woman who opened it was in her forties, pretty, with
thick bobbed blond hair and turquoise-blue eyes. She wore a
white eyelet blouse and pink linen pants. "Chloe? Hi, I'm Emily
Christiansen."

I followed her inside and down a hall, red and blue Persian
runner on chestnut-colored wood floors. To my right was a flight
of stairs, white banisters, same Persian runner.

Emily stopped at the stairs. "Sara!" she called up. "Come down.
I need you."

A teenage girl, maybe seventeen, in jeans and a blue denim
blouse came bouncing down the stairs.

"My daughter," Emily said to me. "Named after her aunt. Sara,
this is Chloe."

Sara smiled politely. She was pretty, like her mother, same
blue eyes and blond hair.

"We're going to talk," Emily said. "Maybe you could bring us—" she turned to me. "Coffee? Iced tea?"

"Iced tea would be good," I said. "Thank you."

We went into a pleasant living room, flowered couches, Persian rugs, a fireplace at one end, with bronze fixtures and a painting over the fireplace mantel of snowcapped mountains at sunset. I sat across from Emily on one of the flowered couches and she sat on the other.

I explained to her briefly why I was there.

"Wynn," she said. "Wynn Wykoff?"

"Yes."

She shook her head. "He never came to see me. I would have remembered. I remember everything that was connected with Sara in any way."

"I guess whatever he wanted to know he got from Mel." I was disappointed. "But Mel had the files back then."

She nodded. "I was never really sure if Mel was doing anything much at all," she said. "So I finally fired him. And you think your Wynn's murder had something to do with my sister's?"

"I have no idea. I'm just following up on everything I run across."

"I wish I'd had a chance to talk to your Wynn even if you say he told Mel it was peripheral." She made a self-deprecating little face. "I'll grasp at any straw."

Teenage Sara came in with glasses of iced tea.

"I think of my sister every day," Emily said. Her voice broke. "It's been twenty years and I think of her *every single day*."

"Mom?" said Sara. "You okay?"

"I'm fine, sweetheart. Thank you for the tea. Now go away and let me talk to Chloe."

"There was only two years' difference between us," Emily said after Sara left. "We grew up with all the same references, the same memories. She always knew what I meant, and vice versa."

I nodded, sipping tea. Spicy, Indian.

"They were engaged to be married, Chad and Sara. And Sara changed her mind. Chad couldn't take it. He stra—" she paused and took a breath. "Strangled her."

"Oh!" I said.

"He turned himself in right away, his parents had a lot of money so he had no problem making bail. Then he vanished."

I nodded. "His parents? Where are they now?"

"His mother died of breast cancer a couple of years ago. His father has dementia. He does have a brother, Michael, but as far as I've been able to tell . . ." She sighed. "They're not in touch. I kept a watch on them all for a long time in case he made contact."

She passed her hand over her eyes. "Chad stole so many memories from me, and what's so much worse, he stole Sara's whole life. Her chance to get married, have children, grandchildren. Sara was— Oh, I can't explain."

"You're doing a pretty good job," I said.

She stood up. "Come on," she said, "I want to show you something."

I followed her up the flight of stairs, caught a glimpse of bedrooms, then we went up another flight. She opened a door and we went into an attic.

"I call this Sara's room," Emily said. "The case files I got from Mel are in here somewhere."

I looked around. The room was small, with only one window that looked out on a big oak tree. The walls were hung with photographs of a beautiful blond girl, obviously Sara; children's drawings; framed report cards; some scrapbooks were stacked on a table.

"I have everything," said Emily. "Everything of hers I could find—it wouldn't fit all in here, there's more in the basement." She sat suddenly on a little upholstered chair.

I looked at the photographs, Sara ranging in age from babyhood to right before her death. The later ones had part of them cut out. I pointed to one. "What's this?"

"Chad. I cut him out of every photograph I had of the two of them."

"Don't you have any pictures of Chad?" I asked.

"None."

"Oh," I said, disappointed.

There was a silence. Outside somewhere a blue jay cawed noisily.

"My husband is a very responsible man," Emily said, "very practical. He cares a lot about me and his family. And he doesn't have one ounce of charm." She laughed. "That's why I married him."

I drifted, looking out at the oak tree. Emily's story was sad, and I'd heard many stories like this as a victim advocate and they always made me sad. But right now it didn't seem connected to Annie Glenn—or if it was, I didn't know how to find the connection. Maybe there would be a connection in the files when Emily got around to showing them to me.

Emily closed her eyes. "I went out with Chad briefly before Sara did." She opened her eyes. "She didn't, um, steal him away or anything, Chad and I just didn't click. But, you know, he could really be extremely charming. He had pet names for people, not mean but funny or silly or sweet."

"Ah," I said.

"Rosalie," said Emily.

I looked at her. *"What?"*

"Rosalie." She shrugged. "He called Sara Rosalie. Chad called all his girlfriends Rosalie."

And so did Teddy, so did Teddy.


Scottie and Rachel were sitting in the common room at the Oliver House. Rachel was wearing her pink capris and a black T-shirt with a rip in the neck seam that belonged to Max. Scottie was dressed for court in khaki Dockers and a blue-and-white-striped seersucker jacket.

"I didn't know about that woman getting murdered," Scottie said. "That yoga teacher. I still don't understand why you didn't mention it when I was here before."

"Because." Rachel sighed. "We went over this last night."

"What about Flynn—he's not worried?"

Rachel shrugged. "He's not a bodyguard, he's a detective."

"And Chloe?"

"Chloe went to Salt Lake City. On a lead. I'm not supposed to tell anyone. She was supposed to come back yesterday but she stayed over."

"Why aren't you supposed to tell anyone?"

"Just on general principle but I guess it's okay to tell you. Plus Max blurted it out at Central School. So Kurt and Teddy and Billy know anyway."

Scottie looked at his watch. "Almost eleven," he said. "I've got to go." He stood up and walked down the hall, wheeling his carry-on. Rachel followed.

"I don't know what's gotten into you," he said. "You were scared of everything before and now it's like you're scared of nothing."

"I'm still scared," said Rachel. "But I just ignore it."

Outside the front door, Scottie stopped and looked at Rachel pleadingly. "Sweetheart. I'd really like it a lot if you'd come home." He paused. *"Please?"*

Rachel looked past his shoulder, not meeting his eyes, and at that moment her cell phone chimed. She punched it on.

"Max!" she said. She turned away from Scottie.

"A picnic!" she said. "That would be so fun. Of course. You can stop by here or I can stop by there. Central School? Why not."

She closed her phone. Her face was flushed and she looked very happy. "We're going on a picnic later today, in the afternoon," she said. "We're going to this cool place up in the mountains. You can come too, Scottie, if you want."

"You know I can't come, I have to be in justice court at one-thirty. I already missed morning court." He turned away and bumped the carry-on down the porch steps. Just before the bridge he turned and looked at Rachel. "I worry about you," he said. "I can't help it."

"We'll be *fine,* all of us. Kurt's going and Billy, too." Her voice lilted upward. "And the whole thing was organized by Teddy. I mean, how much safer can you get?"

# chapter thirty-seven

*EMILY WEPT AND WEPT, TILL HER DAUGHTER*
and I got her organized enough to start calling around to newspapers, his university, whatever, for pictures of Chad Sommers
to send to the Dudley PD, then I left hurriedly to catch my flight
to Tucson, which was two hours long but at least I gained an hour
with the time difference. All the way to the airport, a menace to
the other drivers, I'd tried to contact Rachel and Flynn, but every
time I just got their voice mail. In the airport lounge waiting for
the flight to be called, I managed to reach Lois.

"He's not here, honey," she said. "He's tailing Tanya—in Tucson, probably in a mall. If he checks in I'll have him call you."

I checked my messages as soon as we landed but nothing from
Flynn or Rachel. I tried calling them again with no luck as I
walked through the airport on the way to catch the bus to Park 'N
Save where I'd left my car but neither one answered. It was two
o'clock in the afternoon, sun pouring down out of a cloudless sky.
When I finally got to my car, the seats were blazing hot.

I found an old newspaper in the back seat and sat on it while
the air-conditioning kicked in. I tried Rachel's cell once more but
still nothing. I couldn't see that she was in any immediate danger, I mean, what did she know? And what did Teddy know—not

that I'd gone to Salt Lake City, we'd told Rachel not to tell anyone. I'd done everything I could right now.

I drove out of the Park 'N Save down to the freeway. It wasn't till I'd turned off at the Sierra Vista exit and gone another fifteen miles, halfway to Sierra Vista, that Flynn finally called me back.

"Hi," I said. "Where are you?"

"In Tucson, about to get on the freeway."

"It's about time. I've been trying to reach you for hours. Listen—"

"You and Scott Macabee," interrupted Flynn.

*"Listen,"* I said.

Flynn rushed on. "He's been trying to reach me too. I turned off my cell on the way to Tucson. Sometimes I have to do that, to focus. Scott's worried about Rachel. He didn't know about Camille/Sonora until yesterday and he got so upset he drove to Dudley to be with Rachel last night."

"Where is he now?" I asked. "Still with Rachel?"

"No. Back on the job, had to be in court. Rachel's going on a picnic with all the guys sometime this afternoon. By the way, Macabee knew about you going to Salt Lake City."

*"What?"* I said, suddenly alarmed. "We told Rachel not to mention that."

"Well, she told Scottie. And she told Max." Flynn laughed. "And according to Scottie, Rachel said Max told everyone at the Central School—Billy, Kurt, and Teddy."

"Oh, my god. This picnic, who's going? When? And *where*? Flynn," I said urgently. "Just keep your mouth shut from now on and *listen* to me."

The cool place in the mountains was up over the hills and down and up again. It was a place Billy knew about because the band used to go there. And Kurt had gone there sometimes with Annie and Rachel. There was a sort of path but only for a little while and then it ended. The mountains were carpeted with green plants that only ever showed up in a good rainy season, and flowers bloomed: fiery red penstemon, cool blue lupines, delicate pink fairy dusters.

There were no clouds in the sky and the crows wheeled up above like dark punctuation marks.

Billy Dodds led the way, Kurt just behind in case Billy forgot the way, and Max and Rachel were the end. Max was carrying the picnic basket, which was actually a tote belonging to Alice with a picture of Frida Kahlo silkscreened on it.

Frankly, the picnic itself wasn't exactly a feast—just some bottled water and cold pizza: artichoke hearts and mozzarella from the High Desert Market. Everyone agreed they liked pizza cold as much as when it was heated up.

After a while Billy got confused and Kurt took over, striding ahead, then coming back because everyone was walking slowly as if they didn't really care how long they took.

Teddy wasn't with them, he was meeting them there.


Flynn and I converged at the High Desert Market just across from the courthouse. Flynn had called ahead to Dudley PD and told them the situation and he'd tried to reach Jack Nelson but hadn't been able to. He followed me up to my house, where I dropped off my car and got into the Land Rover. Our first stop was Central School. The door was unlocked and we climbed the steps but no one answered when we knocked on Teddy's door, no marijuana smell either.

We knocked on a couple of other doors too, in case someone there knew where they might have gone, but no one answered.

*"Rosalie,"* I said. "Maybe she stayed behind."

We hightailed it up the cement stairs and there she was, sitting on the porch with her iPod and her earbuds. When she saw us she raised her arm languidly. "Not here," she said. "Picnic."

"Where?" I said.

She went into the house, got paper and a pen, and drew a map for us.

The noise of the blades, the engine, whatever, was so loud that Rachel and Max stopped and looked up at the helicopter, hovering like a bumblebee in the air and not that far way from them, really. The blades of grass near the helicopter bent and bushes swayed in its wind. The noise, the wind, shattered the peaceful atmosphere, making things seem really urgent. But what?

Billy had stopped in his tracks when the helicopter appeared in the distance and now he walked back to Rachel and Max. Kurt had gone on ahead and Rachel couldn't even see him anymore.

"What are they looking for?" Billy shouted to Max over the racket. "Drug smugglers?"

"Or illegals," Max shouted back.

Rachel put her hands over her ears, the helicopter was deafening and the grasses bent in front of it; it was sort of thrilling in a way. She laughed giddily.

Kurt sprang across the crevice and landed not quite perfectly on the other side, twisting his ankle slightly, not enough to worry about until later on tonight. He remembered that very crevice, which was actually more like a seam, a crack, not too wide but lots easier to jump than walk down and up again, from the days he and Annie and Rachel hiked out here. Back then he'd jumped across like a cat, now it was more like a fat bear.

He could hear a helicopter—he was out of sight of the others, he'd gone fast. He'd had a bad feeling about this whole picnic thing from the minute he'd heard about it. A really bad feeling: a chest-pain, back-tension, gut-rumbling kind of feeling. He didn't know where it came from exactly but he was going to trust that feeling.

It was maybe a quarter mile to the cave, which was where they were meeting Teddy. Kurt kept his eyes on the ground until he spotted something that might do for what he was looking for. A mesquite branch, not too twisted. He picked it up, then swiped a rock with it to make sure it wasn't rotten, but it didn't break. It wasn't a gun, exactly, he thought, but it was the best that a gardener could come up with on the spur of the moment.

When he got really close to the cave he circled around and up, so he was above it, then came down the other side so he would arrive from an unexpected angle. Very close but still hidden, he stopped, listened. Mercifully the helicopter was farther away, it wasn't hard to screen out its noise. He heard: cicadas, a couple of crows, the slight purr of a breeze in a creosote bush, but no human sound, except his own breathing. He held his breath and still heard nothing.

Maybe Teddy wasn't there yet. He waited some more and still heard nothing. He inched around so he had a view of the cave. At the mouth, sitting cross-legged and reclining back against a rock, unmoving, totally silent, was Teddy Radebaugh, wearing sunglasses that were aimed right at him.


The men in the helicopter waved at Max and Billy and Rachel and they waved back. Billy had the bright idea of emptying the tote bag with the silkscreen of Frida Kahlo so the men above could see they weren't carrying drugs. The helicopter hovered, then sidled away to the east.

"Where's Kurt?" Rachel said suddenly.

"He went ahead," Billy said. "I hope he comes back soon, 'cause I've forgotten how to get there."

"We're lost in the desert!" shouted Max hopefully.

"Someone's yelling at us," Billy said. "Do you hear?"

"Yes. Yes, I do," said Rachel. She turned because it seemed to be coming from behind.

"Why, it's Chloe!" she said. "Chloe and Flynn!"


Teddy stared right at Kurt, at least it looked that way from the angle of the sunglasses, but maybe for some reason he couldn't see him, because Teddy had not said a word, nor moved one inch, since Kurt had spotted him. The angle Teddy was lying was odd, as if someone had pushed him backwards, but as far as he could tell, Teddy was holding no weapon—actually, Kurt was starting to feel stupid and overly paranoid, carrying his mesquite branch behind his back.

"Hey, Teddy?" he said,

Teddy still didn't move. Kurt came right around the slope and smelled alcohol, whiskey maybe. Teddy was drunk? He walked over to him. The alcohol smell got stronger. Teddy didn't move, nothing about Teddy moved, not even his chest, up and down. Kurt leaned down and removed the sunglasses.

Teddy, he realized belatedly, Teddy was dead. Dead, dramatically so, posed, wearing, he noticed now, a white Indian kurta and jade beads around his neck. In front of him on the ground was a small white envelope addressed to someone named Michael Sommers. And a large envelope addressed to *All Who I Have Hurt*. Kurt figured he qualified, so he tore it open.

*I'm sorry about everything,* it said, *and I didn't plan to kill Camille. I didn't want to kill Annie and Wynn either but they found out about Sara, so it was that or a prison cell, maybe even later a lethal injection. It looks like Flynn and his assistant have found out about Sara too, so I decided to give up. I will love Sara forever. Rosalie gets everything I own. The other envelope is for my brother Michael who lives in Watertown, Massachusetts.*

*Peace.*

Peace, thought Kurt. *Peace? The nerve. The total nerve, you lousy murderer. Hey, Teddy, what's with the white kurta and the jade beads—you're a holy man now?* He'd actually staged this whole thing: an egomaniac to the end. Goddamn him, and the kids would be here soon. *Just what they need in those lives of theirs you screwed up.* Well, at least he could put a stop to that part of the hypocritical drama.

# epilogue

TEDDY'S BROTHER, MICHAEL SOMMERS, FLEW in after the autopsy, which had determined that Teddy had died from a lethal dose of a combination of alcohol and barbiturates. Per Teddy's instructions, Michael wanted to build a funeral pyre for Teddy out in the desert but was unable to get a permit to do it, so instead Teddy was cremated. Michael managed to get together a group of musicians to play Gram Parsons music, and a lot of Teddy's fans from the St. Elmo's, undaunted by a murder or four, came too, to watch Michael scatter Teddy's ashes over the desert.

We were all invited—Billy, Alice, Max, Rachel, Kurt, Flynn, and myself—but none of us went.

Instead of seeing Teddy's ashes scattered, we all went to a party at Alice's: Max, Rachel, Kurt, Flynn, and myself. Billy didn't come, he'd already left for Vermont and his seven-year-old daughter and his pretty wife and his general store, adamant that he would never come back to Dudley the rest of his life. Besides the people already named, Jim Rasmussen came too.

But not Jody. To this day I don't know if Jody knows about her husband and Annie.

Max selected the music, of course, so the occasion was a little somber, which was appropriate, though things got merrier as the afternoon turned to evening. I even heard that much later out back in Alice's garden, Kurt leaned over and kissed Alice, something he'd always wanted to do but never had, out of respect for Annie.

Then he kissed her again.